9TH STORY PUBLISHING

THE WICKED LIBRARY PRESENTS

13 WICKED TALES

EDITED BY DANIEL FOYTIK, NELSON W. PYLES, AND SCARLETT R. ALGEE

Cover art & interior illustrations: Jeannette Andromeda

Logo design and formatting: Daniel Foytik

ISBN: 978-1-7340624-0-3

Please visit us online at thewickedlibrary.com to learn more about The Wicked Library and hear the recurring audio production featuring stories by the authors featured in this collection and many more.

9th Story Studios | PO Box 97925 | Pittsburgh, PA 15227

Reviews of The Wicked Library Podcast:

The Wicked Library has an average 4.7 stars (out of 5) rating on Apple Podcasts. With 421 ratings as of this publishing. Here's what some of the listeners have said:

If you're looking for a high-quality horror fiction podcast you need to check this one out ★★★★★
I recently discovered this genre of podcasts and started off by binging all of the no sleep podcast. I had a hard time finding a podcast of similar quality to listen to next and was excited to discover The Wicked Library. The background music and sound engineering are awesome, and the stories are consistently well written. Highly recommend check this out!

My Favorite Podcast ★★★★★
I'm always waiting for the next episode. I love the stories. I love the interviews. Thank you for all you do. This show got me through a deep depression and it's everything to me.

The Librarian is awesome ★★★★★
Love the Private Collector arc and the stories told. Very reminiscent of Tales from the Crypt, keep it up! So good

Excellent! ★★★★★
The stories are well-written and the Q & A sessions with the authors offer great insights on the entire writing process.

Keep the lights on…. ★★★★★
I have specific taste when it comes to podcasts, and for the past few years, I stopped listening completely. I knew what I was hoping to find, but I just couldn't track it down. I don't remember how I stumbled across The Wicked Library, but from the moment I pressed play, I found what I had been looking for. The show allows me to just shut off my mind and absorb myself into a world not too different from our own. I wish there were new episodes every day, I simply can't get enough. Keep up the amazing   work!

A WORD FROM YOUR LIBRARIAN

Hello Kiddies,

I have been your Librarian for seven years now; the blink of an eye for the *living impaired* such as yours truly, and certainly the requisite length of time for *bad luck* upon the breaking of a mirror. It has been my honour and privilege to help bring you tales that terrify, and it is an absolute privilege to continue this dark avocation.

It is also a sheer delight to scare the absolute hell out of you all!

What you are holding in your hands (*or claws*) is the very first anthology for The Wicked Library. It is quite overdue and almost mildly ironic that it was released almost to the day of the very first episode and the first public appearance of...well, *me.*

So, sit down and relax! Your Librarian has seen to your pending entertainment. Be advised-this is going to be a dark ride. Thank you all from the bottom of my dark (*yet full*) little heart.

Remember-keep the lights on; no one is reading these to you this time...at least, not quite yet...

It's story time....

Your Constant Librarian...

TABLE OF CONTENTS

INTRODUCTION
BY DANIEL FOYTIK

Learning and growing always require that we face and move beyond our fears—whether it's overcoming common fears like heights, public speaking, rejection of ourselves and our work, or more esoteric fears like what's beyond this mortal coil or learning how to embrace our true selves.

Fear and horror go hand in hand, of course, and horror is arguably one of the oldest forms of storytelling—finding its roots in ancient traditional tales, like fairy tales.

Fairy tales are, at their core, horror stories. They incorporate typical horror elements that any modern reader would recognize, like the supernatural, monsters, the unknown, dark, lost places, and the potential for great evil we all carry within us. They also tend to carry a lesson (as twisted as that lesson may be) leaned only after some really awful and horrifyingly Wicked things have happened.

Storytelling lets us understand who we were, who we are, and who we wish to be. It's how we pass on knowledge, ideas, and truth to others, and it's how we come to understand those who came before us.

If you're reading this, I assume you love story, and have a special place in your heart for horror. I spend a lot of my time thinking about horror (obviously)—all its variations, the common, and uncommon themes, the similarities, and the vast differences.

Since I took the keys to *The Wicked Library* from my dear friend, Nelson W. Pyles, and started to get cosy with The Librarian, I've made it my focus to bring the listeners of *The Wicked Library* podcast a variety of great horror fiction from multiple independent horror authors.

We explore many varieties, from classic ghost stories, to cosmic horror, occult rituals, blood-soaked crime scenes, and psychological minefields. As long as it's Wicked and well written, it's fair game.

It's a good thing – the listeners are entertained, discover a new author, a new horror sub-genre, and perhaps end up changed by a captivating tale, while the authors, voice actors, artists, and composers who help bring the stories to life expand their fan bases and have their other work found.

It's great fun to make, but I have to admit, to me it's more.

As a result of producing the show, I've changed in ways I never could have anticipated over the last few years. I've become I've become a better writer and storyteller, but more importantly I've become more understanding, more balanced, and I've made some amazing friends I never would have met otherwise.

And, *The Lift* wouldn't exist without *The Wicked Library*. To be fair, *The Lift* was created well before I took ownership of *The Wicked Library*, and I had even recorded a couple of pilot episodes but, without the amazing writers, artists, and voice actors I met through the ongoing process of creating *The Wicked Library*, *The Lift* never would have become what it is today.

Over the last few years The Librarian and Victoria have become more real to me than I could have ever imagined. Both started as just voices from the dark – mascots really – but, like all of us, they each wanted to be more.

They are now my constant companions, each edging me forward beyond my own fears in their very unique, but equally firm, ways. If we're lucky, and we learn from the stories we consume, I think that's what happens to all of us: we face our fears, take a long look at ourselves, accept what we do like, and learn how to change what we don't. The characters we meet (or sometimes create) within the confines of a story become our guides and help us to find our way when we feel lost, confused, or need a nudge.

Stories are very personal experiences, and they often reveal more about the reader than they do about the author. The same stories resonate in different ways with each reader and depending upon where you are on your own path and what you bring with you, your experience will be different than anyone else's. Isn't that cool?

The stories that follow are written by some of the very best horror and speculative fiction writers I've had the pleasure to work with. These are writers who take their craft seriously. They all have other work out there to enjoy, and many have been nominated for and won awards. But, most importantly, they each know how to capture within their tales those things that make for good horror, and leave you thinking long after you've read the final word.

The following tales, written just for this collection, all explore libraries or places of knowledge, and each story accurately represents the variety of styles and subgenres we deliver with the podcast. So, if you enjoy this anthology, we encourage you to seek out the podcast for more stories by the authors herein, and many, many others.

Now, let's get Wicked,

Daniel Foytik
Story Monkey
September 2019

THE BOOK FOR YOUR NIGHT CLASS
BY STEPHANIE M. WYTOVICH

Fluorescent light cuts through the scratches of chalkboard
wounds, each gash a reminder of conjured words, all those
slip-tongued curses that bleed broken teeth and stolen time,
their dead skin dusting the pages of our books.

It hurts to read it, this tome a pound of severed flesh,
a man-made obscenity with teeth sharpened into fangs.
My brain pulses, the building migraine in my head
a symptom of the witchcraft pumping through my veins,
all that boiled blood and hysteria blurring my vision,
a throwback to the night my body first hanged.

But sometimes, if you hold still, the rage of broken quills
and angry women will etch itself into your palms,
a masquerade of alchemical sigils dancing across
your wrists, its scripture an army of bound wrath,
its voice a mirage, an act of desperation, each note
a carefully written dirge.

I choke on its spells, breathe magic into a box
of dead crows, swallow the spit of aging wolves.
A bell rings and the screams of bloated corpses
echo throughout the vents, their wails an autopsy report,
a toe-tag bouquet. It takes everything in me to rip
myself from this desk, my skin melting into the chair,
this story, my fingerprint a scribbled soul song
disappearing into the teacher's grimoire.

DEATH STALKS THE LIBRARY

BY K. B. GODDARD

I t all began with the death of Mr. Hewell, head librarian at a college of a certain university, which must remain nameless. Hewell, a man of sixty years of age and suspected intemperate habits, was found one morning in the library at the foot of a ladder with books strewn about him. His neck was broken. It did not take long to conclude that he had fallen from the ladder in the act of replacing books while working late. The slight odour of whisky created a certain inevitability about this conclusion. The most disturbing feature of the business was what had become of Mr. Hewell after his fall: There were signs that the body had been disturbed by rats. It was then that the powers that be decided that the library should have a cat. They had made use of cats in the past, but there was no current feline incumbent.

This tragic event left open the position of head librarian. It was supposed by the library staff that Mr Grantham, Mr. Hewell's immediate deputy, was likely to be promoted. This, however, did not come to pass, much to the chagrin of Mr. Grantham. Instead, an outside man was brought in, one Mr. White. White was a well-spoken man of about forty-five, short in stature with a shock of thick, prematurely whitened hair. He had a curious habit of peering up through his pince-nez with his head thrust forward, but he was an amiable man and had a very quiet, unassuming demeanour.

Mr. White was accompanied in his new post by a feline companion. The cat was his own, and he wished to bring the creature to work with him to act as a library cat. He said that he always found a cat to be a very useful

4

presence in old buildings, where rats were not uncommon. This, he said, was particularly so in libraries, where books were often the victims of these uninvited visitors. Besides, he stated, cats were such a soothing influence, and so quiet and light of foot as to cause no disturbance to the academic pursuits of the students and professors.

For that reason, previously stated, permission was readily granted; indeed, to be able to fill the positions of librarian and library cat in one move was deemed highly fortuitous.

She was a fine specimen, that cat. A beautiful Persian with a coat of pure snow-white, rather like that of her master. She was an elegant creature; she padded silently about the place, never troubling anyone but always answering the pattings and fussings of the academics with friendly purrings.

She seemed especially fond of the young students, rubbing against their legs and making friends all round; in fact, she seemed to produce an almost mesmeric effect upon them, her mere presence seeming to calm any attacks of examination nerves. In no time she was as much a part of the library as were the books.

'She is such a gentle creature, Mr. Bennett,' said Mr. White, 'but she is a regular terror when she is after her prey.' I could well believe it, for since her arrival we had scarcely seen a rat or mouse about the place; not alive, at any rate. I think she acted as a deterrent to rodents more than anything else, and yet there was the inevitable consequence of the occasional dead rat to be dealt with. She must have been a very precise and skilled killer, for she never tore them apart; the only injury was a single bite mark.

I got on well with Mr. White, for he was a likeable sort of chap; he got on well with everyone, except perhaps Mr. Grantham, who was just a little inclined to be resentful. One afternoon when the library had closed, I went into the town to run some errands and was returning to my lodgings when I bumped into Mr White in the street with a young lady. He greeted me cordially and introduced the young lady as his younger sister, Mary. Indeed, she seemed much younger, she being his half-sister by his father's second marriage, as he later explained. She was an attractive girl with fair hair, which shone almost silver in the afternoon sun, and her eyes were a vibrant emerald green. There was a delicacy about her that suggested recent illness, but for all that, there was still a rosy glow to her cheeks that was most becoming. She smiled upon me very sweetly as her brother introduced us.

We fell into easy conversation, and as my lodgings and their cottage lay in the same direction, we walked homewards together.

We had gone a little way when White pulled up suddenly and said, 'There is Professor Sanders. I did just want a word with him. Would you be so good as to excuse me? I shan't be but a moment.'

'Of course, Henry,' answered his sister. Miss White turned and watched her brother as he trotted nimbly across the road and hailed Professor Sanders.

As she turned, something arrested my attention: on one side of her neck, mostly concealed by the collar of her dress, was a portion of a scar, like that produced by a burn. She turned back and caught my curious gaze. Instinctively, she raised her hand to cover the mark. Then she smiled and let her hand fall again.

'You were looking at my scar, Mr. Bennett,' she said placidly. There was no note of reproach.

'I am terribly sorry,' said I. 'I did not mean...' I floundered.

She saved me from my awkward apologies. 'That is quite all right. I'm afraid I was once the victim of a vitriol throwing.'

'Good heavens! Are you serious?'

'Quite serious. A young man I knew wished to marry me, but when I refused him...'

'Miss White, you horrify me. I hope the scoundrel received the full penalty of the law.'

She smiled a thin knowing smile, with just a trace of bitterness. 'Oh, rest assured, he received the appropriate punishment; do not fear on that account. As for this,' she said, touching her collar lightly, 'it grieved me at first, but I have since grown used to it. It is what it is and cannot be undone.'

'You are a very brave young lady if I may say so, Miss White.'

'You may say so,' she said playfully. 'Whether you are right or not is not for me to say.' She smiled at me again; it was a very pretty smile. At that moment her brother returned to us with his apologies, and we resumed our walk. That evening I found my thoughts turning more than once to the beautiful Miss White. I found myself hoping that we should meet again.

The following morning, I was approached in the library by a certain Dr Andrews. He was a graduate of the college and, therefore, retained the right to use the library. He was semi-retired, keeping on only a few patients and acting as a visiting physician to the small private infirmary attached to the university. His rooms and small practice were in the town, so we saw a good deal of him in the library.

Though his hair was grey, he still maintained all the liveliness of youth, and his dark brown eyes would often twinkle with a hint to the mischievous nature within. During the course of our frequent interactions, we had struck up something of a friendship. I, therefore, greeted him warmly when I saw him that day.

'Ah, my young friend,' said he. 'How are you this fine morning?'

'I am well, I thank you, Doctor, and yourself?'

'Good, good. I am hoping you can help me. I am after a particular book; I have the name of it here.' He reached into his breast pocket and produced from it a slip of paper, which he handed to me.

I took the paper and, looking over the details, said, 'This should be in the folklore class upstairs at the far end. Would you like me to go and look it out for you?'

'If you would be so kind; you will be quicker than I, and I am on my way to pay a call.'

I went on my errand, and when I returned, I found the doctor in conversation with Mr Grantham. 'I am sorry, Doctor,' said I, 'but I'm afraid the book is out. I have checked our records to make sure, and it seems the book was due back yesterday. I am really very sorry.'

'Not at all, my boy. I can easily come back another time.'

Mr. Grantham was frowning. 'Overdue, eh? Who took it out?'

'Professor Perkins, sir.'

'Well, really, I might have guessed it. Professor Perkins is an excellent man, no doubt about it, but he is prone to be a little absent-minded,' said Mr. Grantham apologetically. 'Mr. Bennett, would you be so good as to step across to the professor's rooms and remind him, please?'

'Certainly, Mr. Grantham,' I replied.

The doctor laughed. 'I shall go with you, my boy. As a matter of fact, it was Perkins I was on my way to see. His forgetfulness is not one of the vagaries of age: we were in one or two of the same societies in our youth, and he was just as bad then.'

So, we set out together, the doctor and I, on the short walk to the building that housed the professor's rooms. As we approached the professor's door, we were nearly flattened by a youth descending from the floor above at great speed.

'Oh, I do beg your pardon, gentlemen,' stammered the flustered youth. 'I need help; it's Webber; he is ill or dying, I don't know.'

The doctor sprang into action. 'I am a doctor. Where is he?'

'Follow me.' The youth turned and darted back up the stairs to the landing above, with us at his heels. He threw open a door and beckoned us inside. We passed hurriedly through the sitting-room and into the bedroom. Lying prostrate on the floor was another student. His face was deathly pale.

The doctor rushed to his side and took his pulse.

'Help me get him on to the bed, Bennett,' said he. We each grabbed the stricken youth under an arm and hoisted him onto the bed. 'What has gone on here? What has happened to him?' the doctor demanded.

'I don't know, Doctor,' said the excitable youth. 'He was perfectly well when I left him last evening. We arranged to meet in my rooms this morning to study a new text together, but when he did not come up, I came down to see what was keeping him. The door was not locked, and he did not answer my calls, so I came in and found him like that. I say, is he going to be all right?'

'You swear to me that he has met with no injury?' the doctor asked, looking sternly at the frightened youth.

'None to my knowledge, sir,' the youth answered.

'All right, then. Be a good lad and run down to Professor Perkins and ask him for a little brandy. Tell him Doctor Andrews sent you; it will be quite all right.' the doctor instructed. The youth was off as fast as his feet would carry him.

The doctor removed his patient's collar, which was already half unfastened. As he did so he gave a gasp, and I fancied I heard him curse under his breath.

'What is the matter?' I asked. 'Is it serious?'

9

For answer, he pointed at the throat of the patient. I looked and saw two angry red spots on the pallid skin. He undid the young man's waistcoat and the top buttons of his shirt, then bent forward to listen to his heart. I was about to ask him what it meant when the other student returned with the brandy.

'All right, my boy,' said the doctor to the youth as he took the brandy. 'You can leave it to me now. You might be so good as to step across to the library and give this note to Mr. Grantham.' He put the brandy down and, producing a notebook and pencil from his pocket, scribbled down a few hurried lines before tearing out the page and handing it to the student. The youth nodded and left the room without a word.

'I thought it as well to let Grantham know that I am now borrowing you,' he said as he rubbed a little of the brandy on the patient's lips. 'I may need your help; the friend is too shaken up to be of much use in the sick room. Ah! He is reviving.'

The patient groaned a little, and his eyelids fluttered open. 'What happened?' he asked, looking from one to the other of us.

'I was about to ask you the same question,' said the doctor. 'My name is Doctor Andrews. We just ran into your friend, or rather he ran into us; he told us you were ill. Do you remember anything?'

'No. I was all right last night. I stayed up for a while studying. Then I remember nothing until I woke up this morning, but I was still dressed, as you see. I must have fallen asleep or passed out without undressing, but I don't remember going to bed. I felt pretty terrible, so I just stayed where I was for a while. Then I remembered that I was late to meet Rogers, so I made the effort to get up, but I came over sick and dizzy and...well, I suppose I must have fainted,' said the youth, his cheeks reddening slightly under his pallor. 'I say, I am sorry to have given so much trouble. I'm afraid I must have given Rogers a fright: he is a nervish sort of fellow.'

He tried to sit up, but was evidently still weak. The doctor pushed him back down gently. 'Just lie still for the moment. I have some questions I want to put to you. Do you wish Mr. Bennett to wait outside? He has been assisting me here; he works in the library, so he is quite used to fetching and carrying and maintaining silence,' said the doctor with a smile and that familiar twinkle in his eye.

'Yes, I have seen the gentleman before,' said Webber with a weak smile. 'No, that is quite all right; I have no objection.'

'Very well, then. I am concerned about this loss of time you have experienced. You say you have no recollection of coming to bed?'

'None whatever.'

'Do you have any pain anywhere? No headache or tenderness?' asked the doctor as he made an examination of his patient's skull.

'No. Other than feeling a little weak and dizzy, I feel quite well.'

'You have some marks on your throat. How did you come by those?'

'On my throat?'

'Yes. You do not recall how you got them?'

'No. Let me see.' I passed him a shaving mirror from the washstand in the corner. 'Why, so I have,' he said in surprise. 'I suppose I must have caught a pimple or two in shaving. I cannot think how else I came by them.'

The doctor said nothing further about the marks. He turned to me. 'Now, friend Bennett, if you will step into the other room with me a moment, I should like a brief word with you before I send you back to your duties.'

We went into the sitting-room once more and closed the door behind us. The doctor said, 'You may return to your library now, but I wonder if you would be good enough to call on me this evening? Come for dinner. There is a matter I would wish to discuss with you, away from here. Will you come?'

'Certainly, I shall.'

'Excellent! I shall see you at about seven o'clock? Good, good. Now, you had best be off before Mr. Grantham reprimands me for failing to return you.'

So, I returned to my work, and thought no more about the fainting student until the dinner hour. I was under the impression that it was something to do with that case that the doctor wished to discuss; something about the wound on the student's throat had evidently disturbed him. Yet he made no reference to the matter during dinner.

Much of the meal was passed in discourse about books, which was only natural given our common interest. It was not until after dinner, when we were ensconced in his study with a decanter of port, that he raised the subject which was foremost in his thoughts.

'What did you make of our young patient today? As a layman, what would you have said was wrong with him?' he asked.

'Well, to the layman, it looked like a simple fainting fit,' I answered.

'And the memory loss?'

'It did occur to me that he might have been drinking. He would not be the first.'

'No indeed. In fact, I put that very question to him myself after you left. He swore to me very earnestly that he had not touched a drop, and I believed him. Besides, you heard him say that he had no headache or pain of any kind. I was young myself once, and I know that it is not likely that a man should drink enough to affect him so and yet escape the consequent headache.' He smiled.

'I suppose a head injury could not be to blame, for the same reason,' I said.

'Just so.' He looked down into the depths of his port glass in silence for a moment, as though he sought the answer to his conundrum there. Finally, he spoke. 'Would it surprise you to know that he was suffering from considerable blood loss?'

'Blood loss? But I saw no bleeding, nor any signs of it on his clothes or on the floor. Did he bleed elsewhere?'

'No, I do not think so. I examined him more thoroughly after you left; except for the marks on his throat, there was no injury at all on his person.'

'Yes, I wanted to ask you about those.' I said. 'They seemed to trouble you. I could see nothing in them, but I suppose your physician's eyes saw more than I did.'

'It was not through the lens of my medical experience that I viewed those marks.'

'How then?' I asked.

'Ah, we will come to that. So: we have a patient with considerable blood loss, yet the only injuries he has sustained are two puncture marks on his throat.' He must have seen the expression of surprise on my face, for he said, 'Oh yes, you did not see as closely as I; they were punctures, not pimples. How, then, did he lose the blood? and if he bled so considerably, where is the evidence on his clothes and bed linen?'

'I cannot imagine,' I answered, bewildered. 'A bite of some kind might account for the marks, perhaps, but the blood loss I cannot understand.'

'A bite, yes. I believe you are nearer the mark than you think when you say that.'

'But the blood; what could have caused that? What kind of creature could drain that much blood with so little injury?'

'What indeed?'

'I have heard of certain bats that live on blood,' I mused.

'In England?'

'The zoo might have lost a specimen.'

'My boy, such bats, although they do occasionally bite humans, could never take enough blood to cause a man any real bother. No, no, it will not do.'

'What, then, could take so much blood? Without it being deliberately withdrawn... What is it?' The doctor's eyes had a strange light in them. 'You are surely not suggesting that someone deliberately withdrew this young fellow's blood?'

'Why not?'

'But for what end? Why are there no signs of assault? A fit young chap would surely put up a fight. Why does he remember nothing?'

'You have not, perhaps, seen what a skilled mesmerist can do.'

'Mesmerism! Doctor, you are quite making my head spin.'

'I am sorry, my boy. Have some more of this very excellent port, for I fear I may yet spin your head so far as to unscrew it.' He smiled at me as he poured me another glass. 'Although, before the night is over,' he said, 'you will likely believe it is my head that has come unscrewed.'

'Never,' I laughed.

He looked at me steadily and said, 'You say that now, but I was once in the position you are in, so I know how outlandish my words will sound. I myself refused to give credence to what I was told, until such proofs were before me as I could not deny.'

'What are you saying?' I asked, full of wonder and a growing sense of unease.

'You proposed two theories just now: one, that a bat sucked out this young man's blood, and two, that a person drained the blood for some purpose of their own. Supposing I told you that both of your theories were half right?'

I frowned in perplexity. 'I don't follow,' I said.

'Ah, you do not yet see. By the way, those bats you spoke of just now, you know that their common name is vampire bats. Do you see now what I'm driving at?' He watched my face as he spoke and saw the sudden start of comprehension there. 'I see that you do,' he said.

'My dear doctor, you're surely not seriously suggesting that this young man was attacked by... by a vampire? Why, I might be talking to Doctor Polidori rather than Doctor Andrews,' I said, smiling, for I thought he was jesting with me. 'Such tales belong to the world of fiction and folklore.'

To my astonishment, he answered me very seriously, and there was real emotion in his voice. 'Ah, did I not tell you that you would come to doubt my sanity? I, a man of science, claiming my patient was the victim of a vampire?'

I was at a loss for words. 'I do not doubt your sanity, Doctor, but how can you give credence to such a thought?'

'Did I not also tell you that I too was once in your position?' He put his glass down upon the table as he spoke, his hand beginning to shake. 'Nay, more than that, my boy,' he said, and to my surprise, in a sudden and swift movement he unbuttoned the collar of his shirt and exposed to me the bare flesh of his throat. I leaned forward. Old and faded as they were, I could clearly see the two white scars in the corresponding place to the student's wounds. There was moisture in his eyes now as he cried, 'I too was once the victim of a vampire!'

The silence hung heavy in the air, and time seemed to halt. Only the ticking of the clock on the mantelpiece told me of the passage of the seconds that ran into minutes. What was I to believe? What was I to say? The doctor rebuttoned his collar and gradually regained his composure with the aid of another glass of port.

'I think,' said I, 'that you had better tell me all.'

The doctor nodded. 'It was in my youth. I was a young man in love. She was the most enchanting girl I ever knew, but she was frail. When a sickness swept through the town, she was carried off. Though it was not wholly unexpected, it was, nevertheless, a devastating blow.

'There was in the town an eccentric old chap by the name of Hawkins. He was a scholar and a voracious reader. Any obscure subject you cared to name; he would know something of the matter. His house was full of rare and obscure volumes. So when he came to me, when my grief was still raw within me, talking of vampires, I spoke harshly to him; I told him his studies had turned his brain. I was hurt and angry.

'How we argued and what was said need not be dwelt on. But I tell you this: all my doubts were ended when I stormed out into the night and came face to face with my love, walking towards me through the darkness. There had been no doubt about her death, yet there she was, with an apparent strength and vitality, a robustness of health that had been absent in life.

'I was incapable of movement, incapable of any rational thought. Every fibre of my being was caught up in the horror and the wonder of she who was before me. I felt the almost irresistible magnetism she worked over me as she beckoned to me. My steps never faltered; in a moment I was in her arms, listening as she promised me immortal life. I did not care for immortality, only for her. I felt her teeth sinking into my flesh and the cold tingling of my veins as she drew my blood from me.

'It was then that Hawkins appeared. God rest that good man, my saviour, for he drove back the fiend that wore my sweetheart's visage, drove it back with prayers and the cross he held before him like a shield. Once the spell was broken, I was horrified at the fate that had nearly befallen me.

'At the break of dawn, we were in the churchyard, and there we unearthed the grave of my love, working in haste, for no one must see us. There we found her. Hawkins drove a stake through her heart. She screamed when it pierced her heart, yet no one in the neighbouring houses looked out, for none who heard that cry could ever have mistaken it for human. Beneath the flesh of the girl, it was possible to see something else moving and writhing, the parasite that wore her skin. Then I saw the look of peace, of love and contentment pass over her features, and I knew that in death she was once more the girl I had loved. I could not stay for the next part; God help me, I could not. Hawkins told me it was necessary to remove her head, that she may not rise again.'

I had listened in silence; now I started in horror.

'Yes, you are appalled by the thought of it,' said the doctor, 'but imagine what it was to me, who had loved her in life.'

'What do you propose to do?' I asked after a further spell of silence, in which my thoughts weighed heavily upon me.

'I have advised young Webber to spend the night with friends. I do not know if he is in any further danger. Whoever this creature is, it could have killed him, but it did not. It is well, for to die by the bite of a vampire is to rise as one of them. I must know who the vampire is before I can defeat it.'

'But why tell me all this?' I asked.

'Because I am not as young as I was the last time I faced such a creature. If I should fail, or worse, I need to know that you will finish the job... and do whatever needs to be done.'

I understood his meaning. If he was to die, he did not wish to join the tale of his enemies.

'Are you with me?' he asked.

'I trust you, Doctor. If you say it is so, then I must believe you. But I must be sure that the person you believe to be responsible is really a vampire, or I cannot sanction what you suggest. If an innocent should be killed in error, I could not live with that; nor, I think, could you.'

'You wish for proof; that is fair. It is the way of the scientist. I promise you, you shall be sure.'

'I must think this over,' I said as I rose to take my leave. 'You have given me much to think on.'

'Yes, my boy, think on what I have said. Take care on your way home: the night grows dark, and it is in the hours of darkness when these creatures are at their strongest. But do not drop your guard even in the daylight, for though the night is strength to them, they may walk by day or night. Now go.'

I slept little that night. What had I committed myself to? The marks upon the doctor's throat and the utter conviction with which he had told his story had forced my belief; yet could I, now that I was alone, in the light and reason of the nineteenth century, really believe in vampires? Yet I believe there is a region in the minds of most people that still reserves a place for the primordial fears of our ancestors. If one could accept the presence of a benign influence on our lives, then why should one not also acknowledge the workings of a malign and opposite influence?

The following day, I was about my work in the library when the nervous student of the previous day, Rogers, came in. When he saw me, he came over and thanked me for my help. I enquired after his friend.

'Oh, he is going on much better now, thank you. Your doctor friend says he will be perfectly all right. I think there must be something going around. Campbell's not well this morning, and I'm not quite up to the mark myself.'

I looked at the young man. Owing to his general nervous demeanour, I had not observed at first the pallor of his face. I noticed now; I noticed too how he fidgeted with his collar.

I decided that I should tell the doctor about this development. The man himself appeared during the course of the morning. He spoke cheerfully to me and said, 'Ah, I wanted to ask you about a certain book.' As he spoke, he led me away to a less populated corner of the library. When we were alone, his face suddenly became very serious. 'I have been called to see another student this morning. Same symptoms,' he said.

'Campbell?' I asked.

'Yes. You have heard?'

'That nervy chap, Rogers, was in earlier; he mentioned it. By the way, I think you ought to take a look at him. He wasn't feeling well, and he was pretty pale,' I said.

'His throat?'

'I couldn't see, but he kept rubbing at his collar as though it was bothering him. There may be nothing in it beyond an excess of starch.'

'In light of what we are dealing with, I had better be sure. I will call on him.'

'No need,' said I. 'There he is, over there.' I pointed out Rogers, who was making for the desk to take out a pile of books. He was evidently still weak, for he swayed and staggered under the weight. The doctor left my side, and an instant later was standing with a hand on the unfortunate student's shoulder. He helped relieve the young man of his burden, and they left together.

I felt something touch my ankle, and I looked down to see the cat watching me intently.

The doctor called on me that evening to tell me that I was right about Rogers: he too had been afflicted with the same wounds that his friend had suffered.

'I have communicated with some of my colleagues to see if they have any similar cases, especially any in which the patient has died,' said the doctor. 'We must find this vampire before things go any further. It is no easy task, for it is not true that they must sleep in their graves, as some would have it. True, the grave is often the safest refuge, but it is not a necessity.'

'So, it could be anyone?' I asked.

'There are certain clues, peculiarities that may give the creature away, such as its aversion to the cross. But take care: if it knows it is exposed, it could mean danger; it may strike as a cornered animal will. Those fangs are deadly and efficient.'

'Like Mr. White's cat,' I mused aloud.

The doctor started. 'What is that you say?'

'Sorry, I was just thinking how like Mr. White's cat your description sounds. She never leaves a mark on the rats, except for a couple of teeth marks. Swift and deadly.'

'What does White feed this cat of his?'

'I've no idea; I have never seen it eat.'

The doctor's face had grown very grave. 'I mislike this, Bennett.'

'Why? What do you mean?'

'It is another peculiarity of the vampire that it can take the form of an animal when it wishes.'

'Are you suggesting that Mr. White's cat is a vampire?' I asked incredulously.

'The attacks started shortly after his arrival, did they not?'

'Well, yes...' I admitted.

'Or perhaps before.'

'Before?'

'I am thinking of Mr. Hewell.'

'But White came because Hewell died,' I countered.

'Did he? Or was it the other way around?'

'But that was an accident. His neck was broken.'

'Just because a vampire can kill by its bite does not mean it cannot kill by other means. If the creature fed first, who would know? The damage done by the rats would obscure the traces.'

The thought made the bile rise in my throat. 'Will the rats become vampires too?' I asked as the sudden horrific thought presented itself.

'Thankfully, no; the vampire can only turn humans.'

'Well, thank heaven for that, at least. Do you suspect White too, then?'

'I cannot be sure; he may know nothing or everything; he may be one of them, or only this thing's creature.'

The doctor left me that night with instructions to observe White carefully. It was only after he left that I realised I had neglected to tell him about Miss White. It could surely make no difference, for how could anyone suspect a young woman as lovely as she of being a blood-sucking fiend?

The following morning brought two more victims amongst the students. It could no longer go unnoticed by the college authorities, and the doctor gave orders that anyone with the reported symptoms of the "sickness" should be admitted to the infirmary. I, for my part, observed White carefully, but he never betrayed any sign of being anything other than a perfectly normal, mild-mannered librarian.

Later that day, things took an unexpected turn. I was engaged in replacing a number of books when the silence of the library was shattered by a startled cry from the far end of the upper gallery. I left what I was doing and ran up the stairs and along to the far end, in the direction of the disturbance. The sound of echoing footsteps reverberating around the gallery told me that several other people had the same idea. We converged on a scene that sent a thrill of terror through my heart. Standing in stunned silence was a student; at his feet was the body of Mr Grantham, dead and ghastly pale. Upon his throat were two familiar puncture marks.

The implication was terrible. If the doctor was right, Grantham would rise again as one of the undead. My friend spoke earnestly to me that night of our duty. The body must be staked and beheaded; it was the only way to prevent his rising. In spite of my reservations, we made our arrangements.

The doctor gave orders that the body should be placed in a side room in the infirmary building. As Grantham's sister was his only relative, and she was abroad and unable to return before burial must take place, there was no difficulty in hastening the arrangements. It made our task easier. The doctor placed a cross on the body in the meantime, which he hoped would guard against its rising until more permanent measures could be taken.

Once the body was coffined and ready for burial, we acted. Despite my doubts and protests about the necessity of what the doctor intended to do, I found myself in the infirmary after dark, holding his bag while he worked away to unscrew the coffin lid. It was a dubious position to be in if we were caught. I wondered what the penalty was for the decapitation of a corpse.

'Think what further harm we may prevent by our actions,' the doctor reasoned. 'What harm can we do if we are wrong? The man is already dead.'

As we had been leaving his house that night, the doctor had stopped suddenly in the doorway, fumbled in his pocket with a shaking hand, and brought out a bottle. He had looked at it for a moment before taking a long drink from it.

'What is that?' I had asked.

'Something which may save our lives. Here, drink.'

I had taken the bottle from him and drunk deep. 'Why, it is only water!' I had said in surprise.

'Holy water. It is just an idea I had. It may come to nothing.'

I could not understand his actions, but now that we were about our macabre duty, I felt oddly comforted by them.

In a short time, the lid was off. The doctor's sudden hiss of breath told me of his surprise. This was a development we could not have foreseen. Someone had been there before us. I fought the feeling of nausea that welled up in my stomach. The head had been stricken from the body, and a wooden stake had been driven through the heart. The task we had come to perform had been performed by another!

'What does this mean?' I asked, averting my eyes from the grisly spectacle.

'I cannot say. We are in dark waters here, dark and dangerous.'

He looked around and found the cross he had left with the body on a side table. The undertakers must have removed it when they placed the body in the coffin. He looked at it for a moment, then put it into his pocket. His expression was thoughtful. Working quickly, he replaced the lid once more and we left the ghastly room.

As we emerged into the air, a movement between the shadows caught our attention.

'Look,' I hissed. 'It is the cat.'

'Quickly, let us follow it.' We followed silently for some time, keeping to the shadows, as the cat made its way between the buildings toward the library. Then the doctor seized my arm and whispered, 'Look, it is entering the library; the door is open.'

As we tiptoed into the library, all was dark save for a streak of moonlight that shone down the central aisle of the ground floor. The cat was padding along the aisle. As she moved away from us, a change came over her. Instead of receding from view, she seemed to grow the further away from us she got. Then the outline of the feline began to morph into the silhouette of a woman before being swallowed by the shadows.

I could not fathom what I had seen. The silence of the vacant library felt thick and oppressive. The air pulsed with an ominous stillness.

'Who is she?' the doctor whispered.

'It is White's sister.'

'You did not tell me he had a sister!' he said reproachfully.

'I forgot. Then I did not think it mattered. You said it was White or the cat or both. I did not know she was the cat! Oh, my head. This is too much. She seemed so gentle, so innocent.'

'Ah!' he exclaimed. 'You have forgotten that a beautiful face can mask a face of evil.'

'That is so,' came a voice from behind us, cold and hard as steel, 'and the face of virtue may be ugly as sin.' It was White. He had entered silently behind us and was standing, grinning at us with a look of utter malice. Gone were the genial expressions and good humour. He was blocking our exit.

'You know, gentlemen, it is really bad manners to follow a lady,' said Miss White as she stepped back into view. The sound of her footsteps echoed around the deserted space.

'You are no lady!' cried the doctor. 'You are a fiend.'

'A fiend, is it? What harm have I done? I have taken a little blood from your young men. They can spare it. They are so strong and vigorous. I needed them to regain my strength. You see, Mr. Bennett, I did not really lie to you. I was injured by a young man who had once wished to marry me, but it was not vitriol with which he burned me; it was holy water. I have not truly hurt anyone, so why should you oppose me?'

'Not hurt anyone? Hewell and Grantham are dead!' I cried.

She frowned. Her beautiful features hardened. 'Hewell was necessary. We needed freedom to move around the university so I could find suitable prey.

Grantham was not my doing.' She threw a withering look at her brother. 'You got careless, Henry,' she growled.

'I was thirsty! It gets so dry and dusty in here, and he was becoming a nuisance, trying to undermine me,' White answered. 'I did not mean to kill him, but he was weak.'

'Then it was you who staked him. But why?' I asked, my voice faltering. 'Was he not one of you?'

'He was, or would have been if permitted to rise, but we could not risk an unseasoned vampire exposing us. Besides, more vampires mean more competition. I was protecting our interests and cleaning up my brother's mess. But why are we arguing? I could make an exception for you, sir,' she said, fixing me with those emerald eyes. She came towards me in the moonlight, beautiful and alluring, and I could not in my heart reconcile the undead fiend and murderer with that vision of loveliness. 'We could share so much; we could share eternity together. Come to me,' she said enticingly, and the words oozed like honey from her full pink lips. I felt myself drawn to her in powerless rapture. In that moment she held an irresistible attraction. I found myself walking towards her.

'No!' cried the doctor's voice. He grabbed my arm and threw me aside. He held out the cross before him, and the she-devil drew back in alarm with the hiss of an angry feline.

White launched himself at the doctor's back. The cross went flying.

'Go, Mary,' White shouted. 'Save yourself.' She skirted around us and fled through the door behind him. I began to look around for the cross to go after her.

'I advise you to forget any foolish notions you have of trying to fight,' said White. He was standing once more with his back to the door, with his hand around the doctor's throat. 'If you struggle, it will be worse for you, and it does so impair the flavour.' To my horror, I saw the two great fangs descend, and before I could act, he sank them into the doctor's throat.

Then came the screaming; it took a moment before I realised it was coming not from the doctor but from White. Smoke was rising from his mouth.

'The holy water in my bloodstream,' cried the doctor.

The air filled with the smell of burning flesh as the corrosive blood ate away at White. He fell to the floor shrieking, clutching at his burning mouth and throat.

The doctor reached into his fallen bag and grabbed the stake meant for Grantham. He drove it into the writhing creature's heart with all the strength of his fury. Then, acting quickly, he took his instruments from his bag and removed the head. At first, I watched the proceedings with a mixture of horror and a kind of morbid fascination before I had to look away. The grisly deed accomplished, the body collapsed in and disintegrated until only the skeleton remained.

'What happened?' I gasped.

'He has been dead longer than Grantham,' the doctor said simply. 'He has returned to the state that death would naturally have rendered.'

There is no room in these pages to go into the details of how the skeleton was found in the library and the subsequent confusion it caused, along with the unexplained disappearance of Mr. White. I think I can safely leave that to the imagination of the reader. Suffice to say, it was a talking point for some time to come.

As for me, my next chapter is as yet unwritten. I live in hopes of one day finding the fiend with the beautiful face, who so nearly cost me my life and my soul, and of giving to her the same peace the doctor gave her brother. If the opportunity should arise, I pray heaven I have the strength to do it.

FASHIONED CREATURES
BY MEG HAFDAHL

The heavy tote bag, with Joe Camel printed in dull color on either side, created a throbbing crescent in the flesh of Eddy's shoulder. She stopped at the entrance steps of the South Minneapolis library to adjust the straining handle.

Evening light, a rare and potent magenta, flooded the stone stairs as Eddy hiked upward. Joe Camel slapped at her sweaty, polka-dot t-shirt. She navigated around a group of teenagers on the top, cracked landing. They smelled of clove cigarettes and honked in immature, oddly rhythmic laughter. Eddy didn't care about them. Or about the summer evening coming to a close in a spray of artful beauty.

She cared only about the enormous folder of papers inside her bag.

On his way out, a man, dressed rather formally in a bowtie and sweater vest, held one of the glass, front doors open for Eddy. She whisked by him, grateful for the cool, vaguely musty air of the library on her hot cheeks. The scent, of old books and moist bricks, gave her the first good feeling of the day.

And it had been a rotten one. The kind of day which, before that precise moment, had made her both furious and exhausted. Dr. Ambrose had given her his smug look. He had tapped his pen on his bony knee, speaking to her as though she were an infant. As though she hadn't done her research. The nurse, the one with the tight bun and the cat-eyeglasses, she'd even rolled her eyes at Eddy.

Rolled her damn eyes.

This memory sent a rapid, sharp slice of anger through Eddy's gut.

But the library, in its familiarity, quickly soothed.

It was grand, old building that had gone through a number of transformations since its birth in the early twentieth century. There were still remnants of its former glory; like the jeweled, though dusty, chandeliers which hung over the homeless and barely-dressed with twinkling irony. Olive green carpet, more fashionable in the last decade, gave way to hulking shelves that did their best to block out anything but the yellow, unnatural light from above.

Eddy turned at the front display of new fiction, ignoring glossy hardcovers by Danielle Steele and Isaac Asimov. She nearly bumped into an elderly woman dressed in clodhoppers who held a Dean Koontz.

"Oh!" The woman clutched the book even tighter to her chest.

Eddy shrugged as she determinedly made her way to the quiet, far left section of the first floor.

"Good evening, Eddy." Richard stopped pushing a metal cart full of reference books in order to wave in her direction.

Eddy kept moving. "It's a scorcher."

"That's why I stay in here." He gave a slow, rumbling laugh that made her feel at home. Richard was *always* there.

"I might just sleep here tonight," Eddy said over her throbbing shoulder. "My place doesn't have AC."

Richard continued his reliably affable laugh. "Yes, ma'am. I wouldn't blame you."

She heard the squeal of the cart's wheels as he moved forward.

"Say," Richard stopped again. "How's your health, Eddy? On the mend?"

At the honey-sweet sympathy in his tone, a burst of soothing relief, more potent than the cool, library air, filled her lungs. "I'm up and down. Good days and bad, you know?"

Richard scratched at his patchy beard. "Oh yup, I know. I have a touch of arthritis in my knees. On a muggy day like this they can get up to something fierce if they got mind to. Not too bad, today, I'd say, not too bad at all."

"Ah, sure, sure." Eddy spotted the edge of her favorite table, peeking out from the medical reference aisle. She left Richard, wondering if he'd finished talking as she rounded the corner.

A woman sat in Eddy's chair.

"Wha...?" There was a squeak at the end of the half-word that surprised both Eddy and the bitch who'd taken her spot.

"Sorry?" She scrunched up her young face, creating deep worry lines on her forehead.

Eddy scoffed. "That's where I sit."

The woman's fingers tightened on the orange chair's smooth arm. She glanced at the three identical chairs surrounding the worktable. "We can share, or, I think," she thumbed over her shoulder, "there are a few more tables back there, in the alcove."

Anger, as hot and sticky as the summer day, caused Eddy's chin to tremble. Her evening, it seemed, was not going to improve after her visit to the doctor. It was trundling downhill, headed for a sloppy pile of shit. The last time someone sat in her chair, a meek pre-teen, he got right up at the sight of her. He even apologized, real nice, before slinking off.

"You don't understand..." Eddy grabbed at the cutting handle of her bag.

"Ah, ha. Uh-oh." Richard came sauntering behind Eddy with his cart. "You're in Eddy's seat, dear."

The woman, in her early twenties and wearing a pair of thin-framed glasses, leaned back into the chair. She tapped the end of a pencil on the hardcover of *Netter's Anatomy*, a book Eddy knew well. "I didn't know there were assigned spaces." Her smug half-smile made Eddy want to tear her glasses from her pert nose and stomp them to shards. "I'll move over."

She slid *Netter's*, along with a spiral-bound notebook and a handful of pencils and highlighters, to the next spot.

"I like to see sharing." Richard's husky rumble filled the aisle. "Warms my heart." He rolled away.

The woman changed seats with the careless, fluid motion of youth.

Eddy stared at the open chair. It would be hot from the woman's butt. And she wouldn't have the whole table to spread out on.

Yet, her body ached with the hope of sitting down. She allowed the Joe Camel bag to slip onto the wood surface and away from her beleaguered body. It clanged against the woman's pencils, sending a few on the carpet.

That made Eddy smile.

"I'm Veronica." She bent down and grabbed them without looking. "And you're Eddy?"

"Yeah."

Veronica straightened up and then began to drum her fingers across the open pages of the textbook. "I do understand the struggle. I sit in the same spot in my class lecture hall. It's like muscle memory or something."

"Hmm." Eddy plopped into the fabric chair beside Veronica. A jagged ray of the diminishing sun cut across her sweaty forehead. It prodded her eyeball.

The light was all wrong here.

A black depression caught hold of Eddy, reminding her of what little control she held. She wished for a fever, one that rattled her bones and made her lips turn the color of Papa Smurf. Then they would take her in. Then they would bring her ice chips and warmed blankets.

Then they would place a cool washcloth on her forehead like her mother had.

Eddy pulled Joe Camel closer, playing with the floppy handles of the bag. She peered inside at the mountain of papers, wondering where the key was. She'd been certain that it was somewhere inside, the precise fact she needed to make everything perfect. And if she took it, and connected it with something within the vast walls of the Southern Minneapolis Library, it would unlock her life.

Veronica worked studiously beside her, copying down a passage from *Netter's Anatomy* with the reverent smile of someone who'd read a moving piece of poetry.

"Excuse me." Eddy dumped the over-stuffed manila folders out onto the table. They flooded Veronica's studies.

"Oh, wow." She pushed at the bridge of her glasses. "This is quite a collection."

"I'm chronically ill." Eddy scraped the papers back onto her side. "It's long ago come to my attention that I should take a proactive approach to my health. Doctors are only interested in making money and hearing the sound of their own voices of course. Self-important twats."

Veronica's glossy pink lips spread into a delightfully ironic grin.

"What?"

"You're probably right. We are self-important twats."

Eddy sensed a tingling excitement at the realization. "You're a doctor?"

"Almost. Nine more months."

"Makes sense, I guess." Eddy gestured toward *Netter's Anatomy*.

"Yeah, of course that's only if I pass these next series of tests."

Eddy was now glad she hadn't stormed off, and instead chose to stay with Veronica. She was also glad her impressive stack of medical records were on full display.

"And, I'm sorry." Veronica ran a hand through her thick, brown hair.

"Sorry?"

"That you have medical problems. It's good you're staying informed, though, doing your research."

Eddy nodded. She turned toward the nearest row of books, grabbing the familiar green binding of one titled *Multiple Sclerosis and You!*. She made sure to hold the book's front cover, a picture of a man in a wheelchair holding hands with who was presumably supposed to be his smiling granddaughter, so that Veronica could see it.

Veronica did. Eddy watched as she scanned the title before finding interest in her anatomy textbook.

Pleased, Eddy settled back into her chair. She even ignored the growling in her stomach, too excited by this sudden boon to her otherwise rotten day, to be distracted by the thought of cheeseburgers. So she pretended to read the words on the page. Her heart beat erratically, but not at an entirely unpleasant thwump.

The almost-doctor bent to the side, grabbing a Sony Walkman from a leather bag. She slipped the headphones over her lush hair, placing each fluffy earpiece before hitting the rectangular PLAY button.

Eddy stared an image in *Multiple Sclerosis and You!*. It was an artless diagram of something called myelin that caused her to feel suddenly quite bleak. Her eyes flitted up to the black cord of the Walkman.

Veronica's head bopped along to music that was silent for the rest of the library. Seemingly entranced by whatever song she listened to, Veronica highlighted long strings of esoteric terms in her textbook that even Eddy couldn't decipher.

There was something lacking in *Multiple Sclerosis and You!* It didn't hold quite the same intrigue it had on Eddy's last research trip. She flipped through the pages with the dull sense that it could give her nothing.

Stirred to find something new, Eddy left her files with Veronica. She strolled down the medical reference aisle, heady with its electric pull. Glossy book spines called to her with words like DIAGNOSIS and INCURABLE. She ran her palm, still a bit sweaty, across their delicious letters. Somewhere deep inside she believed the right book would call to her. Not with a robust holler, but with a meek though steady insistence.

I am the one.

Pick me, Eddy.

Eddy obeyed. She pressed the pad of her thumb into the crinkly, plastic edge of the noisy one's spine.

Understanding Crohn's Disease.

Yes! Oh, yes it all made such a wonderful clarity in her mind. White, beautiful light created pathways through her mental cobwebs. Crohn's disease! An autoimmune affliction of the intestine. She would need a colonoscopy, perhaps a bowel resection, and if it was really far gone, she would be fitted with one of those crap bags. What did they call those things? Eddy couldn't remember.

The book would tell her.

Eddy pulled it gingerly from the shelf, enjoying the weight of it in her hand.

A figure shifted to her right.

It was Veronica. Her crimped hair was no longer flattened by her headphones. She held a slender finger to her chin as she thoughtfully perused the books.

Eddy trembled with her new purpose. She cradled the book in the crux of her elbow, curious to discover how it would help her.

"Found what you're looking for?" Veronica turned, jutting her freckled chin toward Eddy's book.

"Sure did!" Eddy grinned.

Veronica gave the title a lingering glance. "You know-"

A peculiar sound, like the tinny whistle of a miniature train interrupted her.

Eddy stared into Veronica's widened pupils, trying to process where a sound like that could come from.

"Did you hear that?"

Before Eddy could answer, the sound came again. It was the shrill cry of wind, trapped and dying.

Veronica raised an eyebrow, studying the single paned window behind Eddy. "It can't be from there."

Eddy glanced over her shoulder at the glimmer of evening. The limbs of an elm tree stood perfectly still. "No wind." She pointed out the obvious.

They waited in the awkward vacuum of their silence, hearing the far-off squeak of Richard's cart. In Historical Fiction, Eddy guessed.

Somewhere a man laughed, the sort of stifled, conscious titter of a person close to the librarian's imposing desk.

This time, when the whistling sound came, it was accompanied by the slightest draft at Eddy's ankles. The sensation prickled the skin above her cork sandals, sending further goose bumps beneath her baggy, linen pants.

"Oh!" Veronica stepped back from the bookshelf, clearly affected by the same gust.

A perfectly pleasant explanation came to the borders of Eddy's mind. The South Minneapolis library had been equipped with some of that state-of-the-art air conditioning. It had kicked in, thank goodness, and soon the stinky sweat between her breasts would evaporate.

But Eddy knew that wasn't true.

Veronica seemed to inherently understand this too, as she crouched down, right beneath where Eddy had found *Understanding Crohn's Disease*, to get a better look.

"A vent or something?" Eddy stroked the cover of her book.

Veronica's curly hair trembled with her strident head shake. "Nuh-uh."

"What...what is it?"

"Look at this," Veronica shimmied down onto her belly. The way she stared beneath the row of books, where there was a gap between the last shelf and the rise of the thick carpet, made Eddy feel hollow. All the good feelings she had about Crohn's Disease dissolved.

The sweat was still there, though. In tacky lines, dribbling from her armpits and stippling her top lip.

"What is it?" She repeated.

"I think if I just..." Veronica yanked at a loose edge of flossy carpet, pulling it back easily.

"WHA..." Eddy yelped. It wasn't; t right. Tearing the library apart. She tripped backward, hitting the opposite shelf with her shoulder.

Ignoring the protest, Veronica swiftly angled up on her knees. She continued to roll back the soft orange flooring, scooting back as it looped its rubbery bottom toward them.

Eddy watched with dumb fascination.

"Do you see that?" Veronica's voice had become a hoarse whisper. "Tell me you see that, Eddy?" She stood, holding a limp corner of carpet.

It was her name, yell-whispered by the pretty almost doctor, which jolted Eddy from her muddy confusion.

Eddy stepped forward.

"Jesus. I see it."

At her toes, right where she had stood as she'd chosen her new book, was a door. It was a crude square made of splintery wood, unlike the smooth subflooring surrounding it. Eddy squatted, noticing how the far-left corner, tucked beneath the shelf, was squished down into a sagging splay of rotting wood.

Another humming breeze escaped from the uneven opening. At this angle, Eddy could smell its must. It was more potent than the old library and its yellowing books. It smelled of acidic soil. And something worse. Something sweet.

"What do you suppose?" Veronica continued to shake her head of curls. "There's not even a proper handle on it."

Eddy snorted at such an insignificant detail. Her knees ached as she rose back up.

Suddenly, a girl appeared at the end of the row. She carried a stack of Judy Blumes and looked as if she were lost in the colorful and distracting thoughts of a preteen. She blinked at the two women and the unfurled carpet, then walked on.

"Should we tell someone? Richard?" Eddy wondered what it might be like to be the person who'd found an important sort of place. Maybe there was treasure down there, a hidden piece of history people had been searching for. Daydreams cloaked her soul. In a matter of seconds, she pictured herself on the six o'clock news, and immortalized in ink in the *Star Tribune*. Maybe she would even be on *Donahue*.

"No!" Veronica hissed. She placed a finger over mouth in the international gesture of *shut the fuck up*. "Not until we get a look."

Eddy nodded.

Veronica's features softened. "You be the lookout while I try to open this thing, okay?"

"Be quiet about it, then." Eddy peered down the row. It was getting late, and thankfully medical reference wasn't exactly the sexiest place to be on a Friday night. Yet, that girl had passed by. What if someone else came? What could she possibly say to divert their attention?

A calming sigh filled Eddy's lungs. She remembered how good she was at stories.

Veronica kneeled down, straining a rip in the thigh of her blue jeans. She placed her hand on the strange door, testing to see if it would be pushed open.

Ancient hinges creaked.

Undeterred, Veronica fit the thumb of her right hand into the crease between door and floor. Disgust rippled across the surface of her face as she dug into the soft wood with her nails. With help from her other hand, she raised the stinking mouth open. It stopped at about her shoulders, prevented from going farther by the lowest shelf of books.

"Oh, holy shit." Veronica breathed. "Look."

Eddy made a quick pass of the row to make sure they were alone. "Is it heavy?"

"Not really."

She crouched beside Veronica, overcome by the gagging scent. "Doesn't that bother you?" Eddy protected her nose with the glossy backside of *Understanding Crohn's Disease.*

"I've been cutting up dead bodies in Dr. Azam's anatomy course. And medical students are the ones stuck draining abscesses, I'm sure you know."

Eddy squinted at the shadows inside the stinking hole.

It couldn't be.

"Stairs?" She squeaked. They were circular and steel. They led to a vast, black void.

"And do you see that, Eddy?" Veronica's stick arms were beginning to tremble under the weight of the door. "It doesn't...there's no sense to it."

"Is that...?"

"Light." Veronica finished Eddy's thought with a giddy hiccup. "It's faint but I see it."

A ghostly shimmer sparkled from below. Every few seconds it was enveloped by the darkness, snuffed out.

"Are we really going to go down there?"

Veronica shifted the position of her hands. "You first. I'll slither down behind you."

That particular imagery made Eddy feel unwell.

"It really stinks." Eddy let her nostrils out from behind the book. The scent hadn't improved.

Veronica shrugged with one shoulder. "I'm not going to let that stop me. What if there are rare books down there? Something we could sell? Medical school is expensive."

"Yeah." Eddy thought once more of the sort of attention this could garner. "Okay, but it's too dark, I won't be able to see my ass from my elbow."

A crackling explosion nearly made Eddy lose her lunch. Veronica rocked backward at the sound, managing to keep hold of the door.

"This is Ms. Mahannah, head librarian." It was the loudspeaker, a relic of the sixties. "I'm reminding you it is now half past seven o'clock. Time to make your final choices, as we close at precisely eight p.m."

Eddy and Veronica shared a relieved glance that a monster had not made that grinding squeal as it leapt from the open hole. It was only Ms. Mahannah and her ancient squawk box.

"We gotta hurry." Veronica set the door's edge on her left shoulder. She pulled a pen from the pocket of her jeans. "Here, take this and lead the way."

Eddy stared at the plain, blue pen in her palm.

"Press the cap down." The eye roll was evident in Veronica's short tone.

Eddy pressed it in, happy to see a rather forceful stream of light.

With reluctance, she set *Understanding Crohn's Disease* on the loose hump of carpet and swung her legs into the hole. The penlight revealed a filigree pattern on the twisting stairs.

Drenched in nervous sweat, Eddy felt for the first step with her sandal. She was surprised by the solid feel beneath her foot.

Cool air gripped at her legs as she submerged herself in the darkness. Eddy took another step, and another, alternatively shining the light at the dusty, clay walls and the dizzying steps as she descended. Veronica came down with a thud, the door snapping closed.

What if it doesn't open?

What if we go missing down here and some janitor kicks the carpet back in place and...?

As if privy to her private panic, Veronica answered; "I gave it a little push, seems like it'll open easy from this angle."

She sounded strange in this cold, secret basement. Eddy turned and shone the light on Veronica's round face. "If we're not quick people'll see that mess up there, and they'll come down. They'll follow us."

"Yeah but we're here first." Veronica was just behind her, breathing hot, eager breath on the back of Eddy's head.

The absurdity of what they were doing ate at the last strands of Eddy's curiosity. She took another step into the abyss, and then abruptly stopped.

Veronica slammed into her, nearly sending them both toppling down the final steps.

Or do these stairs go on forever?

Eddy shuddered. "This is crazy."

A peculiar, breathy laugh tickled her ear. "This is Nancy Drew stuff. If we're lucky we'll find a first edition Bronte secreted down here by that old witch librarian. The worst thing we're going to find is nothing."

Don't be a scaredy-puss, Edwina! Her mother's voice, not all that surprising in this vile, stinking place, filled the inside of her skull.

"I'm not scared."

"Good!" Veronica patted the top of Eddy's head from her place on the higher step. "Let's move."

Eddy shone the slim beam from the penlight on the two final stairs. She carefully stepped down into the soft dirt floor. Veronica joined her, panting from what Eddy guessed was exhilaration. Some people liked scary movies, she supposed, and haunted houses.

Eddy preferred safe, clean places with lots of light. Like the hospital.

"Can you make anything out?"

"That bit of light, it looks like it's coming from over that way." Eddy flicked the pen toward a hallway with a low, sloped ceiling. At the far end there was a smoky, ephemeral hint of light.

"Maybe there's some sort of window or passage that way, causing that wind sound." Veronica reasoned.

"Maybe." Eddy's sweat became cold rivulets. She shivered, daring to walk toward the blackened corridor.

Veronica's feet shuffled behind.

Using the penlight, Eddy glanced up at what was the underbelly of the South Minneapolis Library. Richard and Ms. Mahannah might as well be a million miles away.

Who would make that crude door? And why weren't the stairs dustier? More...more unused?

Eddy turned to look at Veronica.

But her reassuring freckled chin was gone.

Fear beat its strident, thumping drum within Eddy's chest. She swung the light, its illumination weakening by the second, through the entirety of this mud prison. Veronica was not on the stairs, or against the soft walls.

"Where'd you go off to?" She hoped it sounded casual. "Veronica?"

There was only the sound of her own panicked heart.

"Please..." She pleaded. "Where ARE YOU?"

The silence burrowed into her ears. Eddy swallowed down a slow-rising purge of her lunch. She swayed on unstable legs, wishing she'd never come down there. Or to the library. Or, in that awful moment, she wished she'd never settled on Minneapolis. But the doctors had given up on her in Des Moines. And Omaha, and Kansas City, before that.

Whatever the reason, she *was* in the dark. Alone. Beneath the world.

"Eddy." A voice, not in her mind, but a real voice, called for her. It was from the narrow corridor.

"Veronica? How'd you—"

The penlight took one final gasp and then died in Eddy's slick palm.

Complete darkness swallowed Eddy into its cold, inky lair. Tears welled up in the corners of her eyes as she stumbled from one unfamiliar tether to the next. What she thought for one fleeting moment was a stair, was only what felt like a smashed, moldy box.

"HELP!" Fear funneled up her throat, straining at the inside of her cheeks.

Light, uncertain and gossamer, strengthened in her vision. Eddy rubbed her wet eyes with the sleeve of her blouse, then concentrated on the aura.

With nowhere else to go, Eddy followed its promise. She found herself in the low-ceilinged hall, grazing her hands against the crumbling walls.

A door, as damaged and rudimentary as the one that had started all this mess, stood open. This one was larger, and upright. Prickles of light emanated from within.

"Veronica?" Desperation clung to her skin. Eddy stepped into the windowless room, seeing the source of light.

A single, hazy bulb protruded from a battery powered lamp. When her eyes adjusted to the glow, Eddy took in the rest.

There were so many things familiar to her, yet warped in this putrid, dirty room. There was a hospital grade dresser with rotting cans of Fancy Feast littered on top. A broken IV trolley leaned like a drunk against the head of a hospital bed.

Beneath the grimy, yellowed bed covers was a figure.

It breathed with great effort, raising the bed sheet with each hitching gurgle. And, it was, at least in part, the source of that smell.

Eddy frowned, unable to stop the purge she'd been fighting. Her Pizza Hut lunch, three slices of cheese and a large Pepsi, came up in one wet, unceremonious pile.

"Unh!" She fell backward, out into the hall. Her toes were warm from the vomit bath, she noticed, as she struggled to get up.

Eddy stopped, taking in a sour breath while on her knees.

All the questions in her mind had whirred to a stop, too. She could think only of the acid on her tongue and the reptilian fear at the base of her neck.

Something skittered by her.

When she looked up, Eddy saw it had once been human. The dim light from the makeshift hospital room reflected in its tortured eyes.

It moved on amputated arms and legs, hurrying beside her, spiderlike.

It had no teeth.

Eddy tried to scream but only saliva dribbled out, still hot and sticky.

Then, someone had hold of her arm.

She kicked in the dirt, weak with shock.

They dragged her to yet another door, this one shut.

Her shoulder ached from their claw like grasp.

This wasn't happening. She'd fallen asleep in the MRI machine was all, or they'd double dosed her on morphine.

The looming figure used their free hand to knock on the closed door. "It's me."

Eddy cocked her head at the familiar voice.

"Come in, quickly please." A woman, authoritative and from the sound of it, with all her teeth, spoke through the wood.

The door groaned open and Eddy was pulled inside. She was embarrassed by how little she fought.

Bright, sterile light assaulted her eyeballs. She screwed them closed, bringing her knees to her chin in what she knew was a scaredy-puss pose.

Whomever had yanked her through the door left her be. Eddy cradled her legs, rocking back and forth in her infinite horror.

"These are fascinating." The woman who sounded like she was in charge spoke from across the room.

"You're not disappointed?" It was Veronica.

Eddy's eyes popped open. She studied the torn jeans of the med student standing beside her.

Light shone from camping torches.

"Oh, not at all!" The other woman trilled. "Breast cancer, multiple sclerosis, lupus, ovarian cysts, bacterial meningitis...oh let's see here, Huntington's disease!" She gave a pleased laugh.

Anger singed the edges of Eddy's fear. Rage built the beginnings of a fire at the bottom of her belly. She blinked at the large, rather nice desk in front of her.

"Well, hello, Edwina." The proper-looking woman in a white coat stood from her place at the desk.

Eddy arched her neck, incredulous at the sight of her medical files spread across the top.

"I say, you are quite a rare find! All those ailments..."

Eddy furrowed her brow, looking up at Veronica for some sort of explanation.

The young woman grinned down at her with what Eddy now realized was the unhinged pseudo-smile of a madwoman.

"You've really made my day, Eddy. I'm going to learn SO much!" Veronica ran a dirty hand through her curls, leaving a streak of mud on her cheek.

"Yes!" White coat woman sat on the edge of the desk. Her obsidian eyes regarded Eddy with unnatural interest. "A true medical marvel. There will be a vast many treasures to cut out of you."

"No..." The word came out all rusty. "NO."

Joe Camel watched placidly from Eddy's tote bag in the corner. A spark of hope came to her. Her files had come down from another route, surely. And there was that subtle wind, streaming in from somewhere. That meant there was more than one way in and out.

"Don't be modest, Edwina. This is the thickest file I've seen, maybe ever!"

"I have to go." It was a strange thing to say. Eddy tried to stand but Veronica's surprisingly strong grip ushered her back down to the floor.

White Coat took a single, latex glove from her pocket. "The only question is where will we begin? Those cancerous breasts of yours? Or, oh! Shall we examine that diseased spine? Maybe see how you do if we remove it altogether?"

Eddy thought of that creature scuttling through the corridor. She trembled with the certainty of her bleak future.

"I don't..."

"You don't what, dear?"

"I don't have cancer." It was the first time she'd ever said it aloud. "Or...or any of those things."

Veronica erupted in a fit of giggles.

White Coat slipped the glove onto her right hand. "Oh, I know! Lord, I really do know! It doesn't take much reading of those files to understand what I'm looking at."

Fueled by the stoked fire within, Eddy jumped up. She grabbed the door with trembling hands, tripping out into the black hall.

She ran.

Veronica, still laughing, pounced on her back. They tumbled forward, smacking into the bottom stair.

Eddy screamed, reaching for the reassuring steel. Veronica dug her long nails into Eddy's side, yanking her down into the dirt. Younger and stronger, she bested

Eddy. She straddled her, her curly hair tickling Eddy's hot cheeks as she panted noxious breath.

White Coat appeared, carrying an oil lamp.

She kneeled beside the women, with a cool efficiency that scared Eddy more than anything she'd seen that night.

"Why?" She asked, stroking Eddy's lip with a latex thumb.

"Please! Let me go...I won't—"

"Give me a reason, Edwina. Why do you spend your life in a hospital? Why do you tell people you have cancer, hmm? Parade about as if you are sick? Try to convince doctors you have all the diseases of the world?"

Memories of Eddy's mother came to her. The soft touch of her hand, gliding through Eddy's dewy hair. Setting a cool washcloth on her forehead, singing *You Are My Sunshine.* Bringing her tomato soup and saltines.

It was the only time she cared. The only time she noticed Eddy.

It was the only time a girl like her could get any attention.

"I don't know." Eddy lied. "I don't know why."

White Coat removed a hidden syringe from the folds of her coat. "That's what we're going to find out, Edwina. We're going to go in there," she tapped Eddy's forehead with the cold, sharp needle, "and find out."

SAQRA

BY C. BRYAN BROWN

had stood for centuries. Its outer walls, square-cut blocks the size of Buicks that acked and pieced together in the same as the pyramids at Giza, the city of he fortress of Sacsayhuaman, showed t was a single story, the roof as flat as moved up there, and the jungle rose on urely as the sun set in the west. The r in the bright sun, a beacon guiding toward the one blemish, the single d center amidst the flashy rest.

Pamela "Panda" Sayers held up a fist and stopped her team. She surveyed the opening from the jungle. The ground surrounding the structure had been mostly cleared. Here and there roots jutted from the earth. The occasional shrub dotted the landscape; otherwise loose dirt blanketed the area. If Swanson was right—and Panda had no reason to doubt him—no one had been here for nearly three hundred years. Yet what she saw was a well-maintained yard, designed for people to walk around the building uninhibited, free from worrying about a snake the size of a minivan falling from a tree. It was the complete opposite of what was behind her.

It'd been two hard days of hiking through the Peruvian jungle, cutting down weeds taller than her and swatting mosquitoes the size of hummingbirds. They'd made their way northeast from Trujillo to Tarapoto, taking a helicopter over the Andes. From Tarapoto, they'd chartered a boat to take them up the Haullaga toward

Iquitos, but they'd disembarked halfway to the city. The dry season had revealed exactly what Swanson said it would, exactly where he said it'd be.

Stones, similar to the ones used to erect this building, submerged under the water, some fifty feet apart. Their surfaces were cracked and faded from the sun. Plant life had grown up and swayed lazily in the warm water. Panda only saw the top two, but Hamilton counted at least five in his brief dive. According to Swanson, the land here had been much lower all those years ago, and these stones were part of an entranceway to the sacred lands of the Incan Empire.

Panda had remained doubtful until they reached the building, but now that they were here, the familiar tingle in the pit of her stomach returned. Hamilton came up beside her and hunkered down. The barrel of his M4 steadied on the opening. Kneeling, he was as tall as Panda. His shoulders, twice as broad, had taken more than one bullet for her. He shook his head, shooing away a bug zipping around his ear.

"Swanson is chomping at the bit back there," he said. "Stupid asshole wants to run in."

"It's just an old library, right? I don't think a bunch of rotted books can hurt him, do you?"

"For all you know, he's going to run in there and the place will turn into a bad Indiana Jones movie."

"Throw me the whip," Panda smirked.

Hamilton grunted. "How are we playing this?'

"You and me in the door, standard formation. Davis stays here with Swanson and Banks. We'll see what we see, and they can come in once we deem it safe."

"Suddenly worried a paper cut is going to kill him?"

Panda considered the landscape once more and shrugged. "More like the jungle rot he'd get from it," she said. "I'll be damned if he dies before we get our payday on this one."

"I hear that," Hamilton said. He turned away and whistled once, sharply. He used hand signals to convey Panda's instructions.

Panda switched off the safety on her M4 and took a deep breath. She stared at the dark hole, slowly counting off the seconds, and on five she went. Panda stood just over five feet, so her crouched run kept her low to the ground. Her feet danced around the open roots; her hips moved around the shrubbery without touching it. She pressed her back against the wall on the left side of the door moments before Hamilton did the same on the right. She nodded, pivoted on her left foot, and pushed through the opening, sweeping her weapon across the empty space in front of her. Panda continued to turn left and moved further in.

Panda registered many things all at once: the floor was littered with open books, none of which she stepped on; the walls and ceiling weren't airtight, as blades of light speared the darkness, giving it a murky taint; her half of the room was empty; a descending staircase dominated the center space. She clucked her tongue once—their signal for all clear—and when Hamilton did the same, she lowered her weapon.

The air pressed on her with its thick heat, as if the building had condensed it into a translucent paste, and she took a deep breath and let it out fast. Dust motes zoomed in the meager light, rocketing down from above to drown in the sweat on her face and neck. The smell, which she hadn't registered upon entering, stormed her pores, an invading army of overpowering vanilla and nuts. Panda opened her mouth and spat. The glob hit the ground and floated, bubble-like, on the stone.

"This place is creepy as hell," Hamilton muttered. He pulled a glow stick from his pack, broke it, and approached the stairs. He tossed it into the void. The green light tumbled ass over teakettle for longer than Panda liked; the stick landed some forty feet below them and came to rest next to another open book. Hamilton threw two more down, placing them so the three formed a semi-circle of light at the base of the stairs. The heat intensified the glow's output, giving them a good view of the immediate area.

"Nice placement," Panda remarked.

"Too many games of cornhole in my spare time."

They waited a full two minutes, scanning the lower room for movement, listening for sounds of occupation. Panda heard nothing, saw nothing, but giant snakes and deadly bugs didn't make much noise. She looked around one more time, her gaze touching on several of the open books. Something about them...

She shook it off, steadied the weapon against her shoulders. She descended the stairs fast, her boots making minimal noise as she balanced on the balls of her feet. She went left again, avoiding more open books, but this time she stopped at the edge of the light.

The lower chamber was immense, and she couldn't see more than a few feet in front of her. She slung her rifle and pulled out a handful of her own glow sticks, which she broke and tossed in several directions. Behind her, she could hear Hamilton doing the same.

It took Panda a moment to understand what they'd done. The room extended beyond the building's exterior wall. Whoever had built this thing had dug out an enormous hole, lined it with the giant building blocks and, as her glow sticks settled amongst more open books, she noted the thick columns supporting the floor above. How they kept the whole damn thing from falling in, she didn't know. How they'd dug out toward the jungle without the dirt falling in escaped her.

"They probably had help from aliens," Hamilton whispered. "There's nothing here, boss."

The place was devoid of anything living, at least anything larger than a spider or scorpion, but Panda wouldn't call it empty. The books, all of them open, their pages facing upward, were something. Again, a thought tickled the back of her brain, but ran away before she could fully examine it.

"Go on back and get the others."

"You got it."

"And Hamilton?"

He paused, his foot on the lowest step.

"Touch nothing," Panda instructed. "Not the walls, not the pillars, and not a single book."

"Copy that."

Panda broke the rest of her glow sticks and tossed them around the expanse of empty space, illuminating as much as she could. Whatever was here, it was in the hair standing up on the back of her arms, in the clenching of her bladder, the sudden dryness in her mouth and a sock-like tongue sticking to the roof of her mouth. Just because she couldn't see it didn't mean it wasn't there.

Sweat rolled down her face as she paced the room, going around the back of the stairwell. She made sure to stay within the glowing ring of light. The heat made them brighter, but they'd burn out faster than usual. The fact didn't concern her much; she had no intention of being here after nightfall. Swanson had hours to find his book. Plenty of time. Panda finished her circuit at the bottom of the stairs, staring at the closest book on the floor. She tilted her head and smirked. She'd figured out what had been bugging her about them.

The pages, brown with age, were clean, free of creases and tears. The dust, which had settled on the stairs and in the slight seams between the wall stones, had avoided the books. Even the words, written in a language she didn't recognize, hadn't faded, but rather retained a bright, bold pigmentation. It was as if time had given each of the books a mere peck on the cheek instead of a foot in the ass.

She heard the others before she saw them, their voices carrying down the stairs as they moved through the chamber above her. Swanson and Banks murmured to each other, the volume shifting quite a bit as they circled around the opening, most likely going from book to book. Their excitement, telegraphed through the high tones of their whispers, wasn't hard to miss.

"This place is fucking evil," Davis said, making his way down the stairs. "I don't care how empty it is. Nothing good will come out of this."

"Relax," Hamilton called after him. "They're just books, man."

"They're just books, he says," mocked Davis, alighting at the bottom next to Panda. "Just books in a foreign language found sitting in an old-ass temple. Forget the fact that they're all open, ready to be read. This shit isn't right."

Davis stood a couple of inches taller than Panda's five feet, and she had no problems catching his gaze. She shook her head at him, a hard look in her eyes. The message was clear: shut the fuck up and let the others get what they came for. Davis sneered and moved away, popping his own glow sticks and adding them to the others.

Quintessential Davis, she thought, watching him until he left her peripheral vision. Afraid of everything he didn't understand. She shouldn't have expected this to be any different, despite this being just an empty building and a few old books.

"He has a point," Hamilton whispered.

Panda startled at his voice, so close to her ear. He'd come down the steps without her noticing. He looked off into the greenish light hovering over most of the lower room now. The books gave off a ghostly incandescence, almost as if they were soaking in the glow light and reproducing it.

"Stop it," she said. "I've got one triggered soldier. I don't need another."

"He's from Georgia. What do you expect?"

"Discipline? Common sense?"

"You have to admit—"

"No, I don't have to admit anything," Panda said, cutting him off. "Where are Swanson and Banks?"

"Upstairs, geeking out over books."

"Shouldn't you be up there watching them instead of down here freaking yourself out?"

"Yes, ma'am," Hamilton said.

He retreated back up the stairs as Davis finished his circle.

"I'm out of glow sticks," he said.

"Same. You good down here?"

"No," Davis said, "but I'll manage."

"This place is empty. You said it yourself. Just stand here and don't touch anything."

Davis saluted, a half-hearted sarcastic gesture he saved for when he wanted to tell her to fuck off. She'd seen it a thousand times over the years, but he'd always come through. She owed him... she owed him more than she cared to admit, and so she always let it slide. And there was no way in hell she'd tell him the place spooked her as well. He didn't need any help with his conspiracy theories and wild notions.

Panda headed upstairs. Swanson and Banks knelt on the floor, each one next to a different book. They were on opposite sides of the library, their backs to each other. They'd propped their hiking packs up against the temple wall near the door. Hamilton hunkered down a few feet away from the stairs, drawing in the dirt with his finger.

"You find your book yet, Swanson?"

"No, Captain, I have not. But to be honest, I haven't really looked. These are all fascinating."

"Bunch of crooked lines, if you ask me," Hamilton said.

"All writing is such," Swanson replied. "Though I'd say English is more curvy than crooked."

"Maybe," Panda said. "But those aren't written in English. I don't know what language that is."

Swanson turned to face her. "This book is written in English. It is an in-depth study of the *Ardipithecus kadabba* and, I must say, has been enlightening so far. Come, see."

Panda crossed the empty space between and bent down beside him. The book was the same as the others, and she shrugged. Straight lines, long and short, some crossing while others were above or below. Her eyes traced the designs, searching for patterns, anything to make sense of what they saw. She read left to right, down the page, until the end.

"It's nothing," she said. "Lines, not words. Scratches, not sentences."

"You know what this means, yes?" Banks said from across the room.

"Yes," Swanson answered.

"Somebody want to clue the rest of us in?" Hamilton asked.

Panda straightened up, her head swiveling between Swanson and Banks, waiting for one of them to answer the question.

"This is, for lack of a better name, the Library of All Time," Swanson said. "These books represent the entirety of the universe's collective knowledge. It is said their words are only available to those who seek knowledge."

Panda snorted.

"It is not meant as a slight," Swanson said. "We all have our predilections, Captain. There is no shame in yours."

"I'm not ashamed, Mr. Swanson."

"Your books are a joke," Davis said, cresting the top of the stairs. Sweat rolled down his face and soaked the collar of his camo shirt. "Most of them don't look thick enough to stop a steak knife, much less a rifle round."

"Ah, but with the right information, not a shot need be fired," Banks intoned, standing and stretching.

"I need some air," Davis announced and stomped toward the door. "This place is getting under my skin."

"So, what now? You said you were looking for a single book." Panda gestured all around. "How will you know it? Maybe we can all look for it."

Banks walked to his pack and withdrew a leather-bound journal, the kind with a string that wrapped around to keep it closed. He opened it, slid a pencil from between the pages, and turned to face the area. The pencil scratched up and down over both pages. The man's gaze flicked up every so often, each time to a different part of the room. He shifted on his feet and turned the journal sideways, then continued his sketching.

"I fear I may have been mistaken," Swanson said, his Southern Welsh accent singing into the air. "This book is now providing information on how the pyramids were built. It's possible any book will do."

"The book about something else?"

"Yes." Swanson pointed at it. "The words are rearranging on the page like liquid ink. Can you not see it? It's breathtaking."

Panda stared at the book. The lines and scribbles were all the same to her. Nothing moved; nothing made sense. Heat crept up her neck and her teeth ground together. Hamilton walked over and peered over Swanson's shoulder.

"Hey, maybe Davis was right. Maybe this place is bad."

"Stow that shit, Hamilton," Panda barked. "He's pulling our fucking chain."

"Why would I do that, Captain?"

"I'm not sure," Panda said. "Because you think you're smarter than us. Forget your uppity British bullshit, but focus more on the employer/employee aspect. Us simple Americans couldn't possibly understand what you're doing here, so let's have a little fun, shall we?"

Swanson gave a little shrug and had opened his mouth when Banks slammed his journal shut. All heads turned that way. Banks wrapped the leather lace around the outside and tucked it up under his arm.

"I need to see the lower level now," he announced.

"Why?" Hamilton demanded. "If you only need a single book, then grab one and let's leave."

"It isn't that simple," Banks told him. "I need to record this. The size, the location of all the books, the way they're facing."

"What the fuck for?" Davis asked, reappearing in the doorway. "Seems pointless to me."

"Of course, it does, Private Davis," Swanson said. "Come, Mr. Banks. Let's go see what treasures are below."

The two walked, backs stiff, heads high, past Panda and Hamilton and down the stairs. Panda locked her eyes on the side of Swanson's head, urging him to turn and look at her. She wanted to see into his eyes, sure she'd be able to read him, assess the situation better, if she could only look him in the eye. That's where one found the true measure of anything that took breath and had a brain large enough to think. Most people couldn't keep anything from their eyes. Was he bullshitting them?

She was trapped, a ten-year-old little girl again, between her brothers and her parents. The former telling her yes, the boogeyman lived in her closet and he'd come out as soon as she fell asleep. He'd use his claws to pluck out juicy chunks of her arms and legs, stomach and chest, and eat them raw until there wasn't anything of her left. Their parents, of course, told her it wasn't true. But her brothers were persistent, convincing, whispering to her just before bed, keeping everything quiet, without smiles, all earnest worry for her well-being.

"We hope to see you in the morning, Pam," they'd said. And Tommy, her older brother, even hugged her. He never hugged her. And when he did, their father flicked the back of her brother's ear with his finger and told him to get his ass to bed.

"They're lying to you, honey," he'd said. "They just want to scare you."

"But what if it's true?"

"Think about it for a minute," her father told her. "If it were true, why hasn't the boogeyman got you already? You've fallen asleep every day of your life so far and here you stand before me, pretty as ever."

"Maybe the boogeyman takes turns and tonight it's my turn."

"Why would it be your turn? If he were real—and he isn't—and all he did was take turns, there wouldn't be any adults left alive to have kids. Right?"

"I guess," she said.

"Trust me," her father said. "Now go on up to bed."

Panda had done so and lived through the night, as she had every night since. But what she took from that exchange wasn't that her brothers were creeps or that her dad did the bare minimum to help his daughter through a frightful moment, but that she hadn't known what, or who, to believe. She'd gone to the library the next day and looked up the boogeyman; her search results had been varied, but the truth was that the boogeyman existed in all cultures, all places. How could he not be real?

"I'm telling you," Davis was saying, "this place isn't. These books aren't right. We should walk out the door right now, roll a triple set in here, and hightail it to the jungle. Bury the books and those two pompous fucks with them under a pile of rubble."

Hamilton had moved away from them and knelt next to Swanson's pack. He'd unzipped it and was rifling through its contents.

"Then we don't get paid," Panda said, trying to catch up. "What are you doing over there?"

"Just looking," Hamilton said. "What else have they not told us? I mean, we're here to find a book. One book. But now it could be more. These are books we can't read, but they can. On top of that gem, they're books that change subjects on a whim. I'm starting to think Davis has the right idea."

"I'm going down there to see what's taking them so long," Panda said. "Don't do anything stupid."

"My idea isn't stupid," Davis said. "But I won't blow it without your say-so."

Panda stomped down the stairs into the eerie green. Perspiration slicked her throat and ran in rivulets down between her breasts. She was losing her men, she just didn't know to what. Paranoia? Their behavior didn't make any sense to her. Yes, the books were odd, being here, being open, being untouched by time. But that didn't make them dangerous, and certainly not evil. Books weren't evil; knowledge wasn't corrupt. The way people used knowledge, now that was altogether different. In the hands of the wrong person, knowledge was the atomic bomb or Agent Orange; it was Sarin and DDT. But before it was corrupted, there had to be knowledge in those wrong hands. Right this minute, there wasn't any, only people.

Banks stood in the far corner, drawing in his journal. The pencil scraping across the paper grated against her eardrums, rankling down her spine.

"Aren't you done yet?"

Banks smiled at her, the pencil never stopping.

Swanson was near the wall behind the stairs. He held a glow stick over a book and didn't move as she approached. Panda put a hand down hard on his shoulder, and he jumped at the sudden contact.

"Bloody hell, Captain. You should announce your presence."

"I did. Your pet over there didn't stop, and I guess you didn't hear me."

"I did not," Swanson admitted. "I was engrossed in this book here."

"Yeah? What's that one about? The social hierarchy of Sasquatch in the wild? Maybe whether or not Nessie uses underwater caves to stay hidden?"

All Panda saw on the page were the same lines she'd seen in all the other books.

"And here I thought you were different from your men," he said. Swanson's mouth twitched upward in a smile. "They seem quite aggravated at the situation."

"You're scaring them," Panda said. "You're a smart guy, Swanson. Fear and guns don't mix."

Swanson switched the glow stick from his right hand to his left and pulled it up close between them. His eyes flared yellow, alien-like, the pupils slitting the whites lengthwise. The shadows elongated his teeth into fangs. Panda stepped back, slid her hand down to her pistol.

"Perhaps you should be upstairs calming them down, then," he said, moving the light closer to the wall. He was just Swanson again, eyebrows raised. If he noticed her hand on the pistol, he didn't acknowledge it.

"Perhaps," Panda said, letting out a shaky breath. She released her grip on the gun and wiped her palms down her legs. "But I prefer to address the root cause of an issue."

"I see. Proceed, then." Swanson nodded curtly at her and bent down to examine the book at his feet.

"Mr. Swanson," she said, "you're the root cause. Specifically, the bullshit about reading these books. We both know all you see are the same lines we all see. You're not reading anything, unless you know whatever language this may be, and the books certainly aren't switching topics."

Swanson put his finger in the middle of the page. He began to read:

"Approximately twenty-seven percent of the universe is comprised of dark matter. It does not consist of exotic particles, but baryonic matter and—"

"What you're telling me is you're not going to cut the shit, then?"

"There is no shit to cut," he said. "These books are perfectly legible to me. Their contents mold to whatever questions I pose."

"Then let's grab a book and leave."

"It is not that simple," Swanson said. "Mr. Banks has been compiling notes on this place for decades. There are references to a Saqra, a devil, which will appear if any of the books are taken beyond the temple walls."

"And let me guess: this Saqra will kill to make sure the books stay."

"We took the information about a devil with a grain of salt, as you can imagine. Indeed, we took them all that way until we found this place. And then the things we witnessed upstairs happened, which were also detailed in the extensive research notes Mr. Banks has. Only those who seek knowledge will be able to comprehend what they have to impart. The books will respond to the questions posed by the seekers."

"And now you're leaning toward this devil being a real thing."

"The facts support it."

"Your facts," Panda corrected him. "I haven't seen anything that leads me to believe any of this."

"I cannot help that, Captain."

"What are we looking at, then?" Panda asked. "If you can't remove these books, what's your plan?"

Swanson removed a cell phone from his pocket. "This, for tonight. Tomorrow, Mr. Banks will bring out the camcorder he brought. We'll record the books and see what happens."

"Great," Panda said. "We'll set camp outside in the empty space between the temple and the jungle."

"As you wish, Captain. Our safety is in your hands."

He bent back to his book, roaming the light over its surface. Panda sighed and went back upstairs. Hamilton and Davis stood near the door, smoking. They passed the cigarette back and forth, each taking a puff before Davis flicked it out into the sunlight.

Panda walked to the nearest book and picked it up. The lines blurred for a moment as it moved, but then solidified as she flipped pages. They remained unreadable from start to finish, nothing but fucking gobbledygook. She turned it upside down and shook it. Nothing fell out. Panda dropped it and stepped to another one.

"Fuck me," Davis said.

"What?"

The book she'd dropped landed face up, open, in the same position it had been in before.

"I told you. I fucking told you."

Davis pulled his pistol and aimed it at the book. Hamilton took a step back.

"Private," Panda barked, looking him in the eye. "You will holster your weapon. It's a fucking book and nothing more."

"It's a whole lot more," Davis said. "There's nothing right about this place. I need to take it down."

"You're acting like a superstitious moron," seethed Panda. She held up a hand and took a step forward.

Davis pulled the hammer back. "I'm either going to shoot you and then that book, Captain, or I can just shoot the book."

Panda's eyes flicked over to Hamilton. He drew his gun and pointed it at Panda.

"I'm sorry, Captain," he said. "I'm with Davis on this one. I'm going to need to you to disarm."

"Don't do this," Panda said. "There's no way Swanson is reading those books. This"— Panda kicked the book at them—"was a fluke. You're screwing the pooch on this one."

"Your weapons, Captain," Hamilton repeated.

Panda used her thumb and pointer to drop her pistol at her feet. She tossed her rifle to the side. She undid her belt last and dropped her grenades and extra ammunition next to her pistol.

"Now move away," Hamilton instructed.

"You're idiots. I don't know what else to say. Believing Swanson's bullshit like this."

"Bullshit?" Davis said. "How's this for bullshit?"

He picked up a book and pulled his arm back. He grunted, putting his back into the throw, and released the book into the air. It spun end over end for only a few feet—not nearly as far as it should have gone—the covers flapping like a bird's wings. It fell, a paper rock, and flipped on its way down, landing face up, pages open.

"You see, Captain?" Hamilton said. "Whether or not Swanson can read the books isn't the point. What just happened there is something else."

"A weighted spine," Panda said, though the book she'd picked up hadn't felt weighted to her. "It's not evil. There is an explanation, if you'd just take a moment to think it the fuck through."

"I'm done thinking," Davis said. "It's time to act."

"Fuck it," Panda said. She picked up another book and held it up. "You want to shoot a book? Fine. We'll shoot this one. Come on."

Panda strode toward the exit, the book held loosely in her hand.

"Where are you going?"

"Out there," Panda said.

"No," Davis warned her. "That's a really bad idea."

"I'm beyond caring, Private. This is ludicrous."

She didn't stop walking. Davis told her to halt again and still Panda refused. Her feet moved, one in front of the other. Hamilton yelled as well and Panda sprinted, pumping her arms. She'd locked gazes with Davis, right after he pulled his gun on her, and seen her fate played out in that second, understood what she had to do.

The first bullet hit her high in the shoulder and spun her. Panda kept moving, stumbling, when the second one sliced through the base of her throat. Blood welled up, gagging her, and she slammed into the exit. Her back braced against the stone frame of the door. Two more bullets pierced her chest and she couldn't breathe.

Panda groaned, her chest a volcano of fire erupting upward and out the hole in her throat. With the last of her strength, Panda used her toes to topple sideways out the door. She clasped the book to her chest as she fell. The sun above her, bright and red and beautiful, blinded her with its glory.

Panda landed hard on her side, her booted feet still within the temple doors. The book slid from her chest and landed, face down, on the ground. Below her, the earth began to rumble, shaking furiously. Dust rose as the giant stones loosened, the bond between them weakening. They scraped together, sliding like tectonic plates, until they met no resistance.

She'd never been able to see if the boogeyman was real. How could she? He only appeared when one fell asleep, a convenient way to avoid detection and therefore confirmation. Panda didn't believe for an instant that Swanson's saqra would appear when she brought a book across the threshold. His demon had already arrived, presenting itself in the two forms closest to her. It wasn't some ancient evil, at least not the horns and cloven hooves variety, but in its own way, just as scary. It couldn't be reasoned or bargained with, and it was blind to logic, pursuing only its own thoughts and desires, always to everyone's detriment.

Pamela Sayers closed her eyes and let the trembling earth rock her to sleep.

TONGUE-TIED

BY KELLI PERKINS

I was sure someone was playing Satan's recorder outside; accompaniment to the banshee wail of wind through the eaves. Winter was a live, writhing creature whipping the hotel like the tentacles of the Kraken against some unfortunate ship. Sharon continued her less than subtle mating dance, laughing and flipping her recently blonde hair at the silver fox into whose bronzed flesh she no doubt wished to sink her perfect pink claws.

I wondered if I just *willed* it, as *Malcolm* had suggested, if I could get her to stop fawning over him just long enough to glance out the window. Her car was easily visible, one of the two that remained collecting ice crystals in the side lot. The other, much more ostentatious sports sedan must have been the thin veil behind which our benefactor concealed his almost certainly microscopic penis. I stared at him, too. Surely, he would want to press his own remote start, mitigate the cold it too hoarded in its interior.

Spoiler alert: he didn't.

All I knew was the longer we stood outside that conference room, the more likely I was to run into my boss. Embarrassing enough that this was held at my workplace, let alone how little I wanted to be there on my day off.

Whether by will or not, she was at last cast from his spell and he from hers; us all into the wind's icy clutches. The interim between the resonant thud of her car door and the heat squealing through the vents drew out across space and time, the heat death of the universe expressed in my aching fingertips.

"What's wrong with you?" She sneered at me in that way people do when your company has grown tiresome, as if to say, *Are you still here?*

Kinda think your "self-help 'shop" might be a cult, Sharon. It was on the tip of my tongue, but the words died in my throat, so I shrugged and said "It's cold" instead.

"I know what would warm me up." She practically purred, a visible shiver sent down her spine, the more jiggly parts of her anatomy doing so beneath her faux fur coat. I had an inkling it had little to do with the cold.

I loved her once. Unspoken, thoroughly unrequited and, in hindsight, unwise. Call it Sunk Cost Fallacy, but some of that sentimentality lingered yet.

I declined the invite to further swoon over Malcolm (he was married after all) and kept my eyes forward, resting them on the traffic light barring our passage home.

"If you're still cold, you should speak up." She turned the blower up. *Way* up, past what was comfortable. "That's the whole reason I brought you to this class," she said. "You should be more assertive; ask for what you want."

I laughed inwardly, sweating inside my coat. Somehow, I didn't think she'd much like her end of that monkey's paw agreement.

Gwen was, predictably, passed out on the couch when we walked in, her phone dangling precariously in her hand over the laminate floor. She should be glad it was not lava. The front door slammed against the cold clawing with icy fingers at our backs and the phone fell with the same ferocity of sound and vibration, Gwen sitting up with a start. Pieces of her dark hair whipped her shoulders from the purposely messy bun it hung from as she searched her surroundings for what made all that racket, amber eyes pausing on Sharon and myself.

"Oh, goddammit," Gwen growled, scooping her phone up from the floor. The screen was already cracked from many such a mishap, but she inspected it anyway out of habit.

"What was it this time? Over-exuberant pro-lifers?" Sharon asked in a shrewish tone. "Or did somebody take issue with your resting bitch face?"

"Shut up, *Karen*," Gwen riposted.

If I had to pick two primary traits to best describe Gwen, they would be: narcoleptic and super aggressive.

It really freaked people out at parties or game nights. She could be laughing or mid-point during one of her more impassioned debates one second; the next she'd be flat on the floor or slumped where she sat. And the crazy thing was she didn't really drink or do drugs, although other people probably made their assumptions. At least until she jumped back up like nothing happened.

So, it was out of character for Gwen to burst into my room the way she did later that night demanding I drive her down to Clancy's Bar.

"Why the desire to let everyone know what you think?" I asked her once we were settled in a booth.

"I don't know." Her eyes plumbed the depths of her colorful cocktail, fingers fidgeting with the tiny stir-stick straw.

"Just seems like, considering your condition, you might want to avoid getting so worked up."

"Well, that's the thing, isn't it? Social media: it's so ubiquitous it's practically unavoidable. Plus, it's an outlet. Ever since *Karen* got started with that bullshit, she's been insufferable."

"Is that why you didn't invite her?"

"Are you kidding me? She's the one driving me to drink. I'm serious, Willow. I've had enough. Let her take her cookware or cosmetics or dildos, or whatever cockamamie scheme she's got herself wrapped up in this week and get the hell out of our house."

"But..."

"What?"

"Well..."

"Spit it out!"

"Isn't her name on the lease?"

"Yeah, well, therein lies the problem. Which is part of the reason I dragged you out here tonight." Yeah, beside the fact she needed me to drive, which also meant she probably shouldn't have kept insisting on shots. "I mean..." She stopped to suck her straw. "Aren't you tired of her pushing you around?"

It was my turn to fidget, pushing on the unsunk lime slice I was too shy to ask the bartender to help with, wedging it tighter in the bottleneck it blocked. "I guess she can be a bit of a bully."

"But that's only 'cause you let her. Come on, Willow," she said, swiping the beer bottle from me. She sunk the lime with well-rehearsed ease and slapped it back down in front of me in a slosh of beer. "Do a couple shots with me, loosen up and we'll bang our heads against this together."

Between the darts, robbery via jukebox and the lemon drops I couldn't believe I ever once liked, the only thing I managed to bang my head against was the bathroom door. Or, more accurately, it banged into me as another woman blew past me without so much as an excuse me. I let it go, mostly on account of the feet obviously facing the wrong direction in the singular stall and the all too familiar splash of vomit. There was another woman waiting. The type of girl who sexts via Ouija. Which, of course, meant I was instantly drawn to her.

"Hey," I stammered, complete with an awkward wave. "She, uh, been in there long?"

She spun on one boot-clad heel and leaned against the sink, illustrated arms folded across her concert T-shirt clad chest. I didn't recognize the band.

"Long enough, yeah," she said. A stacked bob of blue-black hair framed features outlined in the same stark color, the sides and thick bangs shaping her face into a pale heart.

"A friend of yours?" I felt one corner of my mouth quirk upward in a half-hearted smile. The back of my neck burned and prickled with embarrassment and I rubbed at it absently; probably the only thing standing between me and looking like some kind of stroke victim.

"Nah," she said. "Just have to pee, same as you." She swept a gesture at my jimmying legs. "Say, I've got an idea, now that there's two of us."

"What?"

"Well, one way or another, we have to pee."

Oh no. "Right."

"We're both women, so...no surprises here."

Don't. "Uh huh."

She patted the sink.

No. "So..."

"One of us watches and one of us goes, and then we switch."

"Watches?" I blinked at her stupidly.

"The door."

"Oh, riiight. So, which of us—?"

"Look, I'll go first. Just so it isn't weird."

She was hopping onto the counter before I'd completed my swift and dutiful spin towards the door. Even with the foam of tipsiness bubbling around my brain, there was no way this wasn't going to be weird.

The tinkling sound of liquid down the drain followed so quickly, I wondered if she was wearing anything under that long skirt. A question happily dashed on the rocks of the pangs of an overfull bladder. I was never so relieved to hear the thunderous roll of a paper towel dispenser.

"Your turn," she said, hopping down.

I felt like I should have been more embarrassed but, hey, which was worse: pissing in the sink of a public toilet, or down my leg in front of a pretty girl?

The girl in the stall started heaving again; a nice buffer between the muffled music outside and the eventual torrent I was terrified to unleash. I was never more grateful for the pinch of performance anxiety.

The way my jeans tied me at the knees only added to my apprehension but, despite one attempted entry (thwarted by a well-timed shout of "shitter's full!" from my lookout), I was able to wrap up my business without incident or injury.

"All done?" She asked the slap of my far less stylish boots on the tile.

"Yeah," I answered, and she joined me at the sink. "Thanks," I said. "Kinda feels like we should at least know each other's names...or is that weird?"

She held out her still wet hand to me. "Judy."

"Willow," I said, taking it for a shake.

"Charmed." And, with another thunderous roll of the paper towel dispenser, she was out the door.

Getting her number crossed my mind, but that was probably crossing the bounds of Weird into What-the-fuckery, so I got the bartender instead. I informed her someone might need help in the bathroom and weaved my way back to the booth.

I had just begun the obligatory "You're never gonna believe what just happened" when I realized Gwen was gone, and so was her coat. All that remained was my half-drained beer and my tartan plaid pea coat slung in the corner.

I froze over with anxiety, my chest and veins full of ice. Sobered by sheer panic, I groped through my coat pockets. My wallet and phone were mercifully still there, but my keys were not.

I had one foot outside before I had one arm in my coat and the air bit at me; a cutting wind that nigh sawed me in twain. Would have drowned out Gwen's name too, had I breath enough to call it. On the other side of that was silence and snow and, by some miracle, my car still sitting where I left it. Except something was off. The windows were all foggy.

Beyond the frosty glass, Gwen's coat writhed as though two pythons fought beneath it. When one finally came up for air, it was Gwen's smile that surfaced, a pale hand emerging with a wave that then promptly shooed me away.

Nice. Nothing refreshes upholstery quite like the jism of a stranger.

I felt all that nervous tension fall away; dropped like paper from a balled fist, leaving me just as crumpled. The feeling settled into my bones, nestled into my sinew with gross familiarity.

I propped myself against the brick exterior of the bar and watched the wind steal my breath away like dancing smoke. Beyond the glare of neon, the streets lay dark and empty, with the exception of one storefront. A storefront I had neglected to notice before. Granted, it had been a minute since I'd been down this way any time past dark, but surely a storefront as unique as this would have caught my eye, even without the benefit of a bright pink light-up sign.

Curio, the cursive lettering guttered at me from across the street like a candle threatening to snuff out altogether. And, for a moment, there was no other light. No sound than that of the buzzing sign, all others swallowed by the surrounding snow. True, curiosity killed the cat but, never minding that, across the street I strode, as sure-footed as that ill-fated feline.

The word *Open* leered at me in a tawdry red, the sign propped in the lap of a formidable Baphomet statue inside the window. I strained my eyes against the oily dark oozing from the recesses of the shop and fought the growing crescendo of my heart, all thought silenced by the fairy jingle of a bell overhead as I opened the door.

How quaint.

I edged my way further into the shop, the shapes of it suggested in shadows and candlelight. Stacks of moldering books loomed on shelves like leaning sentries along its walls, stinking herbs brushing the top of my head like spider's legs as I moved beneath them.

Ambient piano warmed the air at its edges. Satie or Debussy, if I'm not mistaken; perhaps one of the Gnossiennes. From the way it seemed to drift on the periphery, I presumed it was piped through on some sort of speaker system hidden in the unknowable ceiling hung with veils of cobweb and mystery. An appropriate soundtrack for browsing the esoteric titles my eyes adjusted on, some of which were printed in characters I'd expect from a game or film trying to mimic ancient or alien text.

I tripped against a low tower of tomes haphazardly stacked by some shelves near the center, knocking a few over. That some of the more lovingly leather-bound books appeared encased in human skin was a nice touch. A little late (or maybe I should say early) for Halloween, but the effort was much appreciated.

"Those volumes are meant for more advanced students of the Arcane," said a gravelly voice from over my shoulder. I turned to see a lanky lich of a woman layered in witchy tapestries reminiscent of a Renaissance fair. She stared at the armload of books I'd retrieved from the floor until I handed them over, stacking them precariously on one spindly arm. "But I suppose that shows me for expecting my niece's help." She clicked her tongue. "Kids, they have no respect."

I slowly sank back into the skin she scared me out of and gave a nod. "No worries. I mean, kids...right?" I shrugged at her.

Her eyes, yellow and rheumy, slid over me and the jitters returned, drying my mouth and clamping hard on my windpipe.

"I apologize for her carelessness," she continued. "They are not safe to be handled by the public. Allow me to make it up to you. Perhaps a Tarot reading? A small sachet to carry with you? Maybe a potion not found across the street, ah?" She jerked her head in the direction of the bar, hair like dirty batting, like that used for cobwebs in Halloween decorations, fluttering in rhythm with her nod.

"It's fine, really," I assured her in a less than sure tone. "I was just looking around. Hadn't seen this place before."

"Perhaps because you haven't had need of it til now." She raised one bony but resolute finger at me and smiled with crooked brown teeth, managing to guide me like a lost puppy to a table strewn with a veritable alchemist's array of reagents.

I sat across the table from this character I was convinced couldn't be real, if for nothing else but the story I was sure was part of some silly gimmick the shop employs to intrigue customers so that they return, and with friends.

She handed me some old musty cards on which I could feel the touch of everyone to which they had been passed before.

"Shuffle," she told my sneer. "And then pass them back to me."

I did as commanded, fumbling with the oversized cards and unfolding the wrinkles on my face resulting from the cloying odor of what I could only presume was a potion not found across the street.

"Not a standard reading, you understand," she said and, to my horror, spat in one hand, rubbing her fingers together before again touching the deck. "Three cards, just to get a sense of who you are and what you're doing here, and then we shall proceed."

"Okay." I nodded feebly.

"The Hierophant." She placed the card in front of me with little ceremony. "A fancy way of saying stick in the mud, and you're the stick."

I barked a laugh I quickly stifled when she shot me a disapproving glance. "Sorry." I shook my head, face aflame with embarrassment, and cleared my throat. "Carry on."

"Next card." She paused to lick her thumb and I cringed inwardly at the reminder of just how much old woman spit coated the cards I had my mitts all over mere moments before. She lay the card lovingly beside the first, the jovial little fella dangling by one foot from a pole announcing its title before she did. "The Hanged Man; I see," she said without further illumination. She stopped and sat back, allowing her choosing hand to hover over the dormant cards, as if coaxing the correct one to the surface.

She turned up the third and set it next to the others with slow deliberation. "The Moon. Very curious." She sat back, tapping her twisting lips with one spittle-laden finger.

I was filled with quite a bit more apprehension this time. "Wh-What does that mean?"

"The Moon," she repeated, nodding her head from side to side. "She can go either way. But I think I know how to nudge you in the right direction. Let's see..."

Through the tink and clatter of her occult accoutrements, I remained focused on that peculiar final card; the face of the moon pitched downward with equally fierce concentration between two ominous pillars at the mismatched menagerie of canines (dog and wolf respectively) and their crustacean companion crawling up between them. A crawfish? A lobster? What the fuck did a lobster have to do with any—?

"Here." I jumped when she covered the card with a small ceramic carafe wafting with equal parts potency and pungency. "On the house—well... All spells are on the house for they cannot be dispensed for personal gain. It is most forbidden. Lots of rules, you understand. As Granny used to say, not just any twit with a twat can practice the sacred arts." She gave a cackle. "Oh, it ain't what it used to be. So commercialized these days—she must be rolling in her grave!"

"I'm sorry." I was still staring at the stinking vessel set before me. "What do I do with this?"

"Why drink it, of course! What else do you do with a potion?"

"But... What's it for?"

She narrowed her rheumy eyes on me, drawing a long ornate pipe from a burnished case on the table. "Just think of one thing. One thing that could make your life better. Maybe it's been weighing on your mind. Maybe it was the map that guided you here tonight." She lit her pipe, the match struck against it casting her craggy face in harsh contrasts of light and shadow.

"But... Isn't that for personal gain?"

"Relax." She puffed, waving out her match. "That doesn't apply to you. You'll be fine."

"Okay." After all, it was probably no more harmful than those vomit flavored jellybeans from Harry Potter...right? "Bottoms up!"

I knew it was unspeakably foul the moment its burnt hair and earwax-tasting contents touched my tongue, which made the choke of surprise when hands clamped on my shoulders all the more harrowing as I gulped it down in one stinking shot.

"Willow! What are you doing? I've been looking all over for you!"

"Gwen," I coughed. "This is—I'm sorry, I didn't get your-" I turned from Gwen's gaping stare to find a cloud of smoke my only companion, candles guttering as if in her wake.

"Do you have your phone? We have to call the police."

"What?" I stood with a start, practically knocking over the rickety old chair fit to crumble under me as it was. "Why?"

"That motherfucker stole my purse!"

"Goddammit, Gwen!" I whipped my phone out of my pocket and began the search for local law enforcement numbers. "Did you even know that guy? You had another episode, didn't you—you're lucky he didn't take off with my car!"

"Hurry!" She swayed, using the momentum to snatch my phone from me. "The longer you lecture me, the harder he's going to be to catch. Yeah, hello?"

As Gwen relayed her plight to the local authorities, I turned my attention back to the table. Still no sign of my mysterious benefactor, except something was sitting on my side of the table I was sure wasn't there before: a little canvas sachet printed with arcane markings I couldn't make any sense of. I picked it up and was looking at it when Gwen grabbed my other hand. I fumbled to pocket it as she dragged me from the shopfront and back across the street to the scene of the crime.

Maybe it was the adrenaline dump. Maybe I should have better followed that rule of not accepting drinks from strangers, but we weren't five feet in the door before I face-planted on the couch. I listened to the low hum of the fish tank and dreamt I was skimming my tongue along the surface of clean water. The little fishes were silver flashes, stopping to stare at me with accusing lidless eyes through billowing pillars of red ink. I inhaled the fishy spray from the slap of fins on my face and withdrew with the taste of copper on my tongue.

I awoke coughing, a grating sourness at the back of my throat. The kind that comes from bile and acid. My tongue throbbed the way it had when I got it pierced a full decade back, one of many poor decisions made in my misguided youth. A quick survey of my surroundings showed no signs of vomit, so I allowed sleep to swallow me once more.

As I languished on the lazy river, my boat rocked beneath me. I peeled open first one eye, then the other, the bleary shape of Sharon's scowl coming slowly into focus.

"Hey," she said, giving the couch another shove. "What happened to my fish?"

"What?" I croaked at her.

"Doc's missing!"

"What?"

"Doc, one of my silver dollars. I knew something was off, so I counted the fish and there are only six. There should be seven."

Right. Seven dwarfs.

"Wait..." I struggled through the haze of my hangover to sit upright. "Never mind that Finding Nemo is the superior Disney reference—they're fish, how can you tell them apart?"

Sharon opened her mouth, closing it back tight when she found it empty of an explanation. She heaved a sigh, shoulders sagging. "If he somehow jumped out and you found him, you can tell me. I won't be mad; it's happened before."

The gleam of silver scales flashed through my mind and suddenly I wasn't so sure what I remembered had been a dream at all. "Excuse me," I said. "I'm not feeling so well." And I clambered to my feet, pushing past her straight to the bathroom.

My stomach flipped as my mind did through all the horrid implications of having eaten a raw, *live* fish. I parked myself in front of the toilet, but no amount of heaving would bring up something consumed that many hours ago. Plus, it was easy enough to presume Gwen was the culprit. Perhaps he had been found dead and rather than deal with the drama of a fish funeral, she simply did away with the evidence and hoped no one would notice.

I stood up and examined my reflection in the medicine cabinet mirror. My mousy bob stuck out in all directions and there was enough luggage under my eyes to plan a trip abroad. I ran my fingers through my hair and the faucet over my hand, cleaning up the smudged parts of yesterday's eyeliner and cupping water into my mouth. I swished and spat, lifting my face to the frown reflected back at me. I could taste blood and bile—but, thankfully, no fish—at the back of my aching throat, but not the water. Not the way I thought I should, anyway.

I opened wide and said *ahhh*.

There was a paleness and rigidity to my tongue I wasn't quite ready for, the only thing I could liken it to as I poked and prodded the cow tongue my paternal grandmother had fixed for Sunday dinner many years back, when my cousins and I were barely tweens. The other kids wouldn't have any part of it, but the culinary adventurer in me would try anything once. Just like that awful escargot during my more recent stint working at a country club: snails taste exactly like you expect them to, and so do tongues...although tongue doesn't taste like much of anything at all.

A few moderately successful runs through *red leather, yellow leather* and I chalked it up to a night of drinking gone awry and the possibility of allergic reaction or oncoming sickness. I had the notion of having Sharon take a look, but she had left for work by the time I came back out to the living room.

✳ ✳ ✳

I awoke on the couch to the screech of Gwen's phone from the other room. Surprising it still worked, recovered from a pile of snow near the bar; likely dumped there in order to avoid being tracked via Find My iPhone or some such app.

My stomach burbled and growled in protest to its emptiness and, as if by the strings on a marionette, I found myself pulled to my feet and shuffling past the fish tank towards the kitchen. Except I never made it past the fish tank.

This time, I was fully cognizant as I lifted the lid; of the flash of fear and fins as my tongue unfurled into the water. Except it didn't wait for the wormy proboscis extending under the surface to entice its prey. I watched it happen, almost as if in third person: this organ of a mind of its own working its way out of my mouth and further into the tank on segmented insectoid—no, not insectoid, more crab-like—legs, whose pointed ends dug into the corners of my mouth. I snapped up, like a bear with a prize salmon from the stream. Returned to the driver's seat of my consciousness, I ran for the bathroom.

Scales scraped my gums, my reflection revealing what my ears further translated to the sucking and squelching of viscera and bone, the horror lolling out from my mouth dripping saliva pink with blood into the sink. It went on...digesting, slurping up all the spilled blood, undaunted by the primal, guttural screams rolling out of me and across its armored back. And all the while it stared back at me with cartoonish black eyes and what looked an awful lot like a smile on its goofy little face.

"What's going on?" I heard Gwen screaming down the hallway, the monstrosity rolling back up and tucking itself away by the time she completed her Risky Business slide (boxer shorts included) into the frame of the door.

"There's a monster in my mouth!"

She angled her neat brows at me. "Did someone slip you some ayahuasca last night or something?"

"No, there's a goddamn Hell Pokémon taking the place of my tongue! Look!" I opened up and pointed accordingly. "D'ya see that? A leg twitched."

One brow dropped, as if to further emphasize her incredulity. "Did something happen with Sharon? Is this some kind of weird guilt metaphor?"

"Do I look like I'm waxing poetic? It's real—I-it ate a fish!"

Gwen gave her chin a doctorly pinch with one hand, her phone clutched in the other. "There's nothing in your mouth that shouldn't be. See?" She raised her phone, presumably to open the camera app, at which point her scientific manner left her. "Holy shit." Her face fell and the rest of her with it as her cataplexy took hold.

"Right? I fucking told you!" Although some of the steam had been taken out of that statement while I waited for her to regain control.

"Wait." She bounced back, on her feet and phone raised again to survey me through its camera's viewfinder. "What am I even looking at—how the fuck did this happen?"

"It was the old lady."

"What old lady?"

"The one at that weird shop!"

"What are you two *shrieking* about?"

I poked my head out to see Sharon in the hallway. She stood with arms akimbo, staring us down as though one of us had murdered two of her precious fish and swallowed them whole.

"Oh good, you're here," Gwen said. "We need a ride down to Clancy's."

It was my turn to angle my brows with incredulity. "Why would we need a ride?"

"Because we let the police bring us home from the bar last night, remember?" She slipped away to her room, hopping into her jeans and back into the hallway.

Sharon scoffed, crossing her arms. "Sounds like a whole lot of not my problem," she said.

"Don't be a bitch, Sharon. Just lend us your keys."

"And let your dizzy ass wreck one of our cars on the way back? No way!"

"Oh shut the fuck up, the both of you!" I roared in a voice barely mine. "Take your keys and shove em up Malcolm's snake oil-selling jizz-tube for all I care. We're walking!" I grabbed Gwen and pulled her down the hall, purposely bumping shoulders with Sharon on the way. I threw the front door open and Gwen her coat in one fluid motion, stopping short of it to say "Oh, and Sharon..." I waited for her to turn and face me, her shocked expression remaining when our eyes touched. "I ate Dopey *and* Doc!" I said, and slammed the door.

Where I had expected to find Gwen waiting I instead came face to face with a smartly dressed man.

"Afternoon, ma'am." He tipped his brimmed hat at me, my attention falling to the tote of printed material and books at his side. "Do you have a moment to-?"

"Wait." I stuck my hand in his face. "Are those religious texts?" I angled my index finger accusingly at the tote dangling at his side.

"Why yes," he answered cheerfully. "I'm with the Church of—"

"Gonna hafta stop you right there, bud," I said, waving my hand in his face again. "I'm sorry; I'm only collecting Satanic bibles at the moment. Unless..." I pointed again to the tote. "Do you have the *Necronomicon* *in* there?"

His eyes were dinner plates while mine flicked to find Gwen behind him.

"I'm sorry," I told him again. "I really have to go." And I joined her on the sidewalk. At least it was warmer. Gotta love winter in Ohio.

* * *

We were blocks from our doorstep and Gwen was still bursting at the seams, spurts of laughter jolting her as electricity through her wiry frame.

"You're not gonna have another episode, are you?" I asked her.

"No." She grimaced in an effort to compose herself. Or maybe it was the guys catcalling from down the street. Either way, my eyes were on them like a school of piranhas. They were the total package: douchey gelled hair, at least one alligator polo; teeth too white. And where I would normally feign ignorance and find a workaround, I found myself laser-guided in their direction.

"Willow, what are you doing? Just ignore them," Gwen pleaded, several paces behind me now. But I was on a mission. These guys would think twice about bothering another stranger ever again, even if their ears were on fire...and I was happy to supply the flame.

"Hey!" I barked at them.

"Ooh," their apparent alpha grunted. "Buzzkill."

My head swiveled like that of a bird—a predatory one—as I surveyed the three of them. "You know what's a buzzkill?"

Almost as a reflex, I reared my head back. I felt my throat swell, expelling my monstrous tongue as a dragon does fire. Their confused expressions morphed into rictuses of revulsion and pain as a spray of acrid green goo arced across their faces.

"Jesus fuck, Willow!" The words came with a hand clamped to my shoulder, wrenching me away from their anguish and acid-seared skin. "Come on, we gotta get outta here!"

I did return to the shop and I did bring a friend. Except, much like the reason for my prospective repeat visit—like me—the shop itself had been transformed.

In full daylight, *Curio* became *Curiosity*. Where oily shadows had danced in candlelight, clean, modern displays shone with glossy book covers and glittering crystals in the fluorescent lights. Instead of the elusive piano, David Bowie's *1. Outside* thumped through a centralized sound system. The delightful jingle of the door had been replaced by two electronic tones, the latter lower than the former, at the sound of which the vaguely familiar figure behind the cash wrap turned to face us.

"Hey!" Her dark hazel eyes sparkled with recognition and my stomach lurched. "That was quite a ruckus at the bar last night. Heard there was a robbery. Glad to see you're all right."

Gwen's eyes ping-ponged between us for a moment, settling on Judy. "There was an old lady here last night," she said. "Seeing as you all already know each other, perhaps you could introduce us?"

Judy knit her neatly painted brows together. "Old lady?"

"Yeah, around... What time did you wander over here last night?" Gwen slapped the back of my arm.

"Wait," Judy said. "You mean from the bar? That's impossible. I closed at nine. It was after eleven when we-"

"Yeah." My hand shot up in a halting gesture. "We don't need a full recap. I just need to see the old lady."

"Well..." Judy sagged against the counter, wrinkling her Joy Division T-shirt. "The only old lady who ever worked here was my aunt Elise and she passed away a couple years ago; used to own the place before it got passed down to me."

My heart and stomach seemed to be in a race to see which would fall out my butt first. "Your aunt."

"Yes."

"Look," Gwen said, bringing out her phone. "Old lady, ghost lady—whatever—can you fix my friend's face or not?"

Judy took the phone from her, unfazed by the image staring back at her with googly eyes.

"Weird flex of Photoshop skills, but okay." Her switchblade gaze flicked back to us. "The homeopathic crystal freaks do all my marketing for me...and I don't think this is very funny."

We stared at each other a while, *The Heart's Filthy Lesson* blaring its finale above us. Gwen looked a little green in the face, but apparently defeat was not one of her triggers.

"Come on," I said to her, taking her phone back. "Let's go get the car."

What a fantastic death abyss indeed, Mister Bowie.

The good news was my car was right where we left it. Not so much as a flyer tucked under the wiper blades, which was great. *Except...*

"What's the matter?" Gwen tilted her brows at me. "What's that?"

I stared at the little sachet in my hand, still no sense to be made of the symbols adorning it or the fragrant herbs within. "Not my keys."

Our trip home was less eventful, mostly because we had the good sense to take an Uber. Sharon's car being mercifully absent upon our return was just a bonus. But our internet searches were less than fruitful and, although some of the symbols contained in some of Sharon's old Wicca manuals seemed at least derivative of some of the ones on the sachet, they were as unhelpful as all the pictures of fish parasites our other searches turned up, no matter how similar in appearance the "tongue biters" were to what had invaded my mouth.

It's not like in the movies. Churches are never goddamn open when you need em. Yank on those ornate doors all you want; there are no saintly chaplains staying late to see to your salvation.

So that left me one option to wait out the evening. Obviously, I'd have to go back to where it all began...and hope the shop rematerialized as I had seen it the night before.

I nursed a room temperature beer in the same booth at Clancy's, rolling the little hand-sewn sachet in my hand, the heat and moisture from which heightened the herbal smell I couldn't quite place. Marginally better than the potion I'd imbibed, at least. It also smeared the rune-like writing, the black ink bleeding deep red in my sweaty palm. I was just about to put it away when a pale hand reached inside my field of vision and snatched it, my goth dream girl seating herself across from me. She twirled the sachet in her fingers, bringing it to her button nose for a sniff.

"What did you wish for?" she asked.

My quickened heart dizzied me. *Surprise!* Some situations still held the power to steal my speech. But I wasn't going to get off that easy...and nor should she.

"You'd laugh," I said, draining the last of my beer.

She shrugged her delicate shoulders. "Try me."

I nodded at my empty bottle, lifting my eyes to hers. "The real question is, if you know what this is, do you know how to fix me?"

"Well..." *Guilty as charged*, her pursed lips confessed with an admittedly cute scrunch. "In order to help you, I'd first have to know what you wished for."

Well-played, mine said back. "Take me to your auntie's shop and maybe I'll tell you."

"Fair enough."

Moonlight Sonata throbbed from a speaker somewhere overhead, half-lit fluorescents bathing us in unflattering contrasts, the memory of those sentry shelves looming in the otherworldly gloom encroaching on the perimeter of its flickering penumbra. I met the glass bottle set beside me with a rueful stare, fully intending to leave it on the little end table bookending the loveseat we sat upon among the shelves near the back of her store, no matter how cozy the seating arrangement.

"Relax." She popped the top off the bottle and took a swig. "It's just sparkling water."

As if I would know; even the beer had little taste on my tongue.

"Come on," she said, smacking her dark lips. "You have to admit you're curious; that you'd like to sample a taste of my kiss." She smiled like a vampire, but she was not wrong. I did, even if only in the warmth left behind on the mouth of that bottle. So I took it from her, let the ghost of her kiss touch my lips and sampled its citrus fizz.

"So," she said when I'd swallowed, sipping from her own bottle. "What did you wish?" She twirled the sachet again, giving it a long inhale.

"You're gonna think it's—"

"What? Dumb? Silly? Selfish? You presume a lot. Just because you want to kiss me doesn't mean you know me." She laughed, knocking one denim-clad knee playfully against mine.

"I don't know." My cheeks burned, but I liked the beat of butterfly wings in my belly, even if I was sure a kiss would end in blood and viscera.

"Let me make this easier for you: if you don't tell me, I really can't help you." She shifted so that her features fell in the shadow cast by her glittering hair. "What did you wish for?"

My eyes were playing tricks on me, the umbra on my periphery in perpetual shift. I took another sip from the bottle, let the bubbles play along my tongue...or maybe more like my tongue among the bubbles.

"A tongue as sharp as my wit." I chuckled, eyes shying away from hers. That's when I felt the pinch of her fingers on my chin; the pull of her gaze.

"I understand," she said, and I really felt she did.

I tore my eyes from her, reaching again for the bottle. So very thirsty. I already felt like my tongue was my own again; if nothing else, that I was adapting.

"Really," she reiterated. "Doesn't sound so bad."

"Yeah, well, it wouldn't be. Except..." I heaved a sigh and let my head fall against the low back of the loveseat. "All I wanted was to be able to stand up for myself...not to spit caustic venom at strangers on the street. Literal caustic venom."

"It's okay." Her fingers brushed my arm, sending electric-charged shivers all the way down, deep in the core of my biology, a longing ache left in its wake. A desire never before acted upon; not in this context. "We can fix this."

My mind fizzed with possibility, how it would feel to touch her; how I wanted her to touch me. How I couldn't let it happen—not just yet—but, *gawd*, how I needed it to.

And it was happening. My skin tingled, gooseflesh spreading beneath her fingertips, mine committing her serpentine curves to memory. As predator pounces prey, her lips were on mine and I in the full thrall of her kiss. No blood; no viscera. Only her tongue sucking mine, swallowing it right down to the stub.

THE SON OF SMOKELESS FIRE

BY AARON VLEK

"**A**mongst us are some that submit their wills to Allah," the grizzled old wretch wheezed, looking over his shoulder as he handed me the steaming glass of tea on a dirty saucer with two lumps of brown sugar, "and some that swerve from justice. Al-Quran 72:14—The Jinn. What do you think that means, my young friend?" he bellowed, ogling me over the tops of his tiny spectacles.

"Beats me, pal, you wanna maybe let me in on it?" was all I could say, beings as I was way out of my depth here and none of this was exactly my usual line.

This was Cairo. That's Egypt, so's ya know, and this was the first time The Librarian had sent me anywhere beyond stateside. I was always game for the new and weird, and this was all kinds of weird. This time I was looking for a book called *The Necronomicon*. It sounded hankier than usual, and if it hadn't been The Librarian talking, I'd have said it was all just a bunch of bunk. I was completely on my own here and The Librarian's parting words still haunted me.

"Be extra careful, Mr. Enfield, I'm afraid this book is beyond your usual expertise, and there'll be no aid of the sort you typically enjoy. Cairo is a terribly old place, and its streets are teeming with very odd magics that don't hide themselves among the shadows and the nightmares of the mad. In my ne'er-do-well youth I made the acquaintance of certain individuals there. Who knows, perhaps one still remembers their Old Friend; we shall see, we shall see..."

The old man, Hamid al-Wasi, shuffled around barefooted on the thick carpets, his long black robe

90

showing his ankles, and I wondered about The Librarian's acquaintances here. There was rugs of all sizes stacked everywhere, and brass trays and lamps, and I swear one of them looked like a genie was going to pop out any minute. Heaps of old jewelry heavy with coins and bells and strips of cloth spilled over glass cases. Canes with weird carvings and stacks of old books and samovars and settees and old leather shoes—embroidered in gold with red velvet inside and the toes turned up—cluttered up the place. There was robes covered with tiny glass mirrors, wooden camel saddles and halters dripping with fringe and bells, and hookahs and amulets with hands on them, hundreds of them of all sizes and shapes

One little rug on the floor facing the wall looked like it had seen a lot of mileage, and I could imagine the old guy kneeling down on it like they do. Prayer beads made out of some yellow stuff like the ones the old guy was constantly fingering hung on a hat rack. All kinds of coffee gadgets and grinders looking like they'd been around since The Flood were piled up and covered with dust, and pairs of swanky French shoes were heaped up in a corner with old uniforms and swords and skinny long-barreled rifles with designs etched on them in white.

I could see crazy-looking horns and big wide drums and long funny-looking things with strings that I figured was for playing somehow, and a polar bear's head on the wall above a set of low, fat stools the guy said were elephant's feet.

There was smells here too, lots of them, most I couldn't place but also old tobacco, and incense smoke pouring from a little pot on a table. Besides the old man, there was somebody else in here too, a funny-looking guy in black robes lounging cross-legged on a stack of carpets. If he hadn't been eyeing me so close with his strange almond-shaped eyes, I would've sworn he was a statue. No introductions were made, and since the guy hadn't uttered a word, I figured he was a mute or just didn't speak my tongue, or maybe didn't want to.

"You looking for jinn?" the old man whispered, looking around. "I have what you need," he added in a conspiratorial whisper as he dug out a dusty book from a pile and shoved it in my hand. "This book, you call up the jinn now, they do your bidding, kill your enemies and bring the woman you love to your bed, guaranteed, my young friend, guaranteed!" he boomed, slapping me on the back.

"Just five hundred American bucks, US greenbacks, a steal, you think? Am I right? Who can put a price on such a treasure? If I wasn't already rich beyond my dreams I would never part with it. What do you say, my young friend?"

I'd been sent here by The Librarian to find this *Necronomicon*, but I knew it would never come this easy. Where was the trial in it? If it was just sitting here in a pile of old books, why hadn't somebody else found it? Nope, I figured the guy sold books every day to schmucks using this same yarn.

"Nah, this ain't the book I'm looking for, it's old," I countered.

"This book is ancient! It's about to turn to dust. You better hurry!" the guy growled; his voice not quite so friendly now.

"Look, pal, I'm not looking for just any old book of magic spells or the like. You ever even hear of the *Necronomicon*? Or you just make your daily bread shilling guys like me, and besides, I'm not even a guy like me. Now, you know the *Necronomicon* or not?" I demanded, getting to my feet and laying out my escape route in case the guy and his buddy got any funny ideas.

The old man grabbed the tea glass and saucer out of my hands and glanced at the stack of carpets.

"Why you keep looking over there? You a crazy man, you seeing things? You say you want to know about the jinn, but you won't pay? Get out, get out of my shop, you got no money, you won't pay for this treasure that could make all your dreams come true, you crazy, get out of my shop!"

I was glad to get out of there, but not thrilled to see the other guy get up and follow me outside. So, this was the game: you can't fleece the sheep the easy way, you follow them into an alley and gut 'em like a carp. Yeah. Except nobody does for old Frank Enfield that way. I stuck my hand in my coat and relaxed as my .38 slid reassuringly into my hand.

"That's useless here, Sadiqqi Amrikki!" The laughing voice was somewhere between a commanding boom and a soft sensuous echo in my left ear. I swung around to face the silent figure who'd followed me from the old guy's shop.

I gripped my gun and glared him down. He was tall, taller than me and powerful, but nimble like a dancer. Dressed in black robes and leather boots, his blue-black beard was braided in two long points with little beads woven into it, and his long, braided hair had sticks and a bunch of little carved whatnots dangling in it. The black smudge they call *kohl* made designs around his eyes and down his chin and on his forehead, and from his neck hung bones and tiny bells on a silver thread and he didn't look like anybody else in this whole strange land teeming with miraculous characters. From the sash at his waist hung a wicked-looking blade that could've carved me up into chops before I even got the .38 out of my coat.

It was the eyes, though, that made me forget the .38. Swimming with murky ink, tinged with bloody red fire around the edges, the eyes were laughing at me. Spidey didn't need to tell me this man wasn't no man, and I'd found my way into what I'd come here to find: those strange old magics that don't keep themselves hid, like The Librarian had warned me about.

"Easy, easy," the man said, his voice calming me almost against my will as he locked me with his eyes. "You cannot hurt me with that gun, and as a foreigner you do not want to make a spectacle of yourself. Too many eyes watching. You want the *Necronomicon*, you follow me. I will tell you about the old shaykh who brought that book into being. It is a long tale, not meant for the streets. Come, come with me to my place, it is not far from here," he suggested. I had no choice but to go with him, and based on the look of that guy's eyes, I tended to believe him when he said I couldn't take him out with my .38.

So, I followed him down narrow streets clogged with ragged kids, beggars, women covered up head to toe, and merchants selling every possible thing under the sun. We'd been walking for what seemed like hours as the crowds thinned, and the street got narrower and everything looked ever older and more primitive. Only furtive eyes glanced at us from darkened doorways as we passed. Now and then the red glow of a cigarette cast a pale glow over a face, and I was glad to be in the company of somebody impervious to the slug of a .38.

"Don't look at them!" my guide hissed, and I obeyed without question.

"Come, Sayyid, I have food and water, come take tea, rest here a moment," a voice seeped toward me from a doorway. Before I could even turn, my guide spun around like a huge black cat and hissed angrily at the voice in the doorway, and the figure flowed deeper into the shadows.

"I said don't look at them," he barked, showing teeth that were very long and razor sharp.

Finally, we came to the end of the street, but it was barred by a massive wooden door carved with intricate designs. There was an iron knocker the size of my fist, and the door swung silently open and closed behind. We were in the courtyard of a ruined palace, fountains still running with water, orange trees heavy with fruit, and dozens of rooms rising all around us, each opening on the courtyard with little wooden balconies. The strangest music filled the air and my guide, whose name I still didn't know, led me a low table and a bench covered with rugs, where we sat. Before long a young boy with the same strange eyes brought us tea and plates of things that were sweet and delicious.

"So, Mr. Enfield," the man said with a deep sigh. "The Librarian has sent you to find the *Necronomicon*. That one will not know a day's peace until he possesses that accursed tome!"

"What? You know The Librarian?" I choked, guessing this was The Librarian's old acquaintance.

"Yes! He sent word you were coming, and I must find you," he said, combing his long thin fingers through his beard.

"Tell me about him, then. Where does he live, this Librarian?" I asked, still not sure what I was dealing with here, but sure that *old magics* might have all kinds of ways of knowing things.

"Aha, just so! You test me! Very good, Mr. Frank Enfield. The Librarian lives on the river that runs to meet the embrace of the sea!" he said like he was reciting thousand-year-old poetry or something. "It is named the Hud's Son!"

"Yeah, thanks. I had to be sure," I added, smiling at the mangled name.

"And what's more," he added, beaming with delight. "His friends, those that fly on black wings, their voices raised forever in song!" he said, standing up and stretching his arms out wide.

"Caw! Caw! Caw!" he boomed, his voice filling the courtyard and causing a hundred faces to peer down at us from those little balconies.

"But!" he continued, sitting back down knee-to-knee with me, his voice low and conspiratorial, his nose not an inch from mine. "When they walk the Earth, they wear the bodies of old men, is it not so?" he concluded with a grin and a wink.

"Ha! Yeah, that's them, the geezers," I laughed and threw back my tea like it was a shot of whiskey.

"Then there is the woman!" he grinned, his eyes glittering. "Ah yes, the woman, the glorious woman! Tall, hair like wheat drying in the summer sun, eyes the color of the sky after the rains of spring. The woman is like Diana of the Greeks, her mighty bow of victory ever ready!" he cried out to the sky. "Her arrows called bolts fly, *fttt, fttt, fttt*! And they never miss. She fires once, twice, ten times or a hundred, she never misses," he said, his voice no more than a whisper, his features animated with joy.

I was speechless. Whatever he was, this guy knew my associates pretty damn well. With this last utterance I wondered just how well he knew Brenda, and I bristled.

"I see. So, you know them," I said sullenly.

"And they know me," he said proudly.

"That's great, pal, but I don't know you. What's your name?" I demanded, wanting to even things up.

"My name is very long," he began, the fire in his eyes flickering wildly.

"Try me," I said with a bit of an edge to my voice.

"You could not pronounce it."

"Try me!"

"I am trying to be kind, Mr. Enfield. Your mouth is not formed to speak my name, and no human tongue may speak the language of the jinn."

"You mean you're some kind of genie?" I said with a grin. Genies I knew, what kid didn't know about Aladdin? "So where's your magic lamp?"

The eyes darkened and I realized genies, the jinn, were not the cute little fat guys in the cartoons and they weren't to be messed with. I thought back on the old guy in his store and the quote he'd read me about jinn in their holy book. So, like everything else, there was good ones and bad ones, but they were all powerful magic.

"Say, those guys in the doorways, were they...?"

"They were. But their tribe means you harm, so you must not look at them."

"Why, how come?

"They are the enemies of your kind. They will destroy you if they can. Do as I say, no explanations on them."

"All right, all right. So what about this *Necronomicon*? You were going to tell me about the guy who has it."

For the next hour I listened to stories about an old priest, my guide called him a shaykh, who had been seduced by bad jinns and a lot worse and by his own lust for power and forbidden knowledge. The guy had wandered out into the desert, killed his traveling companions, and tossed them down some cursed well where a demon lived, as in human sacrifice.

He changed his name from his Arab moniker to Abdul al-Hazrad—still Arab, I guess—and then went on to have a bunch of devilish trials in the desert before falling into a bunch of maniac visions and waking up with this book that he wrote himself while he was under the influence of who knows what, madness, evil genies, weird juju elixirs they cook up out in the desert, who knows.

Thing was, though, this book had the power to split open the cracks between the worlds and the secret places in the universe that people just aren't supposed to mess with. The guy had let loose a string of monstrosities into the world and left a lot of bloody bodies in his wake. The big fear was that there was a curse on the book, and if the right kind of wizard or whatever got his mitts on the thing, he could end the world. There were folks out there wandering around who wanted to do just that, end the world and usher in some hideous new order of things under questionable management.

According to this jinn, folks like me, humans, and guys like him, good jinn, really, really didn't want any of that to happen. It made sense why The Librarian wanted that particular mess of scribbling out of circulation.

"So, where do I find this Abdul al-Hazrad?" I asked, wanting to get the show on the road. The jinn just put his head back and started howling with laughter, but I didn't get the joke.

"Mr. Enfield, Abdul al-Hazrad lived many centuries ago. He still exists, but not in any place where you can look for him. And I will tell you this: there are many *Necronomicons*," he explained, noting my face sinking and my eyes rolling.

"Just so. It has been copied many times, and in so many languages translated. I do not know why The Librarian has sent you to this goose hunt," he explained.

"'Wild goose chase.' Not the first time, but there's always a reason. I can't stop now; I've gotta look for it. If nothing else, find a copy and bring it to him. These little treasure hunts aren't always what they seem, but they're important, even if I got no clue what the Big Guy's up to. Besides, now I'm curious, I want to know more about it. Can you help me?"

"I may be able to. You are here, are you not? I am jinn, am I not? And The Librarian has sent you to me. Be ready at first light. We will go into the desert and see which of her secrets she will share with us. I know of a certain oasis..."

My head nodded onto my chest and I jerked awake, not realizing I had even fallen asleep. It was dark, the place felt empty despite the number of faces that had been watching me from above, and a small fire burned in a brazier nearby. I lighted a torch and started exploring, passing room after room where solitary black-clad figures huddled around braziers, and a couple of larger rooms where numbers of jinn crouched together playing games of chance or telling stories. Each time they turned and looked at me curiously, nodding without saying a word.

On the ground floor I found a room with a bed and my bags heaped in one corner. Stripping down to my boxers, I climbed into bed. The place felt okay, and Spidey hadn't let out a peep. Just the same, I took out the juju doll from my pocket and set it on a table by the bed, and then I knew no more.

Much later I awoke with a start. The place was dead silent, and I wondered what had roused me. Then I heard it: somebody crying outside in the street somewhere. I could tell it was a kid, a little boy. He carried on like that, just sobbing, and it tugged at the old heartstrings and I couldn't ignore it. I went to the window and saw him, just a pitiful little kid in rags bawling his eyes out in the dusty street, and there wasn't a soul in sight.

"Hey, kid, whatsamatter?" I yelled, figuring he didn't speak any English, but it was worth a try. He just looked up at me and then moved on down the road a bit and started in again with the waterworks.

The jinn had said not to set foot out of this place, but there was nobody around, and only a heartless so-and-so would leave a kid alone like that. I got dressed and headed for the front door, but was immediately assailed by hissing in my ear like a horde of bees. It was voices.

"Do not go out there!" I could almost feel the breath on my ear.

"You must stay here, you cannot go!" came another, and then dozens of voices filled the air, all demanding I return to my room and obey the one who had commanded me to remain.

But Frank Enfield ain't no so-and-so, and I was going out there to make sure the kid was okay. Easing my way down the hall with nothing but a candle, I glanced in every room on my way out and saw countless pairs of red fiery eyes staring at me, but no one made no move to stop me. Of the tall jinn himself there was no sign. No problem; I'd see the kid was okay and be back in five minutes, tops.

The massive front door swung open and shut behind me, and I spotted the kid staggering down the street like he was sick or something. He couldn't have been more than five or six.

"Hey, kid, wait up!" I yelled. "You okay?" But he just kept walking, the echoes of his pitiful weeping driving me nuts. I was barely able to keep up, and tried to keep track of where I was going, but then the kid turned a corner and disappeared and I closed in after him.

He was just standing there in the shadows, and then he wasn't, and the ragged little cloak he was wearing just dropped into the street. I rushed up and picked up the heap of rags, thinking my eyes were playing tricks on me, but he was gone. Right about then, Spidey let out a yelp, but his warning came too late. Something cold and very sharp was drawn across my throat from behind, and I knew I'd been played.

A hood was thrown over my head, my hands were yanked behind my back and tied, and the business end of that something sharp poked me in the ribs and I took that for orders to start walking. So, the kid was a mule, set up outside my window to lure me out into the hands of fate. It crossed my mind that somehow The Librarian would know what was happening and the cavalry would show up. But what seemed like hours later there was still no rescue, no flapping of friendly wings overhead, nothing.

I knew we'd left the city because all the smells went away, and the sounds of animals and people doing what they do at night gave way to a gentle breeze. Under my feet was what my trips to Coney Island told me was sand. I couldn't tell how many had nabbed me, but it was a few, because I could make out several different voices. I had no idea what they were saying, not being well versed in whatever these guys were speaking—probably Arabic—so I just held my tongue and waited. Every few minutes the guy behind me jabbed me in the ribs with his knife and then started cackling with laughter, and then they all joined in.

We must have gone on like that for better than an hour or two when somebody up ahead screamed, and I could hear a bunch of scrambling around and more screaming. Somebody grabbed the hood off my head and cut the ropes binding my hands together.

The guy was bellowing something in my face, his eyes wild and not even focused on me as he shoved me in the direction of a mass of black-robed figures flooding away over the sands; and then they were gone. As in a dream, I looked down and saw my feet sinking in what looked like red mud.

A bloody red stain was spreading fast across the sand. I jumped back away from it and saw the tortured, flailing bodies of three of my late captors being sucked down into the mucky red sand, then disappearing completely. I don't imagine I'll ever forget the look of horror and fear on those crazed faces as they were swallowed up, or the gruesome sound of crunching and grinding that followed. Getting clear of the spreading stain, I could see a lot of fluttering around beneath the sand, like things were swimming around down there.

I hightailed it; no way it was the men still struggling for their lives. I knew they were goners and I sure as hell didn't want to tangle with whatever'd got a hold of them, or even get an eyeful of what it was.

I was smack-dab in the middle of the desert, and with no lights in sight, I was a long way from Cairo with no idea what direction to head in. The Moon provided enough light to see, but I just sat there, figuring this was the end of the road for old Frank Enfield. Half-dressed and barefoot, I'd never survive the blistering sun of the next day, and what was the likelihood anybody'd find me? I hoped the jinn would get over being riled that I'd disobeyed orders and come looking for me, if only for his old pal The Librarian's sake.

I kind of felt like a jackass, though. I wouldn't be out here if I'd done like the jinn fella had told me. But God damn it! There comes a time in a man's life when he just can't gall sitting there with his hands under his ass taking orders like a kid. Especially when he thought he was playing the big hero. But where'd it gotten me?

I was knocked out of that line of thinking by a twinge up my backside that told me Spidey was up and nosing around. Yeah, something wasn't right by a Kentucky Derby mile. The breeze was blowing in a different direction, and the smells weren't the same as they'd been just a few minutes ago. But it was the Moon that had me on my feet with a lump in my throat. It wasn't where it had been, and now it was full.

There was smoke in the air too, fragrant and heady like the incense The Librarian burned on certain nights in his office. I loved that smell. There was another smell, too, that brought the bile into my throat, and I hated *that* smell. There was lights now too, off in the distance, and I decided that was as good a direction as any.

I might be able to find somebody to help a dumb lost foreigner back to civilization. I made my way over the sand and a low white-domed building all by its lonesome appeared on the horizon. No town or houses or any other signs of life, just that white dome up ahead, shining beneath the Moon like it was sucking all the light right out of Her.

A few hundred yards more and the smells were suffocating, and the sounds of weird chanting and crying out and other sounds I found utterly loathsome stopped me dead in my tracks. I knew this wasn't someplace I wanted to go, but rather turn tail and run.

The juju-man part of me was certain of only one thing, though; I'd gone over to the other side somewhere between my forced march as a captive and dragging my feet out of a bloody mess in the sand. I was here on The Librarian's business, and just maybe this place right here was exactly where I needed to be. I was deep in Egypt's old magics now; Arab juju by whatever name they call it, where genies roamed the streets and smoked cigarettes from doorways and invited you home to tea.

I stuck my hand in my pocket, grabbing for my juju doll, and came up empty. It was still lying on a table by my bed, back in the ruined palace. So be it, then; I was, for the first time in my life, in the hooha regions completely on my own with no backup. If the jinn hadn't shown up by now, likely as not he wasn't going to. So, I steeled myself and walked up to the front door of what was about the size of a small domed house, all whitewashed and painted up in red with designs and stuff, maybe writing, maybe something else. I hesitated for only a second before kicking the rotted wooden thing off its hinges.

And nobody noticed. I plowed through a crowd of what must have been fifty people in dirty robes seated on the floor, swaying back and forth, mumbling, chanting, crying out in strange guttural ululations that didn't even sound human, and sobbing, the tears a muddy river down their faces. The light from a bunch of candles and a few smoking braziers dimly lit the scene, along with a rough skylight that let in the Moonlight and a trace of fresh air.

The smoke was so thick I couldn't see what the crowd was facing up front, so I just kept on squeezing through the stinking mass of people that sat knee-to-knee, bobbing back and forth and knocking into each other and nobody seeming the wiser for it. One of the guys flailed his arm around, almost knocked one of the braziers over, and got a nasty burn in the process, but he didn't even notice.

Stumbling through the roiling smoke and noxious fumes, I tripped and fell flat on my face on the dirt floor. Looking up, I got an eyeful of a monstrosity that made everything else I'd ever seen in my life in the ways of juju, haint, the black magic—and the white—look like kid's play. I'll never forget that sight, and Lord knows I'll spend the rest of my life trying. It was the image of a man, older than any man should ever rightly live, his arms and legs busted horribly in several places. Even his neck was skewed at an unnatural angle.

The arms were jimmied into the body of some lunatic stick figure, and the legs were twisted down beneath his body and seemed to be growing out of, or into, the earth itself like muscled, bloody tree roots that oozed some kind of unholy sap.

But it was the face that made me almost lose my nerve. The eyes were locked on mine like a howitzer, and the mouth was a twisted toothless grin trembling with some kind of despicable pride. The thing was alive, the priest or shaykh—or whatever they'd call him—of this unhallowed congregation.

In my disgust and horror, I almost didn't notice the book, the massive rotted leather book that was embedded deep into the flesh of the thing's chest, the skin grown up around it. I knew I'd found what I was looking for. This was Abdul al-Hazrad, the man himself in the flesh, and still alive and kicking, in a manner of speaking. And this was the infernal book itself, the *Necronomicon*: first edition and the bilious fount from which all other accursed and hideous copies spewed into the world like weeping spores.

One by one each man staggered to his feet and shambled toward al-Hazrad, and then reached up and locked his mouth on the river of oozing red sap that dripped incessantly from a hundred wounds.

As the sucking commenced, al-Hazrad's eyes rolled back into his head in some sort of ecstatic trance while the book itself pulsed and glowed like a preternatural heart and emitted a buzzing sound as if a million insects nested inside it. I couldn't turn away; all I could do was stare at the throbbing presence and its slobbering sycophants and try not to breathe. I vaguely became aware that I too had gotten to my feet and somebody was shoving me forward into the thick of the worshipping, like they thought I was going to take that withered limb to my lips and partake of that vile sacrament myself.

But no. Absolutely goddamn fucking not. Somewhere deep inside, a part of me dropped into a crouch: cold, menacing, and growling. Its snarling teeth let loose its warning through my mouth, and it flexed its claws. I remember somebody sometime saying, 'your war is not my war.' I knew there was no way I was going to touch that filthy book, and I sure as hell wasn't going to yank the bleeding thing out of al-Hazrad's chest and try to make a run for it. Live to fight the good fight another day, and all that.

So I turned and bolted for the door, knocking sweating, groaning bodies out of my path and shivering as the thing on the dais roared with hollow laughter. I staggered out into the clean cool night air, and took the first deep breath in...I don't know how long. I looked overhead and saw the sky was filled with stars that rained down the sides of the sky all around me, like I stood in some kind of glass dome. I stared at my hands, surprised to not see bloody claws.

Somewhere behind me, I heard a horse snuffle. I reeled around and saw him, the jinn, sitting atop something that *looked* like a horse, except it was blue and made of what looked like fire and water and starlight, all mixed together.

He reached down and grabbed my hand and hoisted me onto the thing's back, and we were off like lightning. The raining stars slowly went away as we rode through what looked like heat waves that rippled over the sand. But I felt good, I felt damn good, and by God, this Arab juju was all right in my book.

The Moon came back to her rightful position in the firmament, and I saw the lights of a vast city appear up ahead and knew we were back in Cairo. I was glad to be out of the desert, wherever it had been, and waited until we were back in the ruined palace to say my piece.

"All right. Sorry if I fucked up, and I'm mighty grateful you saved my hide," I began sheepishly.

"What is this *fuktub*? I don't understand," he said, looking at me like I'd grown a fish out of the top of my head.

"I shouldn't have ignored your warning not to go out, I just—" I began, but his hand shot out in front of my face and I knew better than to open my yap again.

"You have a good heart, Frank Enfield. I knew that would be your weakness, so I sent the boy to lure you out. And I knew your big head; your spirit couldn't resist the call to be the man of heroic deeds! Ha! Am I wrong?" he cried, laughing and slapping me on the shoulder. "Am I wrong? No, I am never wrong when it comes to you Sons of Adam," he added, bristling with obvious pride.

"Sons of Adam?" I asked.

"You humans. I am of the Sons of Smokeless Fire. My tribe, the jinn, we know humans better than they know themselves."

"So, you sent the boy to lure me out, and I almost got killed! I got nabbed out there in the street, and, where were you?" None of this was making sense, but I really wanted it to. For some reason I liked this guy, and I wanted to believe he was on my side in things, that The Librarian hadn't unwittingly sent me flailing headlong into the arms of an enemy.

"I was watching you!" he whispered, the dark red flames at the edges of his eyes darting across his irises like tongues. "And if you had died, ah well, all things must end," he added wistfully.

"Watching me? Why?" I demanded, but he just smiled and sighed.

"Did The Librarian tell you nothing of the jinn?"

"Nothing."

"I am of the Sons of Smokeless Fire!" he said again, like it was a declaration.

"You already said that. Now what the hell's going on here?"

"I never left your side, Frank Enfield. Not from the time you left this house to this very moment. My companions would have never hurt you, not really, and I am sorry some of them have suffered on your account."

"Those guys were your friends? And you didn't think to tell me?"

"Oh, you wanted me to hold your hand during your ordeal in the desert? How can you grow your power if you know your trials before they take you? The Librarian did not mention that you were a child, a beginner in these matters! Is that what you are, Frank Enfield? A beginner, a novice to these magics? How embarrassing for you!" he clucked, pretending humiliation on my behalf.

I was feeling played again, and as usual, it was all The Librarian's doing. But this was no game. *The Necronomicon* was real, I'd seen it, and Abdul al-Hazrad was alive and his worshippers were all too real. I had no doubt that book was as shitty a piece of magic work as there ever was, and I felt that just by being in its presence, I'd somehow lost another kind of virginity I never knew I had.

"What about the book? I didn't get the *Necronomicon*, there was no way to do that and live—or be sane and whole—and so I'll be going back to The Librarian empty-handed. And he won't like it one damn bit."

"Frank Enfield, The Librarian knew you would not bring the *Necronomicon* back to Amrikka! How foolish you are. Did you not learn something in the desert? Did you not find something of yourself in that foul temple? Some dark paths run through all the worlds, and there is no locking them away for safekeeping. They will always bleed their foul mysteries into the world and make monsters of us all. To make ourselves strong, we must fight them, harness our darkness and make it do our bidding!" he hissed through his teeth, his fist in front of my face. "Or we will not remain free of their grasp when they come for us in the spaces between the stars, and in the places within our hearts where it is forever midnight!"

I just sat there, letting it all sink in.

"You found your way to al-Hazrad without my help. Think on that, Frank Enfield. Think on that and wonder how."

I nodded at what he said, knowing he was speaking the truth.

"You must know this too, Mr. Enfield: the woman faced the *Necronomicon* before you, and she prevailed. She took away great power from that dark temple, as you did, if you recall what was awakened within you."

"Yes, I do," I said making a fist of my own and pounding the soft carpets beneath me.

"And there is one more thing. Think of it as a server near."

"A what?"

"This book, one of the children of the Book that dropped its roots into the world. You may take it home, give it to The Librarian if you like, or keep it as a server near of your journey to my lands, the lands of the Sons of Smokeless Fire!" he said, tossing a paperback book into my lap. "Read the first page and wonder upon the power of the jinn!"

The book in my lap said the *Necronomicon* on the cover and bore the name of somebody called Simon. Flipping the first couple of pages open, it said it was published in 1978, thirty years in the future! It was a cheap-looking thing and bore no resemblance to the massive leather-bound monstrosity growing out of al-Hazrad's chest.

"Remember, Frank Enfield, the Sons of Smokeless Fire are not confined to space and time as are lesser...well, the Sons of Adam," he added, grinning. "Give this book to

The Librarian so he will know the jinn showed you good hospitality, and that I understood his joke."

"His joke?"

"Just a joke between old friends. Now sleep. Tomorrow you return to your own lands, and I must retrieve the bodies of my companions from the City of Blood Sands. They will be quite angry I took so long to come for them."

"You mean they're not dead?" I said, glad to hear it even if I *had* thought they had planned to sell my hide. In the end, they had set me free.

"Dead? What do you mean? The jinn do not die. Oh, Frank Enfield, The Librarian has much to teach you, so very much to teach you…"

His words faded off, and I drifted into a place where it was nighttime, but all the stars and the Moon were in their rightful places, and I just sat there in the darkness, feeling something inside me awaken again and stretch its powerful clawed feet. It rose up and started to prowl around inside all the hidden places in my mind, and elsewhere, within the many houses of the mansion that is Frank Enfield. Somewhere, I heard Spidey giving it the guided tour, and somewhere beyond even that, I heard The Librarian laughing.

WHAT MEDICINE ELSE CAN CURE
BY CHRISTOPHER LONG

The crew were positioned far closer than she'd expected. Tucked behind their equipment, she could see they were struggling to contain a very professional variety of boredom. Not that she could blame them. This was nothing new or exciting to add to their CVs. Over the years, they'd doubtlessly filmed plenty of celebrities opening up about their pasts. It gave them the disinterested air of doctors; priests, perhaps.

The director had sat Julia in the small, quiet back sitting room of her old family house, positioned by a window that looked out onto the well-manicured garden. Summer had withdrawn today, cloaking itself behind a cold grey sky. Now, thanks to that seasonal retreat, a breeze was sliding softly past her exposed neck.

I knew I should've worn a scarf, she scolded herself. *This place was always draughty.*

Her father and uncles had built this house after the war. She'd grown up here, before going onto raise her own children under this roof. It was here that her father had famously said *I'm off to make the beds* before heading upstairs to actually build beds for his children to sleep in.

They were here because the director had arranged each group of questions to suit a different location from her past. It had sounded like quite a nice idea, to begin with. They'd sat in her garden back in Kent to talk about her grandchildren. In the kitchen where she'd first worked to talk about life as a professional cook. In the offices of the first paper who published her work, to let her reminisce about writing. Now, however, they'd sat her in the sitting room where she'd once sat with her parents and then her own children, only to ask her about Robin. The niceties of having a documentary made about her life were beginning to turn sour.

"So, you bought your husband the car after your first show was picked up, is that right?"

She tensed. The lens audibly zoomed in. The man operating it looked about as blank as the dark round glass dimly capturing her reflection.

Julia was enough of a pro to know what they wanted. Ideally, you were expected to reference their question whilst answering it. It helped the documentary cut together better.

She took a deep breath before starting to tell the story of the most personal and broken skeleton stashed away in her larder-sized cupboard. It always began the same way, with the joy of realising she'd become popular. That glimmer of a past victory made it easier for her to access the more difficult memories that lay in wait.

In reasonably quick time, she'd gone from a cook hired to demonstrate new recipes at trade shows to someone who wrote articles for newspapers and lifestyle magazines. From there, a few choice daytime TV appearances had revealed that she had attracted the attention of a sizeable audience.

At no point in her life had Julia ever dreamt that she was destined for fame. Maybe that was why the public liked her so much. She was honest. She never clamoured for their attention or forced herself to be something she wasn't. She came across as your friend. Your kitchen confidante. As she'd grown older, that image had evolved into an understanding auntie and then onto a kindly grandmother. Or, as the papers insisted on calling her these days, the Queen of the Nation's Kitchen.

To be honest, it all struck her as little too twee, but her agent clearly had no problem with it. She quietly suspected he'd helped foster it in the first place.

Robin, her loving husband, had always been her loudest, proudest cheerleader during the early years. He'd had people picking up a copy of any magazine that featured her. He'd insisted colleagues buy her cookbooks for their wives and daughters at Christmas and made sure everyone tuned in whenever she'd appeared on TV.

Naturally, he'd been over the moon when she'd been given her first full series. That was why she'd decided to treat him to the car of his dreams. Not that she'd known much about the one he chose in the end. She'd never really been what you'd call a car person. She liked practical little run-arounds. Simple, easy to park, easy to maintain, with room for the kids and everything required to keep them happy. Robin was different. Whilst being mature enough to accept practical and affordable cars all his adult life, he'd longed for a vehicle that could turn heads.

He went for something quick, in the end. Violently quick. As lethal as lightning, in gleaming gunmetal grey. His own runaway rollercoaster. The engine had sounded vicious to her ears, as if it was betraying something primal that lurked beneath the graceful bodywork. She hadn't seen the parallels at first. All she'd seen was a happy husband, in love with his new car.

He'd loved that car almost as much as he'd loved a drink—not that any drink had ever loved him back. No, alcohol did something to Robin. It unravelled him. Twisted him in on himself. After a few glasses, the envy would start to show.

He'd been raised in a world of quiet, agreeable housewives and their loud, proud, high-earning husbands. When he was sober, he couldn't have been happier for her, but when he was drunk, a different truth had boiled out of him. Rose up through him like lava, escaping in muttered comments to begin with. Then his laughter would turn piercing and his hand would slam against the table. His eyes would begin to burn as the anger barged past his gritted, toothy grin.

The shouting normally started when she told him to put the bottle down. After that it was never been long before the children were hiding, and she was fighting to calm him down. Thankfully, he'd always left the house before things truly fell apart. Whether that was some unconscious instinct, trying to steer the beast away from his family, or whether it was just a need to flee from his defeat, Julia could never be sure.

Most times, he'd walked it off. Stalked into the countryside to bellow at the moon. That one time, however, he'd gone for the car, and she hadn't stopped him.

People did drink and drive back then, but she should've known. She had known. Anyone would've known. He could barely walk straight as he'd turned his back and stormed off, marching out of their house. She'd watched him slam the car door and disappear into the night with a roar of precision engineering pushed to its teetering limit, the headlights only coming on once he was on the main road.

In the end, he hadn't gone far before he'd lost control. A few miles at most, out the other side of the village, heading towards the hills. The police had phoned her with the news, but she hadn't been surprised.

Driving here today, they'd passed the tree he'd hit. There was still just a stump there. A stunted, lifeless effigy. A broken splinter of a tombstone.

After she was finished recounting a mildly edited version of the story to the camera, conscious of the fact it would air before the watershed, Julia struggled to catch her breath. She glimpsed the crew through a thin veil of restraint and tears. A couple of them were looking more sombre now, but most were keeping one eye on the clock, all too aware that they still had one more location to go.

She kept to herself as they hurriedly packed away. It was strange to think they were taking her most painful memory with them, captured to share with a primetime audience.

She felt hollow as she stood on weak legs. Scooped out. It'd been so long since she'd truly opened herself up to those memories. Performing the act here had come with a sense of contagion, or lighting matches close to a can of petrol. It had left her feeling strangely spent, returning to ground zero and speaking the words. She'd stirred the air Robin used to breathe.

It was as if that future TV audience had arrived early, curious and cruel. Lingered too close. She'd felt them listening in, rapidly consuming her every word.

Her smile looked too delicate as she clutched at her designer handbag, trying to hide her shaking hands. The bag was expensive. Retro chic. The past dressed up as the present, the years smoothed away with rounded corners and pastel colours. They did the same with cars these days.

Julia took slow steps to leave the house, barely able to make eye contact with all those familiar rooms. She'd awoken something from its slumber here. She was sure of it. She could hear the echo of all those past arguments, the stern tread of her father up those creaking stairs. Heading towards her room, demanding to know why her headmaster had called him at work.

What did you do to that little girl this time?

Hammering on her door, demanding answers whilst she pushed her face against her pillow to muffle her own tears.

That'd been a different time. Little Susan Carstairs, the name forever a catching splinter in her heart.

Leaving the house, she was caught off guard by the current owners. They were hovering close to the front door and pounced as soon as they saw her. They struggled to sound natural. They smiled too much, which did nothing for her nerves.

Julia hated being treated like royalty. She refused to see herself as anything special. It was the television that'd put the airs and graces on her, shaping her into the Queen of Cakes. The Duchess of Dining. The Princess of the Priceless Recipes. As far as she was concerned, she was simply a working girl who'd gotten lucky. If these people knew some of the things she'd gotten up to when she'd grown up here, they wouldn't be so quick to beg for a selfie.

"You're definitely the queen of my kitchen," the lady of the house cooed. "I can't believe we live in the house where Julia Harris grew up."

"Well, it's nice to know it's in good hands." Her voice was wavering, fraying at the edges.

This afternoon had left her holding the pieces of herself together between trembling fingers. The sight of any couple, happy or otherwise, would hurt for a while now she'd dipped her toe back into life at this house, although she had to wonder how these two would feel when they finally watched the documentary.

Maybe they'd stop bragging about living in the house where Julia Harris grew up, once they knew what it meant to her. This place was as much a tombstone as that broken stump by the side of the road, on the other side of the village.

She averted her eyes from the end of the drive as she thanked them again and headed towards the car. Julia couldn't have told you why, but she was certain she'd see his car there. The car she'd bought him. Silver in the sunlight, waiting for her. The sleek, shaped bonnet concealing a banshee that lived to scream at high speed.

Maybe she'd see him tearing off into the emptiness that had claimed him. Or maybe she'd catch sight him of returning from it.

She politely turned down the chance to ride to the next location with the crew and stuck close to her assistant, Kenny. The lad meant well. He was painfully young: all hair product, expensive trainers, and dreams of producing one day. He tried to keep his attitude holstered around her, but it would slip through when the stress overwhelmed him or when he was caught off guard around some of the older men on the crew, thinking she was out of sight. Still, he fussed after her like a mother, checking she was okay, making sure she'd taken her pills.

"Seatbelt on?" he asked.

"Yes."

"Okay then, off we go."

As they followed the van, she recognised every street they passed. It was like remembering a song, each verse coming back to her as she heard the one before it.

The village seemed so much smaller than she remembered. The distance between the houses. Between the roads, shops, school, and parks. It all looked so cramped. Perhaps her eyes had become too accustomed to city sprawls. The long, congested streets that refused to sleep. The tourist traps and the shiny new betting shops too close to the rundown local pubs.

This village had been her entire universe once. It'd been boundless then, the ever-distant horizon ringed and fortified with familiar hills. The tall, teetering, windswept trees full of birds to wake you in the morning.

It'd been a place where the summer dwelt comfortably within the confines of the park and where Sunday mornings always smelt of church hymn books. Where everyone always appeared friendly, and the corner shop never ran out of sweets.

Maybe it was true what they said about childhood. Maybe you truly did only remember the sunny days, or the snowy days. The greyer days were erased, unless they contained something vital. The embarrassing moments. The guilty secrets.

Little Susie Carstairs running home from school, tears in her eyes and blood on her bare knees. Bruises on her arms. The rain beginning to fall as Julia started her friends chanting one word over and over again at the fleeing figure. Chasing her through the streets, with adults watching through their windows and the stones growing slippy in their fingers.

Witch. Witch. Witch.

The rain began to fall again now, the past bleeding back into the present. Leaving little wet tumbledown scratch-mark kisses down the car windows. She could almost see those children. Hear their cries.

"Can you remember the last time you were here?" Kenny asked, hands at ten to two on the wheel, driving as if he was transporting a historic vase.

She'd seen him drive when she wasn't in the car. Windows down. Bass up. Skidding to a halt for red lights and roundabouts. Another boy at one with his toy, barely aware of the world.

"Oh, it was a long time ago. A lifetime, really."

Witch. Witch. Witch.

She'd had a new hip last year. She was walking without a stick now, but by the end of every day, the pain always grew a little too much for her to bear. Thankfully the stitches were out, and the bruises were gone. The dark, hideous, swampy mark on her leg had settled down to a skulking red scar.

The pain of Robin's death was different. It would never leave her. Sprinkled with guilt. Seasoned with sour memories. A lingering burden of their love, refusing to be healed or ignored.

The pain of what she'd done to Susan Carstairs was even closer. It was etched into her bones. It had doubtlessly infected even her new hip joint by now. It steered her every decision. It lingered behind her every step.

"I went along when he bought that car," Julia said to herself, watching the village slide by her window. "I watched him strut around the showroom, sitting behind all those steering wheels like a grinning schoolboy. Choosing the place where he'd die one day."

Kenny didn't say anything. He was keeping an eye on the van as it escaped them at a narrow junction.

"I wonder if he ever knew?" she asked her reflection.

"Knew what?"

Judging by the look on Kenny's face, he hadn't heard a word she'd said.

As they arrived at her old school, Julia saw a few children lingering in the playground. They must've stayed after lessons to meet her.

They ran towards the car as Kenny parked up. The producers must've arranged this. It certainly had their fingerprints all over it.

The kids had all brought along books to be signed, and proud parents to document the occasion. Julia did her best to play along, once she was out of the car and smiling. It wasn't like she had a choice. After all, she was the nation's favourite grandma. The woman who'd introduced a whole new generation to the joys of baking.

She knew she became a different sort of grandmother around strangers' children. A little kinder, perhaps. More tolerant, certainly. A pantomime version of herself. Overly pleased at their achievements. Comically shocked by their funny comments. A sad smile ready for any child coping with a pain she couldn't fix. It always took a lot out of her, but it was worth it to see them happy.

She asked each child what they liked to cook and what they liked to eat. She told them about her grandchildren and about the first cakes her daughters ever baked.

"Why're you here?" one tiny dot of a girl asked from beneath an unkempt mass of blonde hair.

"We're filming a documentary about my life. You see, I used to go to school here too. Of course, it was very different back then."

The little girl nodded sagely before giving her a sudden hug. "I wish you went to school with me."

"So do I, love."

Julia was almost feeling back to her old self when one little boy stepped cautiously forward and introduced himself as Timothy Carstairs. She had to stop herself recoiling from his outstretched hand. Instead she shook it limply.

"Sorry, what did you say your name was again?"

"Timothy."

He didn't offer the surname this time, and she couldn't bring herself to push for it. It was possible she'd misheard him. She listened as he talked about lemon drizzle cakes, his favourite. Her heart raced in her chest.

Had he said Carstairs? It had to be a coincidence, if he did. Had to be. Besides, it was only a name. It didn't mean anything. Not everyone in a village was related. She should know that. She'd lived long enough in this tight knot of families, streets and histories. Carstairs could be like Smith around here now, for all she knew.

"Mummy doesn't like to cook," he said in that earnest tone only children can muster. "But my granny shows me how to bake all her favourite cakes. She knows all sorts of old recipes."

"Yes, grans are very good at that."

Was her tone slipping? Julia tried smiling harder. It immediately felt wrong.

"Mummy said Granny went to school with you, although I'm not supposed to talk about it."

Panic abruptly seized the Queen of the Nation's Kitchen.

"Did she?"

"Granny won't talk about it to anyone, not even me. She said she didn't want me going to school here. She said it'd be bad for a boy like me."

Julia did her very best to change the subject, then posed for a selfie that Timothy took a lifetime to line up and snap with his sticky, pudgy digits. When he finally reviewed his photo, he didn't look happy.

"You aren't smiling," he declared.

She quietly made her excuses and swiftly moved onto the next child, her hip aching from bending down for too long.

For the rest of the time the children were there, she could feel Timothy watching her. Always from the side. Always quiet and close. It could just have been that he felt snubbed, but she read so much more into that lingering silence. The excitement in his eyes had curdled.

Or maybe there was more to it than that. Maybe he'd lied. Maybe his Granny had told him exactly what had happened, all those years ago.

Julia just hoped he didn't ask for an explanation. She could barely make sense of her actions back then herself. At times she'd tried to reason that it could all be filed under 'Childish Misunderstanding,' but she knew better than that.

She could try telling him that mobs might form from people, but they weren't necessarily compromised of each separate person. A mob just required bodies to add to its seething mass of limbs and one opinion. The people within any mob, no matter how small, simply disappear. They blur at the edges. They move as one, people hunting in packs.

She could remember starting some of the jokes about his grandmother. *Little Susie Carstairs cooks with a cauldron. Little Susie Carstairs rides to school on a broom. Little Susie Carstairs sleeps in the graveyard, with all her friends.* She just didn't know exactly why she'd started it.

It was easier now to think of someone standing behind her, whispering all those ideas into her head. Except she knew it'd been her. She'd developed a taste for it. Worse still, she'd seen those little moments of devilment in her own children. Robin used to tell her not to worry.

Everyone has a little troublemaker in them, he'd say, and then, sometimes, he'd shown her his.

As the children around her began to head home, Julia silently prayed for some relief, only it wouldn't come. Her past was too close here. It could reach out at any moment and catch her by the scruff of the neck. To make things worse, she could still feel herself being watched.

She turned and, sure enough, there he was: little Timothy Carstairs. Still holding his copy of *Cooking Up Tricks with Julia*. It was an illustrated book she'd produced for children. Recipes for real cakes, along with some made-up, magical pretend ones. Unicorn's Delight. Slimy Frog Ice Cream. Witch's Brew.

The director was coming over, eager to discuss what was next. The sight of him grounded her. Earthed her. Gave her breathing space to formulate an idea, hopefully one that would readdress some of the guilt she was drowning in.

"I had a thought," she told him. "How about, instead of taking the camera crew for a walk around the school, I give somebody else a little guided tour?"

She nodded towards Timothy. He didn't flinch away as the director mulled it over.

"I like it," her director said. "It'll give us a nice change of tone."

She left him to discuss details with the producers and went over to Timothy.

"Did you hear that?" she asked. "You can be in my programme. Would you like that?"

Timothy nodded.

"Good."

Once everyone was set up, the director talked her through what he wanted. Kenny hovered close by, bottle of water and painkillers in hand. Her stick was in the car, but he knew damn well not to bring it to her in front of other people.

"We want to keep this nice and simple," the director explained. "Just walk your little sidekick here through the corridors and talk about what you remember. Friends, teachers, that sort of thing. And, Timmy, if you have any questions for Julia, then be sure to ask them. Nice and clearly, okay?"

"Okay."

The director went back behind his monitor. The camera and sound guys came closer. Timothy's eyes widened at the sight of them. Julia gave his clammy little hand a gentle squeeze.

"Don't mind them," she told him.

As the director called action, she took Timothy through the front doors and into the reception area. She heard the light tread of the crew behind her.

"It's a lot cleaner than it was in my day," she said, although the smell was still there. Cheap council bleach. School dinners. Dusty, underfunded books. "We didn't have all these glass doors and TV screens back then."

Timothy still looked a little startled. Innocent alienation was holding him back, distancing him from all of this. For her to feel better, she needed the lad to shine in front of the camera, which meant he had to relax. So she told him about her first day at school. About her first assembly. About her friends. She made him laugh as she took him past the classrooms and display boards.

It all looked so different now, yet the muscle memory was there. The tight constraint of the old rules, keeping a watchful eye on her. She would never dare to run down these corridors, let alone whistle or shout. It felt wrong to be talking loud enough for the crew to pick her up, although the further she took the boy into the school, the more she forgot they were even there. The past was becoming far too distracting.

When they passed the little library, Julia remembered the shelves so vividly that it stopped her in her tracks.

"Look at that," she said. "It's exactly the same."

She had to stop herself from kneeling in front of the books and selecting her homework. She recognised every title. Every cover.

They weren't the brightly coloured, optimistic ones she'd read to her children, or the mass-marketed branded adverts for TV shows that her grandchildren loved so much. No, these were the books her generation had been raised on. The ones she'd read a lifetime ago.

Perhaps they laid them out for me on purpose, she wondered.

They pressed on, and the classrooms started to ring a bell. They had actual blackboards in them, little rows of child-sized desks. She told Timothy about her earliest memories of lessons. Spelling tests, which terrified her. Maths, which she'd hated. Art, which she'd loved but been terrible at. As she talked, Julia thought she caught sight of inkwells in those desks, but decided it was just her memory playing tricks on her.

She saw the little cloakrooms. All those empty hooks and cubby holes. The posters for the alphabet and times tables. There was one for King and Country hanging by a classroom door. She remembered that from when she was a girl.

They had to be doing a project on the war. It couldn't have been hanging there this whole time. It would've faded by now, for a start.

A car sped past the windows. Julia jumped as she caught sight of a glint of silver cutting through the trees.

"Are you okay?" Timothy asked.

"I'm fine," she said, speaking softly, hoping she could go back to the hotel soon.

She was getting tired. Her hip was twinging sharply. Her arthritis was starting to seethe through her fingers. She could barely feel his hand in hers.

Julia wondered if the boy could feel the slight shake of her grip. Another subtle sign that she needed to rest, one that only Kenny ever really noticed.

The school was built in a small circle. The front was part of the original school, built back in the 1800s. The rest of the extensions over the years had added wings behind it and then joined across the back, allowing them to have the playground pinned in the centre as a small courtyard area, between the classrooms and corridors.

She spotted the little gardening area as they turned a corner. Her old headmaster had started something like that, an allotment to grow vegetables that the school could use to feed its children. Dig for Your Dinner, he'd called it. Mr Fowler. Her old nemesis. Harder than her father. Younger than her grandfather. A Victorian-principled tyrant, ruled too often by his temper and his lack of patience with children.

If the layout was still the same, then the offices and the staffroom would be at the front. The headmaster's office would be there, set in a little from the corridor, the extra space allowing for a small nook between the corridor and the door. In her time, there'd been a little row of chairs there, ready for children to sit and wait to be judged.

There'd been two little lights over the headmaster's door back then: a red light and a green light. She'd not thought of those in years. It would be red when the headmaster was with someone, and green when he was ready for you.

She'd hated sitting out there, waiting for that light to go green. It was all part of Mr Fowler's little game. He'd loved letting children sit out there, allowing them to hear the thwack of the cane landing solidly against another child's skin, usually their palm. She could remember him looming over her, getting her to hold out her hand.

"Don't close your eyes," he would say, cane poised at the ready. "It's important that you see the consequences for your actions."

She'd heard a lot of people her age talk about bringing back corporal punishment. She'd never agreed with them. She had watched Mr Fowler come in too many mornings with a scowl that told you he'd been saving up all his anger for the first child sent to his office. She'd seen too many children leave here sporting stormy bruises on their palms.

After what had happened to Susie Carstairs, he'd stalked these corridors looking for someone to blame. He'd called parents. Her own father had denied she'd ever have been involved in such a thing, as had every parent. No one could ever believe their children were capable of such cruelty. Even Susie's parents had struggled with the knowledge of what other children had done to their only child.

Realising she'd been quiet for a little too long, Julia tried to think of a question for the boy. "Do you like your teachers, Timothy?"

There was no response.

"Timothy?"

Julia stopped. Her fingers tightened. There was nothing there for them to hold onto. He'd let go of her hand. She twisted around, only now aware of how dark the corridor had become around her.

"Timothy?" There was no reply. No crew watching her, either.

She was on her own.

"Hello?"

Her voice echoed down the corridor. It appeared far too long now. She could barely see the end of it, in either direction. Had she taken a wrong turn? Worse still, was she having some kind of turn?

Her friend Cybil had suffered a stroke mid-sentence when they'd been having dinner together. It'd been like something out of a nightmare, the sight of her friend slowly collapsing in on herself. Floundering in her own skin, unable to ask for help.

Somewhere, perhaps back where she'd come from, there was the lingering call of music.

It was something her parents would've listened to, back when they all lived in the house down the road. Something slow, warm and waltz-like. Dream music. An ethereal, jazz-flavoured lullaby. A big band, sailing away, swaying beneath the unchanging stars of nostalgia.

Unsure, Julia turned and slowly walked back towards it.

"Timothy, are you down here?"

It could be the exhaustion, she told herself. Or her eyesight. Or it could be the pain. She'd not been right all afternoon. This could all be in her head.

Maybe she'd collapsed and, right now, Kenny was fretfully trying to wake her up. As part of her charity work, she'd talked to people who'd suffered from heart attacks or head injuries. A few of them had spoken about slipping into the deepest of dreams. They all said you were best to simply accept the logic of the delirium.

Try to think of it as your brain taking you where you need to go, one of them had said. *You have hope it's leading you back to reality.*

Well, this certainly felt real. This felt all too real. The air was cold. Her panic was palpable. Her footsteps echoed away, retreating to leave her on her own. Her life, her home, her family. Even Kenny. They were all so far from wherever she had accidentally strayed.

There was a light coming from a pair of open double doors. This was where the music was coming from.

Peering through, she saw the old school dining hall. She stepped cautiously inside to find row upon row of empty tables. She knew them immediately, as familiar as all those streets that'd carried her here.

They were set for dinner, but not a school dinner. There was expensive-looking cutlery laid out. Fine bone-white dinner plates. Thick rich napkins. Dark flowers on the table in tall, twisting vases.

The far end of the hall used to have a mural painted on it: a view of the village, smoke rising from the chimneys, the sun blazing overhead. Now the mural showed a night-time rendition, a winter darkness hanging heavy over those fragile roofs. Shadows trying to flee the probing, medical moonlight.

There were figures at the windows, pulling back their curtains to watch children chase each other off into the gloom.

"Timothy?"

The music was coming from the kitchen. The shutters were down, closing off the serving area, but the side door was open. Julia went inside and the cooking smell hit her straight away. Spice and sweetness and something else, not so much meat as flesh. Raw, wet flesh.

There was her little sidekick, sitting up on a high stool at the far end of the room, past the ovens and industrial cooker hoods, swinging his legs, reading a comic. He was close to the stainless-steel countertop, where someone else was standing, busily preparing their ingredients. A stranger, with their back to the door, chopping hard with a big heavy knife, the wide sharp blade turning from silver to slickest, wettest red with each high swinging slice.

"Timothy, there you are. You gave me quite the scare."

Julia was trying to keep her professional face on show: her voice a bit lighter, her tread a little softer.

The figure didn't turn as they spoke. "Sorry, that's my fault. He always finds me if he knows I'm close by." The voice was old, cracked.

The closer Julia got, passing the hobs loaded with large, bubbling pans, the more she could see this person was hunched not by focus but by age. There was white hair showing through a health and safety-prescribed hairnet. Their gaunt body was dressed in a stained, shabby, badly-fitting tabard. She'd had to wear something similar when she'd done her series on commercial kitchens.

"It's not a problem," Julia said, wondering what exactly was cooking in those pots. It all looked so brown. An earthy, heavy brown, like someone was boiling mud.

"Oh yes, Tim always comes to his granny."

Julia stopped in her tracks. From behind his comic, Timothy Carstairs giggled. The pages shook as the short, buckled old woman turned to face her.

"Susie?"

Susie's face was a ruined mess. The skin had healed badly. One eye was white and lifeless. Her lips were pulled back into a permanent snarl, exposing yellow teeth and sunken gums. There were patches, close to her forehead, where the hair clearly couldn't grow back because of what they'd done to her.

"When I heard Julia Harris was coming here today, I just knew I had to come and see you for myself."

"You...you have a lovely grandson, Susie."

Timothy giggled again. Something about the sound of it set Julia's teeth on edge. She wanted to back away. To turn and run. Only she stayed where she was as the old woman walked towards her, dragging one leg behind her.

"Ah, he comes in handy," Susie said. "Don't you, Timmy?"

He giggled again, hidden behind his comic. Was he even turning the pages?

The sounds of the boiling pots grew louder. It sounded like a tide, rising up to wash Julia away.

"I was always so sorry," Julia said, trying to steer into what she'd rehearsed in her head a hundred times during guilty, sleepless nights. "About what happened to you. I never...I mean, it was never supposed to get so out of hand."

She watched the old woman open a drawer. Loose cutlery rattled. Julia saw rusty blades, stained forks and spoons. Old wooden ladles and other implements. More tools than cooking utensils, blunt relics of a bygone era.

"Shush now," Susie said as she reached in amongst the scrap and rubbish before daintily retrieving a little silver teaspoon. "We'll have none of that. What's done is done."

She slammed the door. The sudden noise of it made Julia jump.

In the far corner, Timothy giggled again. Julia was almost certain she hadn't seen him move since she'd come in here. She felt a desperate, irrational need to see his face. To see him smiling. To know that was his laugh. It didn't sound like him at all.

"There are so many secrets in our little village," Susie Carstairs said, dragging herself over to the pots and gently dipping the teaspoon into one of the pots. "There's St Thomas', sitting on top of a far older altar that the Catholics smashed to pieces centuries ago. There are the stones that line Alf Foster's largest field. Did you know they say a new stone appears every time a child dies in the village? And then there's you, Julia. Our local hero. With a husband who killed himself, like a necessary sacrifice for your success. And with a much darker secret about what you did to me."

"I didn't...they weren't my matches."

"It's okay, my love. I'm not spoiling for a fight. Here, try this."

Susie held out the spoon. A thick brown drip lolled over the edge and tumbled slowly towards the dirty tiles. When it hit them, it splattered, the colour thinning out.

Something wriggled in the spill. Slithered away, leaving a grimy little trail behind it.

"What is that?"

"It's the best secret any village has to offer, Julie. A family recipe. Trust me, you've never tasted anything like it before."

Julia felt dizzy, lost. She was sinking into the heat and noise of this kitchen. Had it always been so big?

She was steered by habit as she leant in and took a taste.

It was sour and heavily seasoned. She could taste herbs, wet mouthfuls of herbs. An overgrown hedgerow of leaves and thick, slimy mushrooms, and there was something else. Something that moved about her mouth before she bit down and felt it crunch.

In the corner, little Timothy Carstairs giggled again, his comic rattling.

"What do you think?" the cook asked the queen of her kitchen.

"It's...it's certainly rustic. What's in it?"

"Only the finest ingredients for you, my love. A pinch of guilt. A twist of regret. A fear of consequences and a very special truth. Would you like to hear it?"

The pans bubbled louder. They drowned out the radio.

Timothy began to laugh. Began to howl. He sat back, the comic still covering his face as he struggled to breathe, as he buckled with his own merriment. Pages slipped over the floor, spilled over him as Susie Carstairs leant close, so close that you could smell the sweat beneath her lavender perfume. The dirt beneath her fingernails. The freshly chopped flesh staining the front of her kitchen whites.

"You were right about me all along."

The laughter in the corner disappeared in an avalanche of paper pages. The boy was gone, leaving only empty, soiled clothes behind.

Julia barely flinched. She was hypnotised by the grin in front of her. She watched as Susan Carstairs' eyes began to change. The colour swam away from her good eye, and something boiled up from the depths of them both. Something black and fetid. Something swirling, nebulous and ancient. An angry ink that leaked past her eye sockets and drizzled down her face, triggering a change in her skin.

The old scar tissue danced, writhed, reformed. Her tongue took on the consistency of a slick slug as she began to laugh.

Julia turned and fled. The lights flickered overhead as she fell out of the kitchen, the taste of whatever had been on that spoon still overpowering her senses. Filling them. Smothering them. Her hip gave out, and she crashed into a table.

She struggled back up, looked over to see the old woman watching her from the doorway, the transformation not yet finished. The true face so much worse than the damaged one she'd worn before.

"You've got one reunion left, my love. Just one. I'd remember not to close your eyes, if I were you."

Julia pushed herself up and ran for the double doors. As she rounded past the entrance, she collided with someone and screamed. Tried to fight free as the hands held tightly onto her. As the lights twitched and suddenly...

Suddenly...

Suddenly there she was, back in the front corridor.

Outside the headmaster's office. Kenny tightly holding her. The crew watching closely now, all their equipment trained on her.

"Julia, Julia," Kenny was saying. "It's okay. You're okay."

She tried to catch her breath. She was shaking badly.

"I don't know what you said to that boy, but he took off like a bat out of hell."

"I didn't..."

She could hear him crying, little footsteps fleeing fast. That familiar sound, of retreating Carstairs tears.

Time slowed as she clawed back some sense of herself. The crew packed up and the director said they had plenty they could still use. She was asked if she wanted to watch the footage, but she politely refused. Her reality still felt far too thin to torment with facts.

According to Kenny, she'd stopped in front of the headmaster's office and knelt by Timothy, who'd declared he had a secret to tell her. He'd whispered something in her ear and then, apparently, she'd whispered something back to him.

"He'd laughed at first," Kenny told her in the car. "Then he burst into tears and ran for the hills."

The producers were already setting about smoothing things over, and plans were being made to move the schedule around so she could take tomorrow off. Julia, for her part, didn't tell them what she'd seen. She didn't want to talk about that kitchen, that face, or the taste she couldn't shake from the back of her throat.

A pinch of guilt. A twist of regret. A fear of consequences and a very special truth.

When they got back to the hotel, she left the crew in the bar and made sure there was a little money behind there for them. Kenny insisted on walking her back to her room, but she soon chased him away.

She kept thinking about that strange little boy, who she'd seen disappear, and about Susie. If that had been her.

You were right about me all along.

She tried to cling to the details. The pans. That overloaded drawer. The small, limp bodies Susie had been cutting up for the pot. Had they been birds or rabbits?

Then there were the words that'd followed her out of that kitchen. *You've got one reunion left, my love. Just one. I'd remember not to close your eyes, if I were you.*

Julia did her best to believe it was just exhaustion. She'd been travelling all over the country for weeks. She'd done a series of live shows as well, along with a recent book tour. She needed a break, and today had clearly just been too much for her. The straw that broke the camel's back.

In her current state, she found herself wondering if that was the same camel you were meant to pass through a needle on to get into Heaven. She was rich. Wasn't that the only way she was getting in?

She had a long bath and a cup of tea before turning in. It was barely eight o'clock, but she didn't care. She was too tired to stay awake, even if she was afraid of what her dreams might show her.

She was vaguely aware of voices in the corridor later on, sounding slick with drink. She stirred again when she heard a toilet flush overhead. She rolled over and went back to sleep, that horrible taste still lingering in her mouth.

The next time Julia woke, she was barely conscious at all. She had no concept of what time it was. She simply looked at the foot of the bed and saw a door where there hadn't been a door there before, set in slightly from the rest of the room.

It didn't matter that it refused to match the other doors in the room, or that it was older, from a different sort of décor. She regarded it in the same way as you might any other door.

There was a plaque on the front. The word *Headmaster* gleamed in the shadows.

Over it was a red light. When it turned green, Julia pulled back the covers and got out of her bed. She trod softly towards the door and wasn't awake enough to do anything but respond to the memory written deep in her muscles.

She stopped and knocked.

"Enter." The voice was strict and keen.

She did as she was told and stepped inside, closing the door behind her.

The light turned red and, for a little while after, all you could hear was the sound of a cane being slapped against flesh. After that, there was nothing but silence.

MUERTE CON SABOR A FRESA
(STRAWBERRY-FLAVORED DEATH)
BY NELSON W. PYLES

1

Georgie Turner no longer cared if Daryl Madison was still alive. If he couldn't give a call to say he wasn't coming to work, or quitting, or whatever, then Georgie shouldn't be expected to care. She thought about this as she sat in front of Daryl's apartment complex. She gripped the steering wheel tightly in frustration.

She looked across the sunlit parking lot; it was now midday on a Wednesday, and the lot was nearly empty. Except for Daryl's car, sitting in its little assigned parking spot.

She scowled and called his cell phone for the tenth time. It didn't even ring, just went to the voice mail.

"Hey, this is Big D. Leave a message, but I will probably just text you back. Deuces."

She hung up for the eleventh time and punched the steering wheel. She was going to have to get out of the car and walk up to the door.

She got out of her car, slammed the door, and walked to the entrance to the building.

She listened to her shoes clap against the sidewalk and tried to let it calm her down. She liked meditation quite a bit, but it just wasn't working today. When it came to Daryl, her patience was already thin, and she really hoped he was home so she could do some screaming meditation.

That would do wonders to calm her down.

She stood in front of the exterior panel of the apartment and searched for Daryl Madison's name. Of course, it was the last one, and of course it said *Big D*.

Georgie nearly punched it, but she instead she pushed it hard just once. For fifteen seconds.

No response.

She then pushed it fifteen times in rapid succession.

She closed her for a moment before deciding that she didn't have the patience to even talk to Daryl. Her eyes snapped open just in time to see a mid-twenties-looking man with long dreadlocks and a nice grey suit open the door.

"Hi," he said with a big smile. "Are you trying to get somebody? The buzzers don't always work."

He held the door open for her. Georgie blinked and returned his smile. She nearly gave him a curtsey as she walked into the apartment complex.

"Thank you so much," she said. She smiled at him and thanked whatever higher power there is that her building wouldn't have allowed a stranger inside. Still, whatever would work was fine with her. She just had to find the apartment, fire Daryl's dumb ass, and get on with her day.

She knew his apartment number by heart, and glanced at the numbered doors as she got closer to her destination. There, on the left, was apartment one hundred five. She stood in front of it and took a deep breath. The breath was for strength, but along with it came a smell the likes of which was unusual. It smelled like meat just before it rotted. She envisioned a steak in the fridge, forgotten and turning greyish. You could still eat it, but if it started to smell, you'd be shit out of luck.

Georgie held her fist up to knock, but hesitated a moment. She swallowed and knocked three times.

There was no answer, but she did hear something: a small mewling voice, but she couldn't make out what it said.

"Daryl?" she called out. "Is that you in there? It's Georgie."

She heard the mewling voice again, but she still couldn't make it out.

"Can I come in? Are you okay?

She heard the voice a third time, and she grabbed the doorknob. She gave it a turn and opened the door.

The apartment was dark. The lights were off, and the curtains had all been closed. The room was also hot, adding to the stronger smell of greying meat. She saw the green digital light on the stove in the kitchen. It was the only light in the place, so she went towards it.

"Daryl, I'm turning on a light in here. Where are you? Why is it so dark in here?"

The mewling sound was louder, sounding like it was coming from the opposite side of the apartment. Georgie found the kitchen light and switched it on.

The kitchen wasn't what she expected. It reeked of rotten meat, but it looked immaculate. She noticed that the oven was on, which would explain the heat but not the smell. She found the oven knob and turned it off. The plastic knob was hot and soft. The oven must have been on for days.

She walked to the refrigerator and opened it. The smell hit her like a fist. It was stocked with grey bruise-colored meat and rotten vegetables. A thin pool of cold blood began to seep out of the fridge and collect on the linoleum. She gagged and slammed the door shut.

"Jesus fuck," Georgie said in revulsion. She heard the voice again, and now could at least see from the light in the kitchen that the small apartment was mostly clean.

Mostly.

She started to walk out of the kitchen when she saw a large empty container of what looked like protein powder on its side, abandoned on the counter. It had a black label that read simply DENSITOL XXL-STRAWBERRY. She gave it a quick glance, frowned, and then made her way into the next room. The mewling sound was getting louder, but not anymore clear. She glanced at the wall near the front door and saw the light switches. She turned them all on, but saw nothing spectacular in the living room. It too was clean. She shook her head and walked to what she assumed was the bedroom. There was a bathroom to the left of the closed door. She knocked on the door.

"Daryl, are you in here?"

A sound came forth, nearly like a scream. Georgie opened the door, but it only opened halfway. There was something heavy on the other side.

"Help me," came the reply. It had a wheezy high-pitched sound, but was soft and labored. It was the mewling sound she had heard, and it was coming from the floor.

Georgie reached her hand inside the room, feeling for a light switch, and found it. Light exploded in the room from the ceiling. She looked down and saw a leg blocking the door.

At least, it looked somewhat like a leg.

There was a shoe and a sock and a pant leg, but they looked...empty. The shoe was pointed up as if something was holding it. She pushed the door harder, expecting the pant leg to move, but it just wouldn't budge.

"Stop," the thin voice said. "Please help me."

Georgie squeezed herself into the room with some effort. She looked down at what was blocking the door and screamed.

2

The most unusual part of the paramedic rescue call for Priyanka Choudhry wasn't what the victim looked like, although that in and of itself would trigger future nightmares for the foreseeable future. It was just how much the victim weighed.

The general statistics about the victim, Daryl Madison, were that he was five feet six and roughly about a hundred pounds. However, it took three paramedics and two firemen a tremendous effort to get Madison onto the gurney, and even then, they had to roll him onto it. They never raised it up; they had to shuffle it out of the apartment requiring additional help to load him into the ambulance, which nearly buckled under the weight.

Rolling the man onto the gurney proved to be nearly impossible. Madison was nearly flat. Most of his bones were broken in the most unusual ways, as if he had been crushed under something. How he was still alive and breathing was nothing short of miraculous.

Pri had determined from the amount of excrement around the body that he had been on the floor of his bedroom for nearly a week. The woman who had called nine-one-one had said that Madison had been missing about eight days. By rights, due to the injuries and the excrement, Madison should have died from dehydration at the very least.

In looking around the apartment, for anything vaguely resembling a clue as to what could have happened to him was nonexistent. The woman, Ms. Turner, said that she hadn't seen anything out of the ordinary at all. From her description, the apartment was dark, and she had heard Madison crying out softly from the bedroom.

It seemed to be the only thing that made sense.

Pri sat on the edge of her bed and shuddered. She closed her eyes and saw Madison's tear-streaked face. His expression hadn't changed; of course, how could it? The bones in his face had all been crushed, and he'd looked like a rubber Halloween mask without a head inside it. A deflated head that was still alive and suffering in a most unimaginable way.

She had left the hospital once they had managed to find a room (and a bed) that could hold him. There was another call she and her partner had gone to from there, but she knew that she wasn't going to stop thinking about Daryl Madison for quite some time.

She crawled into bed and shut off her light. She waited a long time for sleep to come.

3

The research and development lab in Pentacorp's own industrial park was tucked away in a large facility in Eastern Pittsburgh. It was a half hour from Monroeville and quite a lot of the employees lived there, game for the heavy commute. Truth be told, the job was challenging and difficult but, most would say, rewarding, especially financially.

Georgie opted to not live in Monroeville, however, and lived in a semi-quiet complex in Penn Hills. The town was full of "yinzers" who got good and liquored up on the weekends and most weeknights. But the rent was inexpensive, and there was a guard at the door to keep the riff-raff out...and some of it in, so to speak.

So, because of her proximity to the R&D facility, she had no trouble getting there before anyone in the department, and simply waited for whoever the first person was to arrive.

And unfortunately for Phoebe Armstrong, it happened to be her.

"Well, good morning, Dr. Armstrong."

Phoebe gasped and dropped her coffee. It splashed onto her beige pants, and she yelped as the coffee poured onto the white tile floor. Her face went from shock to quick anger as she saw Georgie, feet propped up on the lab table. Next to her feet was a familiar-looking plastic container.

"Jesus H tap-dancing Christ, what are *you* doing here?"

"I'm here to ask you some questions, and you had better have some really good answers for me." Georgie took a foot and kicked the plastic container off the table and onto the floor. "For question number one, why the fuck was this in one of our employees' apartment?"

Armstrong looked at the container and her eyes narrowed.

"Daryl," she muttered through her teeth.

"Oh, don't you mean 'Big D?'"

Armstrong blinked and glared at Georgie. There had been a long-standing animosity between the two women, but it absolutely was about to get to worse.

"First of all, fuck you. That's first. Just want to get that out of the way." Phoebe folded her arms and leaned to one side. "Secondly, we were authorized to start human testing. *You* authorized human testing, so what do you think human testing means?"

"Human testing means finding volunteers or college students to sign waivers and giving them a few bucks here and there. You know, so if something bad happens they can't sue us and aren't attached to the corporation. Daryl was a fucking *employee*."

"Daryl is still alive, apparently, and he's also an adult who also happened to sign the aforementioned waivers. I'm not stupid, Georgie. All of the bases were covered."

Georgie kicked her feet off the lab table and stood up. She walked slowly towards Phoebe. "Except, of course, for the base where the subject stays in the goddamn testing facility to be monitored and not massively overdose on the test drug because it's a *goddamn test drug*."

Phoebe sank slightly. "Well, okay. You got me there."

"When I found Daryl, he looked like a deflated balloon." Georgie pulled out her cell phone and showed Phoebe a picture.

"Oh, balls," Armstrong said.

"Indeed. But it took several people to get him onto a gurney. He was unbelievably heavy."

"Like, how heavy?"

"It took five men to get him into the ambulance. Why?" Georgie asked.

"That's pretty heavy, yeah." Phoebe said, and turned away. She whirled back around to Georgie. "We have a problem."

"I would love to hit you right now," Georgie said quietly.

Phoebe ignored it. "We need to get Daryl here to the lab ASAP."

"Is this something you can fix?"

Phoebe looked at her and frowned.

"I'm just hoping it's something that can be *contained.*"

4

If there was one thing Daryl loved more than anything, it was the taste of strawberries. Ever since he was a child, he had loved it, and when the opportunity came to not only try a new weight-building protein powder but also choose the flavor, he'd jumped at it. Well, maybe that wasn't entirely true; strawberry was the only flavor that seemed to mask the actual flavor of the powder, or so he had been told. "Flavor was a secondary concern," Dr. Armstrong had said.

But to Daryl, it was necessary if he was going to do it and stick with it.

And hot damn, it tasted great!

Daryl had been underweight most of his life. He was tall, but always so damn skinny. He'd tried everything, and really hated the protein shakes most of all. They tasted terrible and never added any weight. He was still hovering around the same one hundred pounds he'd been ever since high school. Dr. Armstrong had noticed his efforts and pulled him aside.

"I think I can help you."

"Yeah? How? Nothing works. Nothing has ever worked. I've spent the last six months eating shit like this," he said, holding up the messy burger. "Nothing."

"Come to my lab after you get done with work today. I can help you." Dr. Armstrong said, and got up from the table.

He never would have guessed that help would have been strawberry-flavored.

He never would have guessed that one day he'd be begging silently for death.

Daryl didn't know what day it was. He couldn't hear, he couldn't see, and he couldn't speak. He was unaware of anything except that he was still alive somehow, and the only taste in his mouth was sour: vaguely strawberry and vomit. He knew he was alive, but didn't know how or why. He couldn't even remember what had happened to him.

He'd taken the protein powder home and read the instructions carefully. They were simple instructions: eight ounces of water, juice or milk, a scoop of the powder once a day before working out. Only one serving per day.

One.

Dr. Armstrong had even gone as far as to underline the word *once* three times, as if Daryl were too dumb to follow the directions. He laughed as he mixed his first batch. Grinning, he took a breath when he was finished and took a sip of the thick shake.

The texture was unlike the other protein shakes he'd had. It was somehow heavier, but not in a bad way. It was thick and delicious. Dr. Armstrong had suggested water over milk, but Daryl preferred milk and boy, had he been glad he used it. The shake was delicious. In fact, it was amazingly delicious. He smacked his lips and looked at the shake, all pink and frothy.

It was refreshing too, this shake. It didn't feel like a chore to drink it. It was thick, but also smooth. Not quite greasy, but it really slid down his throat easily. The strawberry taste was sweet, but not overtly so. It was the best strawberry anything he'd ever tasted. He'd picked up the container and looked for the ingredients to see if was artificial or made from natural flavors.

There weren't any ingredients.

He shrugged and downed the rest of the shake in one gulp.

As he put the empty plastic cup on the counter, he let out a loud belch. He chuckled and wondered what would happen if he mixed up another batch. Dr. Armstrong had said he had enough to last him for two months if he followed the instructions.

That had seemed like forever ago.

Where had he gone wrong?

Maybe the second shake that day was what started it, or maybe the other shakes in the hours and days that followed. It didn't seem bad at the time and Jesus, it tasted so goddamned *good*.

By the second day he had begun actively craving it. When he wasn't drinking one, he was thinking about it. He had four on the third day. By the end of the fifth day, he had consumed eight.

He'd also begun to gain weight. He had stepped on the scale in Dr. Armstrong's lab fully clothed and weighed a paltry ninety-eight pounds. She had recommended that he give it a week before starting to weigh himself, and although he didn't follow the instructions for taking the powder, he did almost follow that direction. It was the very end of day five; pretty much a week, Daryl thought.

He got up off the couch with a bit of difficulty. He felt stiff, but really didn't know why. He lumbered into the bathroom and stepped on the scale. The large digital numbers loaded up and what he saw, he couldn't believe.

"One hundred sixty-five pounds?" he said out loud. He looked at his reflection, but other than looking like he had a hangover, he couldn't see the weight. He took off his shirt and stepped off the scale. He looked himself up and down in the bathroom mirror and didn't really see any difference. If anything, he could see his ribs more clearly than before. He realized, looking at himself, that he hadn't taken a shower in a few days.

Or gone to work, or even left the apartment.

He debated getting into the shower, then decided against it.

Daryl felt a pang of hunger. He hadn't really eaten anything, either. Just the shakes. Maybe he needed a shake, and then he'd take a shower.

By the seventh day, it was difficult to even stand, but Daryl managed to make it into the bathroom. He still was shirtless and still looked as gaunt as ever, but he felt so...bloated. He staggered into the bathroom and turned on the harsh fluorescent light.

He looked even more gaunt than before. His shoulder blades looked like they were about to poke through his skin, which was looking a little grey. His eyes appeared to have recessed into the sockets. His teeth, which had always been a point of pride for him, looked as if they were false gag teeth from a novelty shop; they were a darkish yellow. He stuck out his tongue and it was black.

Daryl backed away from his reflection and tripped over something. It was the scale. Almost as an afterthought, he stepped on it, although it took more effort than it should have. He put a hand on the wall to steady himself, and he heard the sheetrock crack under his hand. He looked down.

The scale said 'ERROR" in black flashing letters. He sighed and stepped off the scale. It took a moment, but eventually, the scale reset to zero. He stood back on it again and, once again, it read "ERROR," but this time he heard the scale crack. He gingerly stepped off and grabbed the sink counter, which groaned.

"What the hell," Daryl muttered. He steadied himself and walked out of the bathroom, leaving the light on. He made it slowly into his kitchen and opened the container of powder. He knew it was low, but what he saw wasn't low; it was practically empty. There was maybe a half scoop left.

His eyes welled up. Dr. Armstrong would be furious with him, if she wasn't already. He'd already gone through a two-month supply in what, a week?

He staggered over to the stove, nearly falling. He caught himself before falling and nearly upended the stove. He looked at the green clock and saw that it was six forty-five in the morning.

What day is it?

He had closed the blinds and curtains days ago. He hadn't watched television or checked his phone. He had to struggle to think of what he'd been doing, and couldn't honestly remember. His eyes had begun to widen with a growing panic. Without thinking, he shuffled back over to the counter and picked up the container. He opened it with great effort, and put the container up to his face. He opened his mouth, crying.

Daryl emptied what was left of the powder into his mouth, and he coughed and choked, trying to swallow. He dropped the container back on the counter and staggered out of the kitchen. He was sobbing and trying to not fall as he headed back to his bedroom.

He needed help.

He would get his keys and try to drive himself to the hospital or to the lab, but he needed help. He worked his way into his bedroom, throwing the door hard into the wall. He turned to swing the door back around to get the keys from his coat. As the door slammed closed, he heard a snap come from the floor. He tried to look down, but the floor had already risen to meet him.

He had fallen, but it seemed surreal, like a dream. Daryl was on the floor, but he was still looking at his bedroom door, as if he had fallen through the floor. He looked down.

For a moment he thought he had dropped to his knees, until he noticed that he couldn't even see his knees. What he saw was his shoes and his pants, and a pile of greyish leather spilling out in between them both. It took a quick poke of a finger to realize the grey leather was in fact part of his leg. He pinched some between his fingers and pulled. It was very thick, and the fact that he felt it made him a little nauseous.

What happened to my bones?

He felt his torso fall backward. As his head hit the carpet, he heard a sound like a heavy wet blanket being dropped onto a concrete floor. To his amazement, he realized it was his own head. He tried to sit up, but couldn't. He tried to scream, but all that came out was a mewling sound. His eyes darted around until even they were unable to move. His breathing became shallow as he felt his body seemingly sink into the floor.

No, not seemingly.

Daryl no longer had any concept of time, and had no idea how long he had lain there in that condition. He would come in and out of awareness, each time not able to feel, hear, or speak.

But he could taste, and he wished he couldn't.

He remembered someone coming to save him. Was it Georgie?

Who's Georgie?

He didn't know, because it was a lifetime ago. Or a few minutes, or hours.

All he did know was the taste of rotten strawberries, and the growing wish for death.

5

Georgie was still furious at Daryl, but looking at him now—or whatever was left of him—made her shudder. She sat outside of an exam room in the lab and watched as Armstrong and two other scientists examined Daryl's body.

Daryl was inside what looked like a giant Petri dish. He was naked, but also completely without form. He looked like a cataclysmically deformed grey puddle. Where his face should have been was a toothless gaping maw, with two bruise-colored indents where his eyes had been. There would be an occasional ripple in the flesh and something that sounded like a moan, but not much else. He was alive by some miracle, and although his size wasn't changing, his weight was increasing.

Georgie stared at the thing that was Daryl until Armstrong smacked the Plexiglas window with the flat of her hand. Georgie started and glared at Armstrong. Armstrong mouthed, "Come in here, bitch," and walked back over to Daryl.

It took a few minutes, but Georgie put on a white hazmat suit and entered the airlock into the examination room. Armstrong waved her over.

"Okay, what has no bones and weighs fifteen hundred pounds?" Dr. Armstrong asked.

"How can you make a joke?"

Armstrong frowned. "That's not a goddamn joke. It was a legit question. Daryl here currently weighs around fifteen hundred pounds. All his bones are gone. Absorbed. Along with his teeth, nails, eyes, and hair. This is fascinating."

Georgie shook her head. "How is he still alive? Has he said anything?"

"Near as we can tell, he's still alive for the moment because he isn't done yet."

"Done?" Georgie asked.

Armstrong nodded. "He's changing. Transforming into something."

"Into what?"

Armstrong shrugged. "Your guess is as good as mine." She smiled then added, "Actually, no. It isn't as good as mine, but I've got nothing right now. Running some more tests."

"What's in that stuff?"

Armstrong smiled. "Science. You wouldn't understand."

Georgie's eyes narrowed. "Why don't you goddamn try me."

"Well, the '*stuff*' is a complex chemical compound that's been decades in the making. It's gone through several different test modes. It's a myriad of—"

Georgie took both of her hands and shoved Armstrong against a wall. She held her there and turned her head to the other two scientists in the room. "You two, get out of here right now."

The two looked at each and left through the airlock. Georgie held Armstrong against the wall.

"I always thought you were into the rough stuff, George, but we *are* at work."

"What's in that protein powder, Phoebe?" Georgie said through her teeth. 'This isn't some small side effect. This is physiologically altering his fucking molecular structure!"

"What's impressive is that it smells like rotten strawberries," Armstrong said. "And even though we didn't use any natural strawberries in the powder, its smells like gone-off real-life strawberries."

Georgie blinked. "Are you crazy?"

Armstrong brought her arms up and pushed off Georgie. Georgie staggered backwards and tripped over her feet. She landed hard on the tile floor.

"I'm pretty far from crazy," Armstrong said, standing over Georgie. "And I'm not stupid, nor am I one of your flunkies. You may have hired me, but I don't answer to you."

"Who do you answer to, then?" Georgie growled. "Because you seem to be absolutely off course."

Armstrong smiled and walked over to the tank, where Daryl's gelatinous grey form twitched. She ran a hand over the Plexiglas almost lovingly.

"I am *exactly* on course." Armstrong twirled and stopped, resting her hands on her hips. "Big D has done so much better than I'd thought he would. Just wonderful. We're even ahead of schedule."

Georgie started to get off the floor. "Schedule?"

"I don't stutter."

"You had told me that this was something to be contained." Georgie said, standing up. She brushed herself off as Dr. Armstrong stood in front of her. "But now it's on schedule?"

"*Ahead* of schedule, yes. See, there were a few things we used as an additive for the powder that worked so much better than expected. Like the fact that he polished off the entire five-pound container in a week." Armstrong stopped for a moment and cackled loudly.

"But you had given him instructions that he clearly didn't follow."

"True, but this was the expected result. It just happened faster with him. Guess he loves strawberries a whole lot, am I right?"

"The expected result?"

"Look, can I level with you?" Armstrong reached out and took Georgie by the shoulders. "Since we're so close to the end of this experiment, I feel like we've really bonded."

Georgie pushed Armstrong away from her roughly. "You are fucking *insane*."

"My sanity is irrelevant." Armstrong flung herself into Georgie, both tumbling to the tile floor. "But what is relevant is that this experiment is about to rocket ahead."

Armstrong rolled on top of Georgie and grabbed her head with both hands. It was hard with the vinyl hazmat suit, but she began to pound Georgie's head against the floor.

Georgie counted to three as she tried to fight off Armstrong, but things began to darken when she counted to five. The pain in her head began to subside, and everything blurred into blackness.

6

Georgie awoke with a splitting headache. She realized she was still on the floor, and reached to the back of her head. There was a growing lump and a bit of dampness that she assumed was her own blood. She opened her eyes and saw she was still in the lab examination room, except now she wasn't wearing the hazmat suit.

She sat up and looked around the room. It was just her and Daryl, still twitching in the giant tank. She struggled to her feet, grabbing a nearby examination table for support.

"Hello?" she called out. "Doctor? Anyone?"

There was no answer, not that she expected one. She sighed and turned slowly to the tank. The faceless, formless Daryl just sat there, twitching or breathing or whatever it was doing.

"How about you? You still in there, you poor bastard?"

The form did nothing.

"You know this is all your fault, right?"

Georgie walked to the edge of the tank and looked inside. There he was, Daryl, in all his grey fleshy mush and rotten strawberry stench, a stupid little man who'd made one stupid mistake too many. She felt pity, revulsion, and hot rising anger. Her hands closed into fists.

"Stupid son of a bitch." She leaned over the top of the tank. "I don't know if you can hear me, but if you still had a face I'd punch it. I'm not without sympathy, but I hope whatever you're going through is painful as—"

A thick grey tendril shot out of the tank and caught Georgie under her chin, knocking her on her back. It happened quickly and left her jaw throbbing. She sat up just as quickly and saw that the tendril was still in front of her, weaving back and forth like a cobra about to strike.

Her eyes widened with horror as the grey mass pulsed and throbbed inches from her face. She watched the mass, roughly the size of a fist, widen and expand into the shape of an oval. It grew to the size of her head and she began to whimper.

"Daryl...please..."

From inside the clear Plexiglas tank, the grey mass that was Daryl began to rise and spill out over the sides. It poured out onto the floor, and the sheer weight of it made the tile floor creak and crack.

From above, the exam room PA clicked on, and Phoebe Armstrong's voice boomed into the room. "Oh, George, this shit just got *real*."

Armstrong then began to cackle.

Georgie began to clamber backwards, away from the oval tendril, her gaze never leaving the pulsing thing. The tendril followed her, maintaining the same distance, neither advancing nor falling back. Behind it, more and more of the grey flesh spilled out onto the tiles. The cracks began to snake towards Georgie more and more.

"Oh, Big D is getting so much heavier now. He's about twenty-five hundred pounds right now. Looks like

MUERTE CON SABOR A FRESA

that floor isn't going to hold him much longer," Armstrong's voice boomed.

"Why is it so heavy?" Georgie nearly shrieked, still backing away and rapidly running out of room.

"Density, stupid," came the reply. "The formula was designed to do a lot of things, but putting on weight was one of them. So part of the physiological change was restructuring the particle density of the subject. Do I need to explain that to you?"

"Yes, goddamn it!"

Armstrong let off a small laugh. "Knew it," she said. "So goddamn smart, aren't you? Well, since we're in a lab, and a learning lab at that, guess you're going to learn something today. First, Daryl's mass remains the same. However, his density and volume have been increased. His bones, hair, and nails have been absorbed by his changing physical makeup."

Georgie reached the wall and stopped. She was shuddering, as the grey form was now completely out of the tank and covering most of the floor, save the oval tendril pulsing in front of her face.

"What the fuck does that mean?" Georgie said through her teeth.

"It means the experiment is working."

"*This* is what you were trying to do?" Georgie glared at the tendril, which still hovered in front of her. "You were supposed to be making a protein shake."

"I know what I was *supposed* to be making," Armstrong said through the PA system. "But this was always the goal. Always the plan."

"What plan?"

"An elder god made flesh," Armstrong said. "An elder god brought back."

Georgie tried to slide to her left to get to the door, but another tendril shot out, blocking her path. She tried to go to the right, and the same thing happened. The grey mass creeped closer to her and she screamed. "Please, Daryl, don't!"

"Daryl is gone, George." Armstrong said. "Just a vessel. This is a god, you see. A *hungry* god. Daryl was weak and stupid."

At this last phrase, the grey mass stopped and retreated slightly. A low rumble began to shake the room; the grey mass was vibrating. It felt like an earthquake, but Georgie didn't think that was the case.

From within the grey mass came a sound like a flattened tuba that was rising in volume. Along with the sound, the shaking was increasing. Georgie managed to get to her feet, and the mass continued to pull away from her. She staggered over to the door and tried to open it. It was locked.

"Damn you, Armstrong! Let me out!"

The PA speaker crackled. "You don't really think *that's* going to happen, do you?" Armstrong said. "You've pretty much become the newest thing in the experiment."

Georgie began to furiously pound on the door, screaming. Her voice eventually was drowned out by the sound coming from the grey mass. Chunks of tile from the ceiling began to fall. They landed on the tile, which was also cracking. The ceiling chunks that landed on the grey mass were absorbed into it.

Georgie stopped screaming to look behind her, and saw that the grey mass was trying to form into a different shape; it was pulling itself together, it seemed, and the loud tuba sound was starting to change pitch. The low bass rumble wasn't so low, and started to sound less like a tuba. It almost sounded to Georgie like...

"Daryl?"

The sound changed to a sputter and almost sounded like a word.

"What are you trying to say?" Georgie asked. "You're still in there, aren't you?"

"Why isn't it eating you?" Armstrong said over the speakers.

The sputtering continued as the grey mass continued to try and form a different shape. It was mostly in one place now, almost like a ball of cookie dough. The shaking was starting to subside, but not by much. Georgie, still terrified, moved closer to the mass to look at it.

"It's reforming," Georgie said aloud. "Daryl is trying to put himself back together."

"Bullshit," Armstrong said. "How the hell do you know?"

The grey mass, which was now a large ball, began to reform itself into something that looked slightly human. There were two leg-like things and a discernible torso, two malformed arms and a large blob where a head would be. It twitched and pulsed, and the sound was now starting to sound more human. It sounded like it was saying the letter 'O.'

"Daryl, can you hear me?" Georgie asked. She reached a hand towards it. A grey stumpy arm thing reached out in return as it continued to twitch and pulse.

"It's not Daryl, stupid," Armstrong hissed. "Daryl is dead."

Upon hearing this, the grey, twitching, changing thing reacted. The reaching arm dropped to its side, and a gaping maw appeared on the head-like ball at the top. It was a crude mouth, and although the sound was coming from the entire mass, the mouth was meant to be the focus point.

"*NAAAAAT!*" it boomed. "*NAAAAAAT DEEEEEEAAADAAAAH!*"

Although the sound was deafening, it was clear enough to Georgie, who stood with her hands over her ears.

"I think Daryl disagrees with you, Phoebe."

"*FEEEEEEEEEBEEE!*" the Daryl-thing sounded off.

158

7

Dr. Phoebe Armstrong heard the bastardized version of her first name come not through the intercom system, but through the wall. She looked through the two-way glass at the grey mass that had once been Daryl—apparently still *was* Daryl—and shuddered.

How could Daryl still be in there? This process was specifically designed to overtake the host and eradicate it completely. That was the whole point of the density, literally consuming every facet of the original host until all that remained was the beautiful Void.

...the Goat with a thousand young...

In lieu of the beautiful Void, however, goddamn Daryl was still hanging in there for some reason.

And whatever was left of him was pissed.

Every fiber of her being was screaming at her to run as she watched this living god on the other side of the glass. This was both everything she'd ever wanted and nothing like what she'd expected. It was horrifyingly beautiful, this thing she'd created. She watched it try to reform itself to resemble the human host from which it had spawned, and fail.

Perhaps the Void was trying to release the imprint of Daryl, and this was its way of exorcising the human stain. She smiled at this thought and decided she would sit down to watch this transformation to the end. This was a miracle she was watching, after all. A miracle of her own design.

She was a godmother in the very literal sense.

"FEEEEEEEEEBEEE!"

Her smile disappeared. A large grey lump slammed against the reinforced Plexiglas. It splintered and bowed in, coming within a foot of Armstrong's face. She screamed and threw herself backwards, landing on the floor.

The lump pulled back, taking the broken web of Plexiglas along with it. Armstrong looked in wide-eyed horror as the chunk of Plexiglas was absorbed into the Void. She began to scoot backwards as the Void vibrated, pulsed, and moved toward the new opening.

"*FEEEEEEEEEBEEE*!" it repeated.

Again Armstrong screamed as the Void, her creation, her child wrapped itself around her legs. The tendrils of grey continued to envelop her as her vocal cords were strained to failure. She made desperate pained mewling sounds as over half of her body was not only covered in the grey flesh, but being absorbed as well. It wasn't painful, but that didn't take away Armstrong's awareness of what was happening. She clawed desperately at the grey matter until her hands were taken and absorbed. She became aware that she could hear in her head what the Void was thinking.

Mostly it was hatred towards her, but that didn't stop the urge to scream as she slowly became part of the Void. She would become the Void along with Daryl, and as she began to relax, that one word...*Void*...began to ring in her head. She stopped fighting and allowed herself to become a god.

To *become*.

8

Georgie watched the damned thing consume Armstrong, and although she wasn't sad to see her go, Phoebe was the only one who had any inkling as to exactly what the hell was happening. She was still in a locked room with a mutated thing that just ate the only person that had any idea of what to do about it.

She stood watching the Daryl-thing, half in and half out of the room. It began to ooze back into the exam room.

Georgie noticed that the mass of it hadn't gotten any bigger, but it was moving slower.

And moving towards her.

"Daryl, just listen, okay?" Georgie pleaded. "I can help you."

"DAAAARRRLLLLFEEEEEEBEEEE!"

Georgie was now backing away from it as it came closer and closer. She watched carefully, as it was fully intact and following her as a lumpy ball.

Not trying to look human anymore, Georgie thought.

The more it moved across the floor, the more the floor creaked and cracked. She wondered what would happen if the floor collapsed under its weight as she tried to get Daryl to get far enough away from the control room that she could try and escape through there.

The Daryl-thing seemed to sense this, and divided itself into smaller lumpier balls to fill in the space between Georgie and the control room.

"Bastard," Georgie said.

"BAAASSAAAAD!"

"Daryl, I have to get to the control room to help you. Can you let me through?"

The Daryl-thing divided again into four smaller balls, all connected by a thinning grey tendril, in a semi-circle around Georgie. Each one was forming what looked like a head. A mouth-like slit formed on each one and although the sound came from everywhere, the faux mouths moved in unison.

"NOT DAAAAARRRRRYLLL. NOT DAAAARRRLLLLFEEEEEEBEEEE." It wasn't as loud or as booming, but it was still coming from the entire thing that was Daryl.

"Okay," Georgie said, putting her hands up, trying to address all four identical versions. "You're not Daryl or Phoebe. Who are you, then?"

All four mouths opened, and a pained bellow came from everywhere. Each mass throbbed, and the four things reconverted into each other. It was both repulsive and fascinating to Georgie. She took the opportunity to make a break for the control room. The bellow began to clarify, and the volume reached a quiet level. The thing spoke a single word.

"*Void.*"

The sound of the voice stopped Georgie dead in her tracks. She had made it into the control room, and turned to look at what had just named itself.

"*Void,*" it said again. Georgie thought it sounded like it was trying the name out to see if it liked it. She watched it pulse and move; it seemed like it was preening. Its pallor seemed to darken as it moved around the lab. A low humming began to emit from the thing as it glided around the room.

It bumped into the Plexiglas tank and Georgie watched as the thing...*Void*...began to cover it and consume it whole. Within a minute, there was a circle-shaped exposure for the steel-reinforced floor beneath.

Georgie heard the control room door open behind her, and a sudden gasp. She turned and saw one of Dr. Armstrong's lab assistants, a pretty young woman not quite thirty, with a hand covering her mouth. She was still in her hazmat suit from earlier. She was also carrying a small pint of fresh strawberries.

"What the hell is *that?*"

Georgie turned back to the Void, which was now consuming a side lab table, still humming and now repeating its name like a mantra.

The thing stopped and began to move towards the control room.

Georgie regarded the young lab assistant and her strawberries.

"*Void,*" it said, now adding, "*God.*"

"Apparently, that is Void," Georgie said, "and God. I see you've brought it a snack."

"Um, Dr. Phoebe thought Daryl might like...actual strawberries."

Void heard the word and began to twitch. It moved closer to the control room.

"God. Void. God. Void."

Void was directly outside of the control room. It reached a dark grey tentacle out, found the intercom control panel, and began to absorb it. The steel floor beneath began to groan from the weight.

Georgie chuckled and patted the assistant on the shoulder as she pushed past her. She made her way to the control room door and opened it.

"Good luck with that," Georgie said, and walked quickly out of the control room.

9

The lab assistant watched Georgie leave, and looked quickly back as the dark grey thing that she thought was still Daryl came within inches of her.

"Um, do you know where Dr. Phoebe is?" She held out the pint of strawberries.

A thick tendril slapped the strawberries out of the assistant's hand. She gave a small yelp and noticed the tendril was now wrapping itself around her arm.

"Void," it said. *"God."*

"Um, Cheryl," the assistant replied.

SPOTTING

BY JESSICA MCHUGH

My phone chimes, and I drop the urine-soaked stick onto the bathmat.

"Shit. I'm sorry."

Devin gingerly picks up the pregnancy test and sets it on the sink. He squints at the result window, then at the box, and back at the test. He grunts and shakes his head.

"I don't know what I'm looking at. Is it...broken?"

It sure as hell seems like it. My urine caused a single pink line to appear, indicating a negative result, but it's on the wrong side of the window, where the double pink "pregnant as fuck" line should be.

"It's gotta be defective." My cheeks burn as I add, "It *was* the cheapest one."

"Shit, Maeve. How cheap?"

Pretty damn cheap. As a rookie social studies teacher and part-time tour guide with more debt than credit, I've trained myself to buy store brands, shop secret deals, and coupon like a motherfucker. Devin usually finds this frugality charming. Low-maintenance. Bohemian. Now he's staring at me like I got caught eating a burrito from a dumpster.

I whip the test into the trash and apologize for doing everything wrong. Especially for not freaking out a week ago when my typically torrential period arrived as minimal spotting instead...and hasn't quite stopped.

Wrapping his arms around me, Devin kisses my head, my nose, my lips, my chin. It's calmed me in the past, but this morning it's like each kiss plants a sour seed in my head. I guess there are worse seeds, though, maybe already cracked and spreading parasitic poison.

"Please try to calm down, Maeve. And stop apologizing, okay?"

I nod, but it's easier said than done. I need to say sorry, need to feel it, because even if the test makes no conclusions about fertilization, it makes a monumental conclusion about me. It declares that I, pregnant or not, am a massive fuck-up. Pregnant or not, Devin will never forget I put him through this. No matter how it ends, I'll always have something to apologize for.

"That's my girl. Go on, check your phone."

I shuffle to the bedroom, a heady brew of fear and shame thinning each breath. It's difficult to walk, let alone unlock my phone with anything but stuttering apeish swipes, but I eventually get the pattern right. Sure enough, the EZTour app is hounding me for an update again, so I finally approve it, flopping on the bed in utter defeat.

"I can't even control an app for my side hustle; how am I supposed to deal with a baby?" I moan. "I *can't* deal with a baby. I don't *want* a baby."

Devin looks up from his phone and blinks in slow sympathy, like my childhood cat Ginger did minutes before she died in our cold concrete basement.

I sit up. "I mean, I *do* want one. Someday...when we're ready..."

He nods. He says he's looking up doctors, but I suspect he's checking our bank account too, totaling up what's coming in and going out. I bet he's considering borrowing from his parents, so we don't miss my student loan payment.

My stomach lurches, and bile burns up my throat. I wince as I take a swig from the least-dented water bottle on my wobbly bedside table and exhale slowly, for as long as possible, until my belly calms.

Jesus, Maeve... In this political climate, this administration, God, *in this hateful state...how could you fuck up so bad?*

My phone chirps—a different notification sound, at

least—and I begrudgingly unlock it. It's from the EZTour app again, but it's not requesting an update.

Maeve Bratton, You Have Not Viewed Your Newest (1) Bookings. View Now.

"What the fuck?"

I click on it—doubtful, angry, praying to whatever god will listen for the app to be as buggy as the pregnancy test—and immediately burst into tears.

The guest list for this morning's 11am *Love Langdon Food & Historical Walking Tour* has increased from zero to one.

"What's wrong?" Devin sits beside me and touches my back, and I collapse into myself, away from his hand.

"I have a tour!"

"Today? I thought you said no one signed up."

The booking window closes at twenty-four hours, and the timestamp on Sam Gleason's booking reads 10:33am Friday, so he got in right under the wire. The app should've alerted me right after, and it probably would have if I'd updated it sooner.

I'm awful, I'm lazy, I'm so fucking sorry.

I crawl to the head of the bed and curl into a ball. I don't want to look at Devin when he lies opposite me. I don't want to throw more nets of apologies over his dark brown eyes.

"I just...I don't know how I messed up my pills."

"Honey, we don't know anything for sure."

"Of course we do. With our luck, I have to be pregnant." I roll onto my back and stare at the cracks spidering across our cheap stucco ceiling. "How the hell am I supposed to spout off fun facts about Langdon when I feel like this? Maybe I can call Jen. Maybe she'll cover me." A guilty pang strikes my gut. "But I guess we'll need as much money as possible if I am—" Then a realization. "Shit, did that horrible heartbeat bill pass? Did they end up closing the Planned Parenthood in town? Oh my God, are there even any clinics left in the state?"

"Maeve, please calm down. We'll go to the doctor as soon as the tour's over. We'll figure this out."

The harder I shake my head, the harder it is to breathe. Tears spill down my cheeks, and Devin tries to comfort me, but I feel like he'd spout the same platitudes if I had a fever, or if one of the goldfish died. I don't know what the right words are—or if they even exist—but they certainly aren't "Everything's going to be okay."

But I nod like I believe it. I allow him to wipe away my tears and pull me into his arms. I give him all the little things he needs to feel like he helped: smiles, affectionate pinches, little kisses, and I slowly peel myself from his embrace. I snatch jeans and an oversized wool sweater that narrowly passes the sniff test.

"How big is the group?"

"That's the worst part. It's just one guy."

"Oh jeez, that shouldn't be allowed."

I shrug. "He might be a journalist, or a travel blogger. I've had a few before."

Devin glances between the blinds and makes an "uh-oh" noise.

"Oh God, what?"

"Bring an umbrella," he says, pouting over his shoulder. "Looks like it's gonna storm."

"Awwwwwesome…" I loop my umbrella on my wrist and tighten my bun with a sigh so loud the little girl who lives above us laughs.

Devin squeezes my shoulders. "It's just two hours. You got this."

Half of me is screaming, "Fuck no I don't," and wrapping myself up like a mummy in our bed. The other half is in the car with the motor running, the inconclusive pee-stick in my lap as Devin plugs the doctor's address into the GPS. Not even a speck of me believes this is going to end well.

"Yes," I say, haunted. "I got this."

Sitting in the bathroom at Langdon Pretzel Pies, I'm reminded why it doesn't matter if my clothes stink. Less than two minutes inside saturates every inch of me in the sweet but dense smell of fried dough. Wearing my new pungent pashmina, I pee while texting the tour stops, "One guest, no restrictions," and prepare to take a pre-tour selfie as confirmations from the East Street Cafe and the Baker Spite House roll in.

The door handle jiggles, and I croak the word "occupied" like it's my first time wrapping my lips around the word. The handle springs to a neutral position, and someone grunts on the other side.

As I quickly gather myself, my mind falls into a movie montage of pregnant woman complaining about how frequently they urinate. Is that my future? Am I already peeing more than normal? I didn't drink anything since taking the pregnancy test, but I had no problem peeing just now.

Jesus fucking Christ, Maeve. Shut. Up.

I open the door and fly out, accidentally sideswiping the man waiting for the bathroom. "Whoops, sorry!"

"Hey!" he barks, and I swivel stiffly.

The middle-aged man's Transitions lenses haven't fully adjusted to the interior of Pretzel Pie, but behind the splotchy dark glasses, he squints at me. "Is this yours?"

He points into the bathroom, and I hustle back. I left my *Love Langdon* name tag on the sink—not the first time, won't be the last—and I roll my eyes as I collect it. "Yes, it is. Thank you."

"You're Maeve?" he asks.

I pin it to my sweater and flick it. "That's right."

His lips peel back from his teeth, and he extends

his hand. "My name's Sam Gleason. I'm on your tour today."

"Oh! Nice to meet you, Sam." I shake his hand and fish out my phone to check him in on the EZTour app.

The wi-fi in Langdon Pretzel Pies is terrible. It takes nearly a minute for the app to load, and even then, it won't let me select Sam Gleason's name. I sound like a Luddite as I poke the screen, cursing it, my phone, and technology as a whole. When it freezes, I force quit and make a mental note to try again at the next stop.

It's only 10:50, and Jen doesn't like me starting early, so I suggest Sam take a stroll until 11:00.

"I'm fine here," he says, sitting at the table where I've plopped my bookbag. "How many people are joining us?"

I'd hoped he'd walk around so I didn't have to answer that question yet, but as he lifts his eyebrows in anticipation, I surrender to the awkwardness that tends to follow my telling a solo guest we're all there is. No one seems to like the idea of being alone with a stranger, even their hired tour guide, for two hours in an unfamiliar town.

But Sam Gleason is relaxed, his arms crossed on the table with a black camera bag perched on the chair beside him. I'm tempted to ask if he's from the *Langdon Post* or one of the local blogs, but I don't get the chance.

He unexpectedly pushes up from the table, walks out of the back dining room, and marches to the register up front. I crane to keep an eye on him, assuming he's buying a bottle of water—and I jump to my feet when he suddenly pushes through the saloon doors into the kitchen. There's an immediate outcry from the employees, and the man backs out of the kitchen with his hands in the air, one of which clutches a wad of raw pretzel dough.

"You're not supposed to go back there," I say, and he chuckles, squeezing the dough between his knuckles.

"So it's not an all-access tour?"

"No."

He throws his head back and laughs uproariously. "I know, I know. I honestly just wanted to see what they'd do."

"Well, now you know." I apologize to the kitchen staff, and Sam Gleason slurps a wad of dough from his fingers.

Perhaps in an attempt to hurry us along, a server brings a mini turkey reuben calzone to our table two minutes before the tour's official start time. I'm about to explain how the sprinkle of parmesan brings Pretzel Pie's proprietary flour-blend to life when I realize it's missing and have to sharply cease the script imprinted on my tongue. I can't even warn him about the temperature, because the calzone is clearly undercooked.

Doughy boogers stretch between Sam's fingers when he grabs the calzone like a trick-or-treater with an unsupervised candy bowl, and he plunges it into his mouth. The sauerkraut would've burned the hell out of him if were cooked properly, but he's all smiles and sounds of delight as he feasts.

I rattle off facts about Langdon Pretzel Pie and the early 20th century shoe store that once occupied the building, noting how it became a bootleg gin operation during Prohibition. "Lots of buildings in the downtown area have cool Prohibition-era histories, lots of secret bunkers that were used to make and distribute moonshine, but we'll talk about that more when we get to the Baker Spite House."

"Baker Spite House?"

"It's a fun story about a sneaky minister who spited the city of Langdon by building a house where they were planning to build a road, but they found a secret distillery down there last year. We're actually lucky to be seeing it today because it's technically closed for renovations. That's a little later, though. We're going to head to our next location in a minute, so there's the restroom in case you want to wash your hands."

Mr. Gleason shrugs. "I'm fine. Let's go."

I glance at his hand; it's definitely not fine, but I sling my bookbag over my shoulder in preparation to leave anyway. That's when I realize I forgot to do my opening spiel. I didn't talk about our social media presence or mention the rule about not shopping. Worst of all, I haven't mentioned anything about tips. In my experience, if I don't at least dance around the notion of getting gratuities, I don't get any.

I thank the Pretzel Pie kitchen staff, who look right through me, silent and unblinking, as I plow through the growing crowd to the street. The skies have darkened dramatically, and a pissing sort of rain slaps me across the face. I open my umbrella, expecting Sam to follow suit, but he didn't bring one; his jacket doesn't even have a hood. Sucking on the inside of my cheek, I pass him my umbrella and wave away his cloying gratitude. My phone's vibrating like crazy in my back pocket, but I ignore it, pull my cheesiest smile of the year, and say, "By the way, welcome officially to the Love Langdon Food and Historical Walking Tour."

He claps, and his camera bag swings like a pendulum on his forearm.

I speed through my background as a social studies teacher who's been leading weekend tours for going on four years. I double check that he doesn't have allergies and ask him to refrain from shopping on the tour, so we stick to our schedule. "And if you feel everything has been satisfactory on my end, gratuities are graciously accepted at the tour's conclusion." I wait for some sign he understands me, but his expression doesn't change, so I clap my hands as if squashing a mosquito and say, "Without further ado, let's scoot on down to the East Street Cafe, a three-generation woman-run business where Langdonites like me go for the best cheese in town."

✳ ✳ ✳

I desperately want to check my text messages, but Sam Gleason won't shut the fuck up. His voice snakes further up his sinuses with each question about local architecture—only the ones I haven't researched, of course. I say, "Oh, that's a good question" but provide no answer, distracting him instead with personal anecdotes to fill the drizzly walk from Pretzel Pie to East Street Cafe.

While he's marveling at an art installation of ducks in front of the Lazy Dog Bookstore, I check my phone. There are three missed calls: two from an "Unknown Caller"—debt collectors, probably—and one from Devin.

"Not tweeting, are you?" Sam elbows me, and I think he winks, but I can't tell because his Transitions lenses still haven't evened out.

"Just checking the weather. Looks like it'll be storming on and off, but it should be nice when we're at the creek. At least I *know* it's nice in *here*," I warble and open the door to the East Street Cafe.

Greeting the cafe owner Krista is like trying to serve a tennis ball to Serena Williams. My salutations get caught in the net of her exuberance, and she glides out from behind the counter like a fairytale queen welcoming royal guests to her daughter's christening. Her sheer joy at this opportunity to boast about her business makes me feel like I've never been certain about a single decision in my entire life. Even when the man with the doughy fingers extends them for a friendly handshake, her exhilaration doesn't dull. She doesn't hesitate. She shakes his hand and exclaims, "Welcome! Take a seat! I'll get your samples!"

My phone vibrates as I direct Sam Gleason to his seat and start in on the history of the East Street Cafe. Krista sets a tray of fruit and cheese in front of him and beams as I explain what he'll be tasting. When my pocket buzzes again, I ask Krista if she wouldn't mind filling him in on what's new in the cafe while I take an emergency call.

She jumps into my role with sunshine gusto, and I dash outside to read the chain of text messages from Devin.

They allow me the first full breath I've taken all day.

"Appointment set for 2:30."

"Miss you."

"Love you."

"Everything about you."

Even the piece we want to kill, my brain adds viciously.

My throat tightens, and tears well over my eyelashes, but I wipe them away and force myself to swallow the grim thought as I hustle into the cafe.

The cheese and fruit are nearly gone when I return, but there's a new addition to the table. When I apologize to Mr. Gleason for my absence, the large tidy woman now seated beside him chirps.

"That's quite all right, dear. Emergencies happen, don't they?"

She resembles a stuffy choir director straight out of central casting in her soft pink blouse and charcoal slacks. She extends her hand, cinematically dainty, and introduces herself as Paula.

"It's nice to meet you, Paula."

"You too, Maeve. We were just saying how glad we are that there's a tour like this in town. Weren't we, Sam?"

"That's right. We've been waiting for something like this for a long time."

"He was telling me about the Baker Spite House." She giggles as she shivers. "That sounds like a silly story."

"Oh, it is. Reverend Baker was definitely a character. Most of Langdon's ministers were teetotal in the 20s, but not Baker. He made moonshine and practically gave it away to the citizens of Langdon."

"How interesting!"

"It's one of my favorites. By the way, how did everything taste, Mr. Gleason?"

"He loved it," Paula says. "Gobbled it up so fast I could barely get any for myself."

Panic ripples through me, but I force a chuckle. "Well, he *is* the one that paid for it."

"Oh! Of course! I nearly forgot!" She reaches into her purse and pulls out her wallet. As she begins shuffling through the bills, every muscle in my body tightens.

She's not going to buy her way onto this tour. She can't possibly think that's okay.

Again, I remember the fucked-up situation I'm in, and my stomach rings with pain. It's probably just gas on account of I skipped breakfast, but I imagine a fully-formed fetus jabbing me with a chubby finger. So when she passes me eighty dollars, pulls the world's widest grin, and says, "I hope it's not too much trouble," my shoulders jump to my ears, my lips smash to a bloodless smile, and I reply dryly, "The more the merrier."

I thank Krista, and gesture for Sam and Paula to gather their things and follow me outside. Noticing Paula's significant limp, I'm relieved to find the rain's granted us a reprieve so we can take our time. A faint beam of sunshine breaks through the murky clouds, and as my guests discuss how it must be a good omen, I scoot ahead to call the Spite House.

"Hi, Vicki, it's Maeve from the Love Langdon Tour."

"You on your way?"

"Not yet. I just wanted to let you know I have an extra guest, so I'll need an extra gift bag."

No response.

"Is that okay?"

"You know we're supposed to be closed, right?"

"Yes."

"So, I don't have the gift bag stuff here. It's at my house. I only brought one because you said you only needed one."

"Oh. I'm sorry."

"So now I have to go home and get it?"

"I'm sorry. You don't have to. I'm sure the guest will understand."

Vicki sighs. "No, I'll get it. It'll reflect badly on the museum."

I'm thanking her for being so accommodating when Paula sidles up, links her arm with mine, and asks how long I've been a tour guide. The unexpected contact makes me flinch, and I drop my phone onto the sidewalk. We dive for it at the same time, colliding with one another and causing me to kick it further away. I apologize to Paula and whimper as I retrieve my phone. It's scratched up, but it still works. I heave a sigh of relief as I shove it in my pocket, ignoring two more missed calls from the "Unknown Caller."

Paula grabs my arm again. "So... how long have you been a tour guide?"

"Four years."

"And the Spite House has been on the tour that whole time?"

"Yes, but the current owners only discovered the hidden distillery last year, so the museum is still a work in progress."

I cordially pull free from Paula and direct the pair to a shady spot on the corner, where I launch into a speech about how the Union and Confederacy used the cross street to get to noteworthy Civil War battles. While I'm speaking, a swarthy Marine with one hand stops to listen. He nods along, eyes squinted, and mustache bristled like the whiskers of an inquisitive cat. When I finish speaking, he raises five hairy fingers.

"Yes?"

"What is this?"

"It's the Love Langdon—"

"Thank you for your service," Sam Gleason says, and the young man nods in appreciation.

"Oh yes," Paula says, "thank you for your service."

"God bless you, ma'am."

I also thank the Marine and try not to sound annoyed as I answer his question. "This is the Love Langdon Food and Historical Walking Tour." I snatch a brochure from my backpack and hand it over. "The season's nearly over, but here's all the info you need to book in the spring. It fills up fast, so it's best to book now."

His eyes widen at the pamphlet. "This is great! How much?"

I can hardly believe it when he pulls his wallet from his back pocket.

"$80, but I'm afraid this tour is closed."

Removing his cash proves a difficult task. He fumbles trying to do it one-handed, and Paula offers to help him.

"There's plenty of room," she says to me. "You said it yourself: 'the more the merrier.'"

"We've already finished two stops. It won't be the full experience."

The Marine's teeth are a pristine white stripe between bright red lips as he tells Paula to grab another twenty. Shoving $100 at me, he chirps. "And a tip upfront."

With a sigh, I take the money and gesture for my now three-person tour to continue down the street. As we're shuffling through the crosswalk, the skies darken, and thunder booms so hard that we, and nearly everyone around us, stop in place and gaze at the swollen black clouds churning overhead.

"Uh-oh. It looks like it's going to pour at any moment. Do you mind if we pick up the pace a bit?"

"Not at all," Paula says. "As long as I get to see this Spite House I've heard so much about."

The Marine's eyebrows jump to his hairline. "Ooh, that sounds neat."

"Can we go there now?" Sam asks.

"First the creek."

They groan as we step into a clutch of wet shadow cast by the buildings that lead to Bellevue Creek Promenade. Their disappointment won't last long. Even on a day like this, passing the last building douses us in a soft, almost twilight, luminescence. Groans turn to gasps, and I throw my arms open as I say, "Welcome to Bellevue Creek!"

Their awe is similar to that of Willy Wonka's golden ticket winners entering his glorious Chocolate Room. I hum the beginning of "Pure Imagination" in spite of myself as the guests go skipping to the stony bank. While they marvel at the beauty of the linear park and the *trompe l'oeil* artistry in the architecture, I explain that the creek, while beautiful, and home to dozens of fish and ducks, actually serves as a drainage ditch.

"It was created to prevent another flood like the one that nearly obliterated downtown Langdon in the mid-1920s. It was the worst storm in the town's history. Real end of the world stuff. Plus, a rash of illnesses had broken out around the same time, and a lot of people were too weak to escape the flood waters. They say the town's population was nearly cut in half in the 20s."

"Maybe it was because of Reverend Baker," Paula says.

"Because of all his spite?" I ask. "It *was* the same decade, and this town *is* pretty magical, so I guess anything's possible! Anyway, there were lots of folks who opposed this drainage ditch project because of the cost—"

"Ooh!" Paula squeals and shoves her phone in my face. "Picture time! Take our picture!"

I want to punch her. I want to twist her lips shut and push her into the cold murky water.

"Yeah! Take a picture!" says the Marine.

"Uh...yeah, sure." I collect cell phones from the woman and the Marine and wait for Sam Gleason to take out his fancy-schmancy camera, but he hands me his phone instead. I take three identical shots, return the phones, and resume my speech before I forget where I am in the script.

They aren't listening, though. They're at the water's edge again, watching a massive trout splash around in front of a flock of ducks perched on a slimy flowerpot across the creek.

The birds are quacking and flapping their wings like mad, and when the trout surfaces again, I realize why. Poking out of the fish's gargantuan black mouth is the last webbed inch of a duckling's foot.

The duckling fights to free itself, squawking and squealing as its frantic family panics on the sidelines. The ducks hop and hiss; some even try to divebomb the fish, but in the end, it sinks beneath the surface and doesn't rise again.

"Oh my God," I whimper, hands on my mouth. "I'm so sorry, everyone. Umm...maybe we should move on."

But no one moves on. No one speaks. Even the ducks fall silent as bubbles burst on the surface of Bellevue Creek.

My belly aches. I feel like I could shit my pants if I unclench even one muscle. So, when my tour group looks to me for guidance after such a grisly incident, I turn stiffly and walk in the other direction, holding my breath.

Hard rain begins as we're rounding the corner onto Court Street, and we run the rest of the way to the Spite House. I'm wondering why Sam doesn't use my umbrella when I realize he doesn't have it anymore. Nor does he have his camera bag, which he realizes himself once he's on the covered porch of the large shotgun house George Baker built out of spite.

"I must've left it at the creek," he whines.

"Don't worry. I'll get you set up with Vicki and run back for it." I knock on the door, but she doesn't answer, so

I cautiously enter the house. "Vicki? You here?"

Paint fumes punch me in the gut so hard I nearly retch. I turn on the overhead fan and call for Vicki again, but no one replies. There's only one gift bag waiting in the foyer, and there are still drop-cloths on the furniture.

"I'm sure she'll be back soon," I say, directing them to the museum lobby, where the plush velvet sofas have been replaced with cheap folding chairs. "Just hang tight. I'll be right back."

Cutting through alleys and backyards, my sneakers skid on wet dirt and loose gravel, and I nearly fall a dozen times before I reach the creek. After I cross the bridge, my burning lungs are granted a cool burst of shock when I see Sam Gleason's bag sitting underneath it, sheltered from the rain. I grab it with a whoop, then crinkle my nose in confusion. It's lighter than I expected. Also, wetter. A thick, syrupy liquid drips from the bottom and leaves dark brown spots as I run back through the fading storm.

I'm breathless and crampy when I reach the Spite House porch. My sopping wool sweater weighs a ton, the sticky camera bag isn't helping, and my phone is vibrating like crazy again. With a grunt, I lean the bag against the door, pull out my phone, and scream "WHAT?" at the Unknown Caller on the other end.

"Jesus Christ," the woman replies, "I've been trying to reach you for the last two hours, what kind of cheap-ass organization is this? Seriously, I've been in this goddamn pretzel place forever and I fucking stink now."

"Who is this?"

She sighs heavily. "I'm Samantha Gleason. I was supposed to be on the 11:30am Love Langdon Tour."

My stomach drops. "*Samantha?*"

"It was probably under 'Sam,' but yeah. You said to be at the pretzel place at 11:30."

"The tour started at 11."

"No, no, someone called me and said it got changed to 11:30."

The door to the Baker Spite House swings open, and paint fumes leak onto the porch. The interior is dark and quiet; nothing different from how I left it—except for the doorknob, now dotted with sticky pretzel dough.

"Where should I meet you?" Samantha Gleason asks.

"What?"

"I paid $80 for this thing, and I'm getting what I paid for. So where should I meet you?"

The floor creaks, and I nearly drop my phone. With slippery fingers, I scoot the receiver back to my lips and whisper, "Call 9-1-1. Send them to the Baker Spite House. 288 Court Street."

"9-1-1? Are you okay? What's happening?"

The drenched camera bag tips over with a thud. Something shifts inside, and the flap falls open, revealing a swarthy hand with five hairy fingers.

Stepping into the foyer, the lanky Marine smiles. "Oh good, you found it. I really didn't want to sacrifice another hand."

The man who claimed to be Sam Gleason suddenly swoops around the corner and up onto the porch. I slam my phone against his face three times before he latches onto my wrist and knocks it into the grass.

"Please don't struggle," he says. "You might hurt the baby."

* * *

Seeing as no one knew about the secret stairwell under the pantry leading to a bootlegging bunker until last year, I suspect very few people outside my present company know about the secret chapel behind a false wall in the bunker. It stinks of rotten earth, and black worms wriggle on the dirt floor as my tour guests shove me inside.

The sopping bastards explain how they hacked my

phone, but I don't understand a lot of it: shit about piggybacking apps with fake updates, stealing information, and monitoring people's conversations—especially those laden with the words "pregnancy test" and "baby." The newer the better, they tell me. I'm lucky. I'm the perfect candidate.

Paula sits across from me and removes her right shoe. The gauze around her four remaining toes has soaked through and dyed the rest of the bandage pink. She rolls her ankle and sighs as she removes a bloody Ziploc baggie from her purse. I suspect her toe's in one of the bloody wads of gauze, but I don't have any guesses about the second until the fake Sam Gleason removes his broken Transitions lenses. His prosthetic left eye is obvious now, and he slips it out with a smirk.

Their next explanations make even less sense than the hacker shit. It's a lot of occult nonsense about George Baker's true religious alignment—all demons and dark lords—and how he didn't care about the town's road project; he wanted the cursed earth beneath, upon which to build his demonic church.

"You thought I was kidding about Reverend Baker causing the illness and the flood in the 20's," Paula says, "but it *was* him—and the Dark Lord working through him—poisoning the people who bought his moonshine and raising the river to scrub them from the earth."

I shake my head. "So, what do you want from me? You want me to tell the real story on the tour?"

"We want you to help us resurrect him," the Marine replies. He plucks his mutilated left hand from the camera bag and sets it at the center of a large symbol painted on the dirt. His partners add their pieces; then they all look to me.

"I'm not cutting anything off."

"Of course not," Paula chuckles. "You're the vessel. You will deliver Reverend Baker back into this world. You and your baby."

I smack the ground. "There is no baby, you idiots! It was a defective test! I was being frugal!"

"Oh, sweetie," Paula says in simpering sing-song. "The Dark Lord picked you. He knows you're pregnant. And frankly, lying about it is an insult to his omniscience. You should apologize."

They laugh, and my blood boils.

Fuck these cultists, fuck George Baker and the dark lord, and especially fuck saying "I'm sorry" one more goddamn time.

I stand, fists shaking at my sides and teeth bared. "No."

The fake Sam chuckles. "No what?"

"No to all of it."

Again, they laugh. Louder. Heartier. So hard the Marine starts coughing and Paula's giggle pitches to a squeal. And while they're doubled over in pious delight, I sprint out of the chapel and slam the distillery door behind me.

The Marine catches up while I'm climbing the bunker stairs. He grabs my ankle, and I kick blindly until a delicious cracking sound accompanies my contact. He releases my leg, and his nose pours blood as he collapses backward and knocks Fake Sam to the bunker floor.

I rush up the last steps, shut and lock the pantry door, and slide a large potted plant in front before making a break for the foyer, where my phone vibrates across the floor. I grab it and run toward the red lights flashing outside. I wave at the police officers climbing the porch. I tell them who I am and where the demonic assholes are.

I collapse in the middle of Court Street, in a puddle of sunshine.

✳ ✳ ✳

I'm getting checked out in the ambulance when Devin rushes up and throws his arms around me. "Maeve, thank God you're okay. What the hell happened?"

I massage my head. "Enough for me to think this house should be on the ghost tour."

"What?" His watch beeps, and he grunts at the alarm. "Shit, we're late for the appointment."

"It's okay. We can make another."

The EMT presses her stethoscope to my back and asks me to breathe.

Devin holds my hand, and I do. I breathe. Deep, slow, revitalizing breaths that allow a shallow euphoria to bloom inside me.

I don't see the police remove my tour guests or any of their nasty pieces from the Spite House. I just hold Devin's hand and breathe. As I tell my story to the officers, as I explain to Jen what happened and demand a raise before next season, as I count the $180 in cash from Paula and the Marine, and as I piss on the drugstore's most expensive pregnancy test, I hold Devin's hand and breathe.

The result is clear, and I laugh in relief.

I'm not sorry.

THE NUN'S CAT
BY MYK PILGRIM

SATURDAY

Sister May didn't move the way other nuns did. She didn't glide with the immaculate grace normally attributed to her station. Instead, the leather-faced woman seemed to slither over the library carpet, though this Saturday in particular, there was something truly out of kilter with the cream-clad woman's movements. A certain thunking quality to her footfall, as if she were carrying something too heavy for her bones to bear the weight.

Katie knew she would regret looking up from her desk at the Dreich Public Library to find out what it was, but before she could stop herself, the nosey child within her wrenched the wheel from her hands. She pulled her glasses down from her forehead and in a fraction of a second, realised that she'd been right on *all* counts.

Not only was the nun headed straight for her, but she was swinging a large carrying case on every other step. Whatever this was, it couldn't be good.

Shit. Shit. Shit.

Katie considered her options.

Ordinarily, she'd pull her magical vanishing librarian trick, evaporate into the stacks and get Bet to cover for her, but there was a giant problem with that. Bet had left early to help her nephew with something she had referred to as "Te personal te discuss hen, but if ye dinnae tell anybody, he has the haemorrhoids."

"Aren't you going to ask me what I have in the box?" Sister May said. Her lips pulled into a mischievous smile.

Katie knew a trap when she saw one, but in the absence of a plan B, her only option was to comply. "Whatever have you got in that disproportionately large carrying case, Sister?"

Sister May planted the case on the countertop; something skittered around inside. It sounded heavier, more slithery than a cat in a box should have sounded.

"Well, dear, I heard you'd been going through a rough patch recently. We thought this little fellow could keep you company until you find your centre again."

Katie didn't have to look inside to know that it was indeed a cat inside the travel box. The unmistakable waft of pungent piss was all the clue she needed.

"Thanks, Sister, but I am not a cat pers—"

"Won't hear of it. You do so much for this community."

"Sister May, I appreciate what you're trying to—"

"Katie, my dear, we're praying for you."

Contrary to librarian instinct, Katie raised her voice. "No. I'm sorry, but no. I don't like cats; I don't want a cat. The thought is very kind, Sister, but please, with my *sincerest* apologies, take it back to wherever you got it from."

Sister May stood, aghast, seemingly unaware of the auditorium of eyeballs taking in the spectacle. She placed a white-gloved hand on Katie's, and after a beat of infuriating silence: "I'm so very sorry, Katie. We shouldn't have assumed, but you always hope."

"That's all right, Sister Ma—"

"The trouble is, dear, I can't take him back, not right this minute anyway." The pale nun ignored Katie's tensed temple. "I can, however, come back in a couple of hours and collect him. He won't be any trouble in the meantime, I promise."

Katie begrudgingly agreed, and faster than she had arrived, Sister May was gone.

By the time three pm rolled around, Katie was in no mood for fuckery. She'd been screamed at by some crackhead who'd locked their daughter in the library's disabled toilet. She'd been drawn into an argument over late fees with a man who smelt like he'd been pissing in the pants he was wearing for the last twenty years. Then there was the other Saturday staple: the stray poo nuggets left scattered amongst the beanbags like undesirable Easter eggs.

But worst of all, Sister May hadn't come back to collect the sodding cat. For the most part, Katie had managed to forget that the thing was even there, lurking inside the plastic box next to the age-yellowed CPU under the front desk. But, at the moment she was about to lock the doors behind her, she heard the whining screech.

Katie was a great many things; she might occasionally stick her gum to the underside of the bus seat when she didn't have an old receipt on her, and sure, she wasn't fond of cats, but she wasn't a monster.

Swearing like a trucker, she stomped back through the shadowed stacks to retrieve the carry-case. It was much heavier than she'd imagined it to be.

"Right you, little shit," she hissed. "Let's go find that lying nun, shall we?"

Katie had driven in circles around Dreich for damn near twenty minutes before she'd realised she had no idea where the local convent was, a situation which bamboozled her more than a little. She'd crossed over the River Forth on New Bridge and circled the Stirling roundabout four times before deciding to call Bet.

"Cannae talk noo, hen; our Alley has just gone in fer his wee procedure."

"I won't be long—"

"Ah dunnie know about that, last month Maude said that she's just gonnae pop round fer biscuits an—"

"Bet, do you know where the convent is?"

"Convent? Ah naw, Katie, ye cannae be thinking that. I may have been born auld but ye, sweetheart, well, there's lots fer you to stay on the market fer. There's nae sense in givin' up on men."

"It's not for me. I've got to drop a cat off."

"Why 'ave ye got a cat? I thought you hate cats."

Katie saw a vacant parking space just ahead. "Hold on."

She clicked on the indicator and pulled over.

"Listen, Bets, all I want to do is get rid of this fucking cat, go home, and slip into a steaming bath with a bottle of wine. Do you know where the convent is or not?"

It wasn't often that Elizabet Nicoll went silent. Unlike Katie, she hadn't become a librarian because she liked books; she'd become a librarian because she loved *the goss*. Also, she'd been sixteen at the time, had desperately needed a job, and there'd been nothing else going.

"Bet?"

"I'm still here, hen."

"And?"

"I've lived here as long as I can remember, and honestly, hen, I have nae idea."

"Well, shit."

Katie jumped as the thing inside the carry-box scratched frantically at the inside of its prison.

Bet broke the silence.

"Have you been doon the auld kirk? Surely they would know where the nuns live?"

"You know what, that's a great idea. See you Monday, Bet." Katie disconnected the call, turned up Tosca on the stereo, and headed to the other side of town.

Storming down the church steps, gripping the carry-box handle hard enough to make the purple plastic creak, Katie spat every single curse that she'd learnt from her last three years drinking in Scottish pubs. She yanked the car door open and had to stop herself from flinging the box into the backseat. She jammed the keys in the ignition and, letting free one last guttural "FUUUUUCCCCKKKKKING BASTARD!!!" peeled out of the church parking area and drove directly towards the corner shop.

There might not be enough wine in the world to take the edge off her day, but god-fucking-dammit she was going to try.

She picked up two, no, four bottles of her favourite red and, just for good measure, three family-sized bars of milk chocolate.

The nosey clerk, a youngster of about twenty who had more ears than teeth, asked if she was "avin' a party".

Katie grinned. "Yes, I most certainly am."

The grin lasted until she got back to the car, and realised that she had to go back in and buy cat food.

Home for Katie was a small flat on the first floor. Her neighbours were nice enough; all were pensioners, which suited her just fine.

She fumbled her door open and was standing in the kitchen, two-thirds through her first glass of wine, before she realised that she'd left the cat on the doorstep outside.

"This is why you are alone; you know that, right?"

Katie realised that whether she liked it or not, she'd have to let the thing out. Images of the hairy little psychopath running through her place, pissing everywhere, made her finish her glass, and pour another.

The only way she could make this work was to keep the cat in the kitchen. The floor was washable, the surfaces too, and worst case, the thing would be gone by Monday. Easy. She finished the glass and went to fetch the cat-box.

The hefty plastic case rattled as Katie planted it on the wood-print linoleum and unfastened the latch. It was a long moment before anything happened. The creature lurked in the deep shadows like a bad smell.

Bored with waiting, Katie turned away to refill her glass; when she looked again, there was a hairless scrotal face staring up at her from the case, though 'staring' wasn't the right word at all. She burst out laughing at how ludicrous the thing was, and as if in embarrassment, the cat snapped its head back inside the box.

Katie tore open one of the foil cat-food packets, wincing at the morning-breath reek of it. She squeezed its contents onto one of her less-loved saucers and placed it on the floor, out of reach of the case. She set down an equally unloved bowl with water. The cat didn't go for either. Instead, it seemed to be rearranging its possessions within the box. It was another few infuriating minutes before the emaciated-looking thing skulked out onto the linoleum.

Its body was a skeleton draped in swathes of wrinkled pink skin, but despite that, it moved with the elegance of a midnight panther, its male parts swaying. Katie couldn't discern any actual eyes in its squinting, wrinkled head. The skin bag sniffed at the food saucer before promptly wincing.

"I wouldn't eat that shit either," Katie said, feeling a lot less malice towards the pathetic creature.

Weren't Sphinx cats expensive? The revelation sent Katie's mind reeling. She'd had a bad run of luck, sure, but not the sort that would warrant such a gift, however unwanted.

The cat lapped at the water with a swollen black tongue, ears flapping like windsocks in a hurricane.

Content that she had fulfilled her obligation, Katie scooped up her glass and the second bottle and, locking the cat in the kitchen behind her, went to put her body in the place that her mind had been all week.

Bath salts were something that Katie had discovered far later in life than she'd been happy about. Despite all the "hocus pocus" and "snake oil rhetoric" usually printed on the packaging, it did bring her peace. Baths were wonderful and all, but adding Epsom salts dialled the experience up from a ten to a solid twelve. If she had a favourite time of the week, this was it: wine, candles, pocket digital radio and—if she was in the mood, which had become more common in recent months—the shower head.

Katie slipped out of her clothes, dropping them where she stood, and slid into the steaming tub. A shudder of molten joy crawled up her limbs, warming her insides. She inhaled the sweet tang of lavender as if she'd spent all week holding her breath. Within seconds, the knots that comprised her shoulders untied, her forehead prickling with sweat.

If such a thing exists, heaven is a hot spa.

She sang along with the songs she knew on the radio in between sips from the bottle and hummed the ones she didn't.

She didn't notice padding steps on the hallway outside the open bathroom door, nor the slinking body that scurried across the tiles towards where she lay soaking.

Something frigid batted the tip of her nose Katie shot up, emptying half her glass into the bath. "Jesus Christ!"

The cat hadn't even flinched. It stood upright, bony paws pressed on the lip of the tub. It regarded Katie with its permanent squint.

"Got over yourself, have you, bawbag? How did you get out of the kitchen?"

The cat didn't explain. Instead, it leant over and licked Katie's cheek, her forehead, but when it went for her mouth, she shooed it away.

The cat withdrew, apparently to explore the bathroom. Katie shut her eyes, slid back, submerging her head, leaving her mouth and nose periscoped above the surface. Inhaling, she filled the cavity of her insides with lavender steam. She focused on the rhythmic bass-kick that was her heart. Thump after thump reminding her that despite everything, it was still there, not dead, still beating whether she believed it or not. She was still here; she had survived, she had stood up, she had fought back and walked away.

Katie started awake, sitting up in one thunderous movement and sending a tidal wave of glacial water across the bathroom floor. Her chest heaved with asthmatic shudders; she scrambled for the silver bath handles and, quivering, lifted herself out. The feet she planted on the beige bathmat didn't feel like hers, padded with waterlogged skin, numbed against the sensation of the cotton beneath.

The taste in her mouth was rancid; it was rotten eggs and cold sick. Cigarette butts stirred in with old grease. She cleared her throat and gobbed a full mouthful of viscous phlegm into the cold bath. The black mucus glob floated on the surface, seemingly pulsing in the low candlelight.

She jerked the bath plug and watched the septic mass spin wildly before the cyclonic plughole dragged it down into the darkness of the sewers far below.

"What the fuck."

Katie's mouth was a swamp. She spat again; this time the spittle was more of a grey. She wrapped her shivering body in a towel and frantically brushed her teeth.

When she was done, it was better; not great, but better. Her hands still shaking, she decided it was time to abandon the wine.

Katie snuggled up on the couch, watching crap on TV while she nursed a hot chocolate. It wasn't long before, despite her protesting and shooing; the cat was curled up asleep on her lap. Looking down at the wrinkled, scrotal creature, Katie named him Baws.

"Because you look like a bawbag," she whispered to the dozing kitty.

SUNDAY

Sundays were pretty standard for Katie; she'd catch up on housework, do laundry, and make phone calls while she did.

"So you have a cat now? Three years north of the wall and now you're a cat person. Frankly, Kate, I'm disappointed in you. Why couldn't you just get hooked on heroin like a normal person?"

Katie rinsed the mop in the bucket and continued on the kitchen floor.

"No, Stella, that's not what I said at all. I think maybe all those screaming children have affected your hearing, sister dear. I said 'I am *temporarily* housing a misplaced cat'."

"Oh, well, that's an entirely different story, then. Tell me, lady denial, do you currently have a box full of feline faeces taking up floor space in your kitchen?"

Katie glanced over at the litter box that she couldn't quite recall purchasing that morning. "Of course not. What do you take me for? Anyway, how's mom?"

"She's fine, keeps asking where dad is. I've started telling her that he's nipped out to the pub and will be back later. Her memory is getting worse. You should visit soon. I've got that feeling, you know."

Katie picked up the mop bucket and headed to the bathroom. "I'll make a booking soon."

She tipped the dirty water down the toilet and flushed. Then she sprayed the bathtub with bleach and got to work on the ring of dead skin with a sponge.

"We both know what you mean when you say *soon*—listen, fuck mom, I miss you. Come and see *me*."

"Have you seen *him* this week?" Katie asked.

Stella went quiet.

Katie stopped scrubbing; the silence was enough of an answer for her. "I'll take that as a yes. What happened?"

"He was hanging around in the driveway last night; we called the police."

The wires in Katie's jaw ached from the tension. "And?"

"He was screaming that you killed his son. Let's talk about something else." Stella went quiet again. "So, how's work?"

"The council's been interfering again this week, trying to force meetings on us, after-hours stuff. Bet has told them 'te stick it right up their arse.' I swear, I couldn't survive without her."

MONDAY

It had taken Katie some considerable time on Monday morning to coax Baws back into his travel case, but she'd managed. She arrived at the Driech Public Library late enough that there was a cluster of sour-faced 'yummy mummies' hanging around in the October chill.

They cursed at her under their breath, but she ignored them. Life must be hard enough, she thought, pushing a pram with a screaming sugar-addicted monster *and* believing that painting oneself traffic-cone orange was an attractive look.

She put Baws' carry-case down on the pavement and fumbled with her keys.

A little boy wearing pearly white trainers toddled towards the case. After kicking the box, he jammed his fingers through the wire grid. When the cat didn't come to meet him, the boy pressed his snot-crusted face against the wire grid, drool streaking down his neck.

Baws came, instantly forcing his black tongue into the child's mouth. The boy's shrill shriek cut through the frosty morning like a firework.

Katie chuckled to herself as she watched him sprint back to his inept tango-faced mother. It was nice to see a spoilt manner-less little brat get a full-cream karma payout in real time.

✳ ✳ ✳

After she'd made her mandatory cup of tea and turned all the computers on, Katie drafted her to-do list for the day.

The list consisted of one single item, repeated several times.

Return cat.

Between her shelving and usual patron enquiries, Katie asked around and made some phone calls. It was as if the nuns had evaporated into thin air.

Baws sat quietly in his case under the desk, seemingly content. Katie had never met a cat like him. When she opened the cage door to give him some water, he slithered around her ankles in a figure of eight and lapped up the entire contents of the saucer before slipping back into the box without a sound. Katie half hoped the nuns stayed away, for a few more days at least—as much as it irked her to admit it, she enjoyed the company.

As always, Bet cut straight to the heart of the situation.

"Doesn't he leave arse-prints on all your hard surfaces? He's got nae hair te cover his smelly freckle."

Katie started to protest until the reality of all those *mystery* dabs on her glass tabletop caught up with her.

"Are ye all right, hen? Ye look like shite on a shoe."

"I feel fine. A little tired, maybe."

"Mebbe coming doon wit something? It's that time of the year. You've had yer jags?"

Katie nodded.

"Good, good. With all these wee bastards running around smearing their snotty fingers o'er every book they cannae read, you've got te take care of yerself."

"I know, I know, I didn't start working here yesterday."

"Hen, as long as I'm working here, you will have *always* started here yesterday."

"How's your nephew feeling?"

Three hours later, Katie knew more about the configuration of Ally's genitals and rectal passage than she'd ever wanted to. At one point, Bet had broken out pen and paper and furnished her with diagrams of the procedure while they ate biscuits.

All in, it had been a good day, and even if she couldn't admit it, Katie was glad not to be going home alone.

Her dreams that night were anything but peaceful. The hospital had an onion-skin overlay, moving shapes followed by matching translucent shadows.

There was no kicking from inside her bruised pregnant belly. Her tongue flopped around, exploring the not-at-all-natural configuration of what was now her mouth: a collection of shattered molars lining her snapped wishbone jaw. Tears tore down her face, carving their way through the canyons of dried blood before soaking into her hospital robes. Katie's blinks elongated as she gave herself to the drug-induced silence and slipped away from the image of Alan's rage-contorted face.

She woke to find Baws sitting on the pillow beside her, regarding her in the dark with the slits he used for eyes. Her chest was full of cement, her jaw tingling with echoes. She sat up slowly, needing to do something, anything but lie there like some victim.

The cat, sensing her distress, came nearer, nuzzling his head against the bare skin of her arm. His skin was organic velvet, not quite warm, but not cold either. The contact helped pull Katie back from the spiral she was tumbling down.

She relaxed back into the pillow. Baws waited until she'd settled; then he curled himself up in the crook of her arm. Katie shut her eyes and slid back into slumber.

THURSDAY

"Yer breath is getting bad, hen," Bet said, and proffered a non-negotiable pack of Polos in Katie's direction. "The last time I got a whiff af a smell like that was after me granda had drunk hisself deid."

"Don't be so over-dramatic. Shit happens." Katie took the packet and made a show of popping three in her mouth.

"That may be true, but from what aye can tell, fer you, it's happening oot the wrang end af your body."

Katie elbowed Bet, not entirely playfully.

A bald-shaven gentleman wearing denim shorts and a black shirt came up to the library counter with a stack of books under a hairy forearm. Katie greeted him and started checking out the stack.

Excelsior! A biography of Stan Lee and a worn copy of the *Kama Sutra*, unskillfully concealed between a book entitled *Counting Ribs* by Half Nelson and a *Classic Spider-Man* omnibus.

"So hows yer Baws doing?" Bet said to Katie, without looking up.

The bald man didn't miss a beat. "Much better, thanks, the antibiotics have helped to get the swelling down."

He winked at Katie, slipped the books into a bag, and disappeared.

"Ye know, last week, I was wondering why he was walking around like he had a carrot up his arse."

Katie couldn't contain her laughter.

Sometimes, just around three, Katie heard the familiar slithering of Sister May. Before she'd even had time to raise her view, the woman was there at the counter. Katie visibly flinched.

"Oh, I'm sorry, Katie, my dear, didn't mean to startle you. These shoes are so old they don't make a sound, but I'd be lying if I said I didn't like them that way. Keeps the young ones on their toes."

"Sister—" Katie started, but as seemed to be her custom, the nun cut her off.

"I hear you've been looking for me; I'm so sorry for not coming back last week. There were a few complications, and I had to slip away for a few days—couldn't be avoided, you understand."

Katie shrugged; she was much less flustered by this conversation than she'd expected to be.

"So how did you get on?"

"Get on?"

"With the cat. He's a sweet little chap, isn't he? Got a kindly streak in him a mile wide."

Katie considered telling Sister May about the cat's new name, but decided against it. "I wasn't expecting to like him, but well—"

"I knew it! So thrilled, dear"—she leant her face so close that Katie could smell the coffee grounds on her breath. "There's no company quite like cats. I'm so glad.

You two have fun, I'll be back to check up on you in a few weeks."

She turned on her heels and vanished, her white robes trailing behind her.

Bet slid in from the far side of the desk. "There's something not quite right about her. I dinnae like it."

Katie shrugged and offered to get them both tea.

FRIDAY

Friday had been an unremarkable day; work felt distinctly less worky, though Katie felt like she was coming down with something, and couldn't wait to get home.

Baws would be waiting for her by the door, squinting his eyeless squinty squint as if to say, "Welcome home, darling, I've missed you. Tell me about your day."

And Katie would tell him everything; surprisingly, he'd sit and listen. Then she'd pour out his old food, and replace it with a new pack of expensive food he'd completely ignore. He'd keep her company while she sat and ate her supper, and then follow her into the bathroom and watch when she showered, or lovingly lick her face when she chose to bathe—more often than not, becoming more friendly than Katie felt comfortable with.

Baws had a habit of forcing his tongue in her mouth. She couldn't quite remember the first time it had happened, but he did it every time he got the chance. She'd often start awake in the dark with a septic-tank tang in her mouth, only to hear him motoring across the bedroom carpet and down the hall to hide behind the couch in the lounge.

"Stupid fucking cat," she'd hiss, and go back to sleep.

When it caught her off guard, the pulsing, ribbed tongue left a bitter residue in her mouth. At first, Katie had felt violated by it. But now, as disgusting as it was, it had become cute: one of those things that all cat owners know, but no one discusses.

That night Baws was waiting for her outside the front door; he seemed to sense that she wasn't feeling well. He stretched his soft pink arms up to her thigh and rubbed his wrinkled head on her knee until she picked him up and cradled him in her arms. The heat emanated off his hairless body like a Sahara wind; it seeped through her jumper, crawling deliciously up her arms and into her chest.

Baws affectionately licked her chin as she carried him through the house; lazy gobshite was fast asleep before she had even popped on the kettle. Katie's throat was broken glass, and the thought of eating hard food was more than she could bear, so she split the difference.

A few minutes later, she was curled up on the couch, a snoozing Baws cradled under one arm while she shovelled soothing chocolate fudge brownie ice-cream into her face with the other.

She watched the usual shit on TV, in much the same way absent parents mind their children. Her mind was vaguely aware that things were happening on the screen, but that was it. After giving the ice-cream tub the *coup de grace*, Katie wrapped her other arm around Baws, and for the first time in years, slipped off into a careless sleep.

SATURDAY

Katie woke up on the couch; her throat felt like it had been slashed. Her stomach growled like a tiger beneath her sweater. Its grumbling roused Baws from his sleep, or at least that's what she'd thought until she looked down and saw *them*.

Two tiny pink bodies curled around each other on top of the blanket. Their pink mouths papped open and shut.

Gingerly, Katie stroked the soft velvet head of each kitten with her thumb, her heart almost bursting in her chest.

She leant down and spat an unpleasant wad of grey phlegm into the empty ice-cream tub. There was more blood in it than she felt comfortable with, but when she heard the cries of the implausible kittens, she didn't linger on it.

"Baws," she whispered, "you never told me you were a girl."

Katie smiled. Crust on her chin flaked off and drifted onto her jumper.

Should she buy formula? Take them to the vet?

It didn't matter, either way; she wasn't going into work, not today. This was too special, and if she'd wanted anything less than special, she'd have just stayed in Yorkshire.

Katie dialled Bet, who picked up after a single ring.

"Are ye okay, hen? Do ye need me te drive you to the hospital?"

"Don't be daft, Bets."

"Well, naebody calls this early unless they're leaning towards deid, or they're pished. Are ye pished?"

"Kittens. Baws had kittens. Two of them."

"I've heard a great many excuses for not calling into work, but thas a new one. Ye dinnae have to lie, hen; pished is pished. Happens te us all sometimes."

"Seriously, he"—Katie corrected herself—"*she* had kittens, I woke up and there they were. Could you cover for me today?"

There was a long silence down the phone.

"Bets?"

"Sure, I'll cover for ye, but fer the record I know it's because you've been oot on the pish." She hung up.

Katie lay still on the couch as long as she could before her bladder compelled her to do something about the disproportionate liquid to body mass ratio. As she shifted to get up, the two mouse-sized beans peeped. Baws appeared from nowhere; he, no wait, *she* jumped onto the cushion beside them, apparently saying, 'see, Katie? Look what I made, aren't I clever?' Katie stroked Baws' head.

"You lied to me, you stupid cat."

Once out of the shower and dressed, Katie guzzled down two packets of hot lemon. The sleep had helped, but if anything, fatigue was kicking her arse. Her head was full of cotton wool, her eyes aching, and she couldn't quite shake the churning sensation in her guts.

Her mind flashed to the brief bout of morning sickness before everything with Alan had gone to shit. The memories didn't make her feel any better. Being the practical gal she was, she decided that tidying the house would give her a better grip on the world.

Stella picked up the phone, sounding like she'd run two marathons to answer.

"You will never believe what happened. Baws is a girl, and she had kittens!"

Katie walked up and down the house picking up detritus, discarded clothing, and used tea mugs.

"So, he's a she? I'm a little confused, Kat; you've been handling penises since you were 14—"

"Pot, kettle, black?"

"True as that may be, how have you misread the whole penis thing? Seems like a stretch."

Stomach rumbling, Katie put the last mug on the drying rack and snapped off the marigolds.

"I looked her over earlier, and if you put a gun to my head, I'd have still ticked 'cock' on the ballot slip. Maybe she's one of those hermaphrodites?"

Katie bent down and shook the litter box, uncovering three grey-dusted nuggets.

"You realise how weird this is, right?" Stella asked.

"Oh, I know." She picked one up between thumb and forefinger and popped it into her mouth. "But then again, when has my life been normal?"

Around eleven, fatigue hit Katie like a bus, and she collapsed into bed. Her dream was less than kind; things watched her from the shadows as swells of nausea twisted her guts into knots. Her chest heaved as she threw up buckets of chunky pea soup. Vomit dripped down her chin, down her bare torso, and congealed in the slight tuft of her pubic hair.

She didn't know where the buckets were coming from, but they filed past her as if on a conveyor belt.

Katie awoke and saw the carnage surrounding her: septic grey vomit spilt over the side of the bed and dripped onto the carpet. Baws sat beside her in the mess, licking her chin and yowling like he'd never been fed in his, *her* entire life.

Amid the lake of sick were the kittens. No longer just the two; now there were six pink bodies, floating.

None moved.

None breathed.

Baws wailed.

Katie threw up again; this time, she managed to turn her head away from the kittens and coated her duvet in vomit that was quickly changing shades to an alarming scarlet.

Her mouth burned, the taste of hot iron seeping in between her teeth. When the tide of nausea ended, she drew back onto the cleaner side of her pillow. Peering down at the hamster-sized bodies on the sick-sodden covers beside her, Katie knew they were dead.

She'd killed them, all of them, not even one day old. She had done it. She'd done it again.

The old spiral began: Alan's blind rage, the final animal scream she'd loosed in that impossibly long second before he had decimated her jaw.

Then the real blows came.

Steel fists smashing into her bulging belly, making the water cocoon within her compress into cement. The unborn body shrieked, begged her to peel herself up off the kitchen floor, and escape. But Katie couldn't; the blows rained down on her like a rockslide.

Later, a less than tactful lady doctor would tell Katie that the child within her belly had had its skull concaved, both forearms broken, and every rib snapped. By the time Katie had come to in the hospital, the baby was already long gone.

The real injuries Alan had inflicted that night before he'd fled their two-bedroom flat were on his wife's soul.

He escaped the consequences through the loophole of a noose.

She'd slowly worked through physiotherapy sessions and made an effort to rejoin the world, but Alan's father had made it difficult. Thankfully Stella and her hubby had cleared Katie's house out while she was in the hospital, carefully boxing up her possessions.

Stella had insisted that Katie come stay with them while she 'got her shit worked out'.

At the time they'd thought nothing of it when they woke one morning to find Katie's car tyres flat. Bad luck happens, but things are rarely that simple.

Flowerpots destroyed, clumps of dog shit smeared on door handles, and bricks smashed through windows while they were out. It had admittedly taken them longer to put it all together, but when the written threats came, it became clear. Alan's father blamed her for everything, logic be damned.

Once the police were involved, a restraining order kept him away, mostly, but that didn't stop him exploiting every loophole he could find to make her life hell.

All he needed was a few intrigued locals and some creative whispering.

Once ripples started to show in the community, Katie couldn't even face the clerks at the supermarket or order a coffee at The Bean without finding all manner of unpleasantness in the bottom of her cup.

Small communities are like that; as serene as they may seem from the outside, the rot runs deep.

The endless chorus of 'Murderous cunt!' and 'We know what you did' bled into Katie's already vivid nightmares until she suffered a thermonuclear anxiety attack while driving and wrote her car off.

After that, against all of her sister's protests, Katie sold off everything she had left and moved North.

This all passed through her mind in a fraction of a second as she lay there, chunder particles scorching her lungs, heaving sobs cleaving through her chest like shifting tectonic plates.

The minute bodies beside her had already lost their pink hue and were fading to the shade of chalk-smeared tarmac.

All six were stone dead.

Katie cleared her throat and forced herself up.

She needed to do something, anything, take charge and make her own choices. She scooped the frigid bodies into a towel, cradling them for the first time in their brief lives. She bore them to the bathroom, tears streaming down her face, her stomach still writhing eels. She filled the basin with lukewarm water and placed them in; with shaking fingers she began to rinse the sick off their cold little bodies.

Something nudged the back of her knee; she turned away from the kittens to see Baws staring up at her. A fresh wave broke within her as she leant down to stroke the cat's wrinkled head.

"I'm so sorry, my love, I'm so very sorry."

Katie turned back to the sink and noticed movement. A pink body twitched. She wiped her eyes with her forearm and watched.

The small bodies began to wriggle, sending gentle ripples across the water's surface. Katie's heart leapt; her pulse smashing plates in her ears.

The bodies writhed like corpulent maggots. One close to her opened its mouth in what, at first, Katie thought to be a yawn; it was not.

Pink kitten skin slid back from its twitching black tongue like an impossible foreskin. It was ribbed, with the texture of wet rubber, growing thicker as the kitten flesh folded further back, revealing more.

More bodies followed suit, sliding back their feline countenances until the inverted skins sagged off their slick ebony worm bodies like deployed skin parachutes.

All of them made the change but one.

Their slithering tendrils converged on the stationary body floating near the plug, and tore at it. Tissue paper flesh breaking free, its tiny bones didn't look like bones.

The water changed from mostly clear to pink, then scarlet as their thrashing intensified.

Katie's stomach rebelled again; she spewed into the basin. Something large slid out of her throat and across her tongue, grazing her teeth as it left her body and landed in the water to join its siblings. Viscous paste coated Katie's teeth and gums, leaving her throat rancid eggs and old crusty socks.

The fleshy creature that she had just birthed from *fuck knows where* inverted itself.

She wailed as the black snake-things intertwined, connecting and disconnecting their lengths, false kitten skins flapping behind them, splashing pink foam on the floor. Only fish-food chunks remained of the devoured kitten-sack, fragments of pale skin detritus swirling through the liquid.

She reached over the basin, keeping her body as far away from the *things* as she could, worm-things lashing at her forearm, tearing open circular holes in the soft underside.

She snagged the plug chain in her spaghetti fingers and yanked. It leapt from the sink, and water slurped down into the septic pipes below Dreich.

The worm-things' manic twitching slowed as if falling into slumber; then, as she'd expected, they retracted, re-filling the raw-chicken skins faster than they'd slipped out.

Their tiny legs expanded like balloons until the last miniscule kitten's mouth closed, encasing the final centimetres of its septic black tongue.

Then the mewling began.

The kittens were very much *not dead;* they were also, very much, *not kittens.*

Katie ran and slammed the bathroom door behind her. She flew through the lounge and locked herself in the kitchen.

Yanking a bottle from the fridge, she drank deep, emptying it in seconds, rinsing the bitter aloe taste from her mouth. Leaning her back against the counter, she slid down until she sat on the kitchen floor.

"I always fucking hated cats," she told the empty wine bottle; which didn't need words to convey how much it agreed.

Katie's stomach groaned, and in response, she reached out a hand and snatched up a clump of cat shit from the litter box.

It was in her mouth and smushing between her molars before she caught herself. Once she was aware, it was only a fraction of a second before she filled the litter tray with all the wine that had been in her belly.

Rushing to the sink, she ran the hot tap through her mouth and tried to pick the stodgy lumps of shit from toothy crevices, but they clumped there, solid as chocolate chunks in ice-cream.

Katie crumpled on the floor, weeping, and blacked out.

She awoke, her arse aching from the cold of the linoleum. Looking down, she knew that all of it wasn't some insane nightmare. Five pulpy pink kittens snoozed on her lap. Her temples clenched. A faint scratching sound made her glance at the still-locked kitchen door.

A coral puddle slid under the door and began to expand, as if someone was blowing a not-at-all translucent bubblegum balloon.

The shape expanded as more material slurped under the door. An all-too-familiar round head, slightly bigger than a tennis ball, began to form at the top of the mass. Wrinkles filled out the eyeless sockets; pointed ears snapped up; the rest of the cat's body stiffened into its not-at-all-natural shape. Hanging from Baws' mouth was a lump of pink flesh, which also began to twitch and expand into its public countenance.

Baws slinked towards her and deposited the newly-formed kitten on her lap with the others, before planting both stringy paws on her thigh and nuzzling her neck, frigid nose tip trailing higher up her throat until it started licking with that thing that wasn't a tongue.

Katie turned her head away, her body quivering. Hands hollow, she knew what to do.

She reached out her hand and stroked the thing that she had convinced herself she'd loved. Using the last of her will to fight the instinctive waves of revulsion, she scooped up the mewling younglings, cradling them in a single arm. The kittens wriggled around and over each other until they found equilibrium, one settled with its nose pressed in her armpit.

Katie slid open the drawer and placed the sharpest knife she had on the counter beside the stove, then filled her soup pot almost to the brim with water. Baws slithered around her legs, coiling and uncoiling like a legged snake. She lit the gas, and a halo of vibrant blue licked the pot's base; tiny bubbles formed on the tin-coloured bottom.

The babies in her arm stirred. Katie rocked, humming until they relaxed back into slumber. She needed a distraction; Katie boiled the kettle and spooned twelve sugars into a cup of tea. The sweetness helped steady her more than she dared to hope.

The pot was almost boiling; she readied herself. The air in the small kitchen felt like a swarm of midges chewing at every inch of her. A streak of sweat ran down the furrow of her spine and came to rest in the crack of her arse.

Then she did it.

The kittens splashed into the boiling pot; the kitchen became the site of a million air raid sirens. The worms sprouted, helicoptering desperately as the molten liquid transformed them from ebony black to puckered pink and then, ghost white.

Katie slammed the glass lid on top, catching the ends of three of the worms in the rim. The shrill crying jumped several octaves higher.

Overcome, Katie shrieked; pain tore through her. She wept as she had never wept before; everything, all the death and sorrow that came before was eclipsed by this; the baby that had died inside her, and her dead husband.

Baws pounced on her back, opening gashes with his serrated claws. Still, Katie persisted, as the cat ripped through the flesh of her forearms and punctured her breasts with its sharp teeth.

She was faintly aware of thudding from beyond the realm of her current universe. It rolled in the distance like thunder.

The desperation inside the pot seemed not to slow. Katie held the lid down with everything she had. Baws made a go for her face; the creature's foreskin head peeled back to reveal its real jaws.

Concentric circles of broken bottle teeth, all of which seemed to rotate in its black plasticine gums. Katie didn't even consider the knife; she was too terrified to lift a hand off the pot lid in defence. She was out of options, so she swung her elbow.

The teeth shredded the back of her arm as the creature tumbled head over arse through the air and smashed into the cupboard behind her.

Both hands locked on the pot, Katie scanned over her shoulder, waiting for the next attack. Torrents of merlot poured down her arms onto the pot lid, transforming into blood cream streaks as the dry metal flash-cooked them.

Her head echoed with the dying screams of her children, but the fight was lessening.

Baws came at her again, this time scrambling up the back of her leg. Katie took the chance, snatching the knife off the counter and forcing the blade through the cat's torso, stopping it dead.

Distant thundering grew louder.

The pot stopped shuddering. Although Katie could see the meat froth through the lid, she didn't dare lift her hands.

The kitchen door collapsed, splinters of false wood littering the floor. Police found her still clinging to the lid, hysterically weeping. Once they'd convinced her to let go, they found six boiled kittens and a male Sphinx cat, which had been run through with a knife; they rushed it to the emergency vet.

FRIDAY

Jeanette hadn't worked at the shelter long, but she'd never worked anywhere that had had a nun pop by, especially not one entirely clad in white.

"Morning, uh, Sister?"

"Afternoon, my dear." The nun gestured to the wall clock above Jeanette's head, which read five past midday.

"Sorry, so what can I help you with?"

"I'm here to collect a cat. A Sphinx. My distant cousin was sitting it for me, but it didn't quite work out."

THREADBARE

BY SEBASTIAN BENDIX

L ayne returned to the house a little before noon. It had not been a particularly profitable morning; a couple of cigarettes from another homeless guy down on Colorado, a handful of change hanging outside the Starbucks during rush hour, maybe three bucks in total. Someone gave him a stale bagel to eat for breakfast, plain, no cream cheese. And it was hot, 80 degrees before mid-day, the air stagnant and stale. Damn mountains, always blocking off the breeze; they kept the heat trapped like cigarette smoke blown into a beer bottle. Layne hated this town, and he was pretty sure the feeling was mutual.

Calling it a house was being generous; the squat on Yucatan was barely a cottage, some run-down shack that hadn't been occupied despite the owner being dead now several years. Finally, some questionable but enterprising development group had bought the land and scheduled it for demolition, but they hadn't reckoned on the squatters who had been living in the house for the better part of a year. Layne was one of those squatters, naturally. There were five of them – Dizzy, Alejandro, William, Layne, and Rafaela. But Rafaela was the only one Layne was worried about.

Rafaela.

He had met her panhandling outside the Paseo, hustling that prime dinner-and-a-movie crowd. She was younger than Layne by a good ten years, the rare runaway who hadn't slipped into drugs or prostitution in the few years she had been working the street. She left home at sixteen—abusive drunk of a father, as is so often the case—and just got accustomed to homeless life. At this point she could have cleaned up a bit, gotten a straight job with a cleaning company or at a fast food joint, maybe even rented a room somewhere. But Rafaela liked living life on her own terms, even if those terms were decidedly grim by most people's standards. She made Layne feel like less of a loser, like he had chosen this life rather than having fallen into it due to bad choices, bad luck, or both. Rafaela made him feel like a human being, which made her a rare commodity in his world. And she made that rundown squat feel like home.

He knew there was trouble halfway down the block, before he even reached the house. Boone was there with his goon Cutty, thuggish emissaries of the shady developers. They had been around the place several times now and the idea of going to the cops had been bandied about by the others, but was ruled out for obvious reasons. The law might have been on their side in regards to squatters' rights, but no cops were going to pursue action against these hired goons on the word of a few bums. They were on their own, and despite having numbers on their side, none of the squatters were fighters. Boone and Cutty looked like they had been through more than their share of scraps. They also looked armed.

Layne picked up the pace when he saw Rafaela at the door, wincing as Boone drew close to her, threatening her with more than just a forceful eviction. "Hey," Layne challenged. "There a problem?"

Boone turned to see Layne approach; his lip curled into a vicious sneer. "Yeah, there's a fucking problem," he said. "You and this tainted taco are still here."

Layne felt a flush of anger bloom from his chest to face. His right hand sat, as usual, in the pocket of his well-worn army jacket, fingering the hilt of the box cutter he kept there for emergencies. "We've been over this, Boone. Tell your bosses they need an approved court order."

"Listen to Mr. Lawyer here. You missed your true calling, crackhead. Now pack up your shit here or me and my buddy are gonna have some fun with this lovely lady of yours."

Layne could see William and Dizzy peeking fearfully from behind a ratty window curtain. Useless, as usual. "We've got rights," he said, hand in pocket, defiant. "So step off."

Now Boone was pissed. He grabbed Rafaela by the hair, yanked her close, causing her to yelp—more out of fear than pain. "I'm not playing, crackhead. Get your shit right now or things are gonna get real ugly for your bitch—"

Before Boone could finish the box cutter was out and slashing an arc across the back of his hair-grabbing hand. The cut wasn't deep—the blade was old and quite dull—but it drew blood. Boone let out a hiss, let go of Rafaela. "You little fuck," he hissed, checking his hand. "I'll fucking kill you...!"

Boone was reaching behind his back—no doubt for the snub-nosed revolver hidden there—when a cop car turned the corner, spotted the altercation, and approached slowly. Cutty told Boone to cool it with a panicky shake of his head. Boone left the gun where it was hidden and turned to the patrol car, smiling insincerely. The passenger window of the cop car rolled down and a mustachioed patrolman looked out.

"There a problem here?"

"No problem, officer," answered Boone.

"All right then, move along," said the patrolman.

"Will do, officer." Boone turned his phony smile to Layne. "We'll be seeing you Layne. Real soon."

The patrol car sat idling at the curb as Boone and Cutty walked off down the street. And while Layne was grateful for the protection, he knew it was fleeting. Once the thugs had turned the corner, the patrol car pulled away from the curb, leaving Layne and Rafaela to sit in their anxiety.

"We can't stay here tonight," Layne said.

Rafaela nodded grimly. There was no blame in her face, but Layne felt shame nonetheless. He wanted to protect her, show her that he was a man, that he could provide her with the life she deserved. But right now, all they could do was get moving.

Afternoons at the Pasadena Public Library internet commons were a depressing affair on the best of days, but the afternoon heat had drawn a particularly desperate, odiferous crowd. The musty basement room played host to many a local homeless person, allowing them to while away the hours, catch up on the latest streaming shows, social media memes, and, more often than not, porn. Layne managed to score a computer between an elderly woman looking up psalms and Gabe, an older regular who was obsessed with conspiracy theories and cryptozoology. He also freely ogled Rafaela, which Layne did not appreciate. But literal beggars certainly couldn't be literal choosers.

Rafaela was enjoying an episode of Real Housewives on headphones while Layne sat silently next to her, too concerned with their current predicament to give himself over to entertainment. They hadn't been seated more than ten minutes when Gabe leaned over, catching a glance at the banalities playing out on Rafaela's monitor.

"You know why people watch this crap, right?"

"Because it's entertaining?" Layne hoped his disinterested answer would end this exchange as quick as humanly possible.

"Nah," Gabe said, barely above a whisper. "It's because all of the knowledge is being consumed. Eaten."

Layne shot Gabe a look that he didn't follow, and really didn't want to follow.

"The moth people," Gabe said with a knowing smirk. "The moth people are eating all the knowledge."

"Is that like the lizard people or something?" Layne asked wearily. There was no getting out of this.

"Lizard people are a crock. It's moth people. They're everywhere."

"Oh yeah? Like where?"

"Like here." Gabe's eyes darted nervously around the cramped room. "In this library."

"The Pasadena Public Library is infested with moth people," Layne flatly intoned.

"That's right. They come out at night and feed on the old books, devouring all the knowledge in them. Once all the books are gone, no one will remember anything. Then they'll come for us and feed off of whatever's left in our brains!" It was clear from the crazed look in the older man's face that he sincerely believed all of this. "I've seen them myself, with my own eyes," he continued. "Saw them once when I hid in here overnight."

Now here was something Layne could use. "Hold on... you've stayed here in the library overnight? How'd you pull that off?"

"It's not hard," Gabe said. "I figured out the door codes and I know a good place to hide when this place clears out." His eyes caught a hungry look at Rafaela's shapely legs. "Could show you tonight."

Layne gave this serious consideration. They were in desperate need for a place to hide out, a place where Boone and Cutty couldn't get to them. A night in the library would do them well, provided that Gabe actually knew what he was talking about. Layne touched Rafaela gently on the shoulder. She took off her headphones and looked at him.

"I think we might have a plan," he said.

"The internet stations are now closed," a voice crackled over hidden loudspeakers. "Please make sure your printer sessions are finished and exit the internet commons area."

Layne and Rafaela looked to Gabe. The library page who manned the internet commons desk went into the back to turn off the copy machines and color printers. "Now!" said Gabe.

As the last of the stragglers headed up the stairs, Gabe, Layne and Rafaela hurried over to a side door outfitted with a manual punch code lock that was positively archaic by modern digital standards. Gabe quickly pressed the numbered buttons in a simple four-digit sequence – six, two, two, four. There was a click, and he turned the door knob, opening the door to reveal a back hallway accessible to library staff only. Gabe ushered them in quickly and quietly closed the door behind them.

The hallway led them into an office area with staff mailboxes and a newspaper sorting area. There was an emergency exit door and another door that led to parts unknown, which Gabe presently indicated. "We can hide in there until the cleaning crew leaves." He turned his unsavory gaze to Rafaela. "Then we'll have the place all to ourselves."

Layne felt a flush of anger. There was no way he was staying holed up here all night with this creep's eyes crawling all over Rafaela. Before the older man had a chance to react Layne grabbed him by the lapels of his crusty coat and pushed him out the emergency door. As luck would have it, there was no alarm. Gabe had only a moment to register the betrayal before Layne pulled the door closed with a definitive slam, leaving the old lech in the narrow alley outside the library's east wing.

"Fucking creep," Layne said to Rafaela. She gave him a vaguely disapproving look.

"Babe," she said. "That wasn't nice. He was trying to help us."

"We don't need his kind of help." He led her to the mystery door, the one that gained them entrance to Gabe's coveted hiding spot. "Now let's go before someone sees us."

They stayed in the dusty, unfinished basement room for a little over three hours, listening for the sounds of the Spanish-speaking cleaning crew as they finished their night's work. The room was a repository for books that were being taken out of circulation; old editions, worn out paperbacks, damaged hardcovers—stuff no one would miss. One pile had a stack of books that looked like the pages had been chewed ragged by some sort of large animal, and Layne was reminded about Gabe's ridiculous mothman story. This was likely the source of that delusion. Silly as the story was, Layne had no desire to remain in this dank, dreary room a second more than was necessary.

At last it sounded like the coast was clear, so Layne and Rafaela ventured out of the room, back through the hall and into the internet commons, up the stairs to the first floor reading area. The library was empty and full of shadows cast from streetlights through the large windows, and it took them a moment fumbling in the patchy dark to find the wall-mounted light switches. They were far enough into the building that a few lights wouldn't draw any undue outside attention, and they set about entertaining themselves until it was time to go back into hiding and sleep. Rafaela was naturally drawn to the media room and the extensive collection of magazines.

Layne had already perused an *Entertainment Weekly* and *Popular Mechanics* when boredom set in. He looked across the reading table to Rafaela, who was still deep into the *Vogue* she'd started reading over an hour ago. She sensed him looking at her, and turned her attention to his longing gaze.

"What?"

"Nothing," said. "You're just beautiful is all."

Rafaela smirked and rolled her eyes. "Layne, I'm not having sex with you in the library."

"That's not it, I swear." He reached across the table and took her hand. "I just want you to know that I intend to get us out of this. All of it. I'm gonna get some work, get us a real place where we don't have to worry about getting kicked out or pushed around. A real home."

She smiled softly at him, squeezed his hand. But something in her eyes told him that she didn't believe him, that she had heard this all before and that these were just more empty promises. But this time he meant it, he really did. He would do anything for her, whatever it took. Still, that vaguely patronizing look made him feel worthless. More worthless than he already felt. "I know you will, baby," she said, and went back to her fashion spread.

"Seriously Rafaela, I'm—"

A crashing sound shattered the moment, causing them both to jolt out of their seats. It came from the cavernous main hall outside the media room, where the new books where shelved and where the front desk sat like the bridge of some anachronistic starship. The first thing Layne assumed was that there was someone still in the library, an after-hours security guard or lingering cleaning crew member. But Gabe assured them that the city would not pay for graveyard shift security, and if the cleaning people were still around, they would have heard them by now. No, whatever made that noise was someone—or something—else. Something that shouldn't be here.

Rafaela looked to Layne, frightened. He put finger to his lips, indicating that they should remain silent. Stepping softly, he crept over to the media center entryway to sneak a look into the main hall.

The vast hall was dark, lit only by the moonlight filtering in from high windows above the bookshelves. At first Layne noticed nothing out of the ordinary, just the long tables reserved for readers, their stiff wooden chairs tucked neatly under the tabletops. But then he heard a rustling, a soft, sloughing sound, like heavy curtains dragged on linoleum. Reflexively he reached into his jacket pocket, grasping the sole possession that had any real worth—an antique lighter given to him by his long dead father, a family heirloom passed down over three generations. Layne had debated selling it many times—it was valued at several hundred dollars—but he just couldn't bring himself to do it. Selling the lighter would be the final defeat, and he just wasn't ready to throw in that towel just yet. But some part of him knew that the day was fast coming when he'd have no choice.

He flicked the lighter's pinwheel wick with his thumb, igniting the flame, casting a flickering nimbus around his upheld hand. The acrid sting of cheap lighter fluid tickled his nostrils, a strangely comforting smell. Keeping the lighter filled was one of the few indulgences he afforded himself; a working lighter was a useful form of social currency in the homeless world as someone was always needing a light. And you never knew when you might be stuck in some dark, treacherous place.

The sloughing sound resumed, startling him, causing him to nearly drop the lighter. The flickering light of the flame caught something at the edge of its range, a large, human-sized form lying on the floor draped in what looked like an old gray shroud. Layne's first thought was that it was someone wrapped in a dirty old blanket, some other stowaway encroaching on their territory. He fought back a rush of indignation, traded it for a healthy dose of fear. The thing on the floor twitched, a shudder that ran from its center all the way to the edges like a ripple on still water. Layne's throat felt suddenly dry.

"Gabe, is that you?" The thing did not answer, stayed flat on the floor, its back twitching spasmodically. The rustle of its form on the hard floor made a fluttering sound. Like wings.

"Look man, I'm sorry about pushing you out, but I didn't like the way you were looking at—"

The thing rose at the sound of his voice and Layne recognized right away that it was not Gabe. It was not a man at all, in fact. A misshapen head emerged from the curtain of its shroud and Layne saw the light of his lighter reflected back a thousand times in large, segmented eyes. A clutch of fingerlike mandibles drummed where a mouth should have been, a wet, clicking sound emanating from inside its ghastly insectoid skull. The body itself was no bigger than a child, but its legs were as long and thin as a deer's, inverted at the knee and ending in a clawed footpad. The wings, however, were the worst part—long feathery scales of dusty grey, fanning out in a span of at least fifteen feet, like those of a giant butterfly coated in fuzzy soot. It might have been beautiful were it not an affront to all that was decent and sane.

Gabe's moth people were real.

Boone had spent the better part of the day going from one homeless encampment to another, searching for the fucker that slashed him, hoping to take out his frustrations on that hot little girlfriend of his. The fact that the cut was little more than a scratch didn't matter—no lousy gutter rat was gonna cut Boone Daily and live to tell the tale. If he had to comb every train yard and underpass, so be it.

Cutty had been complaining about being tired, so Boone scored some crank off a local dealer and now they both were wired and good to go. Unfortunately, that also meant that Cutty wouldn't shut up. The guy had been going on for an hour about nothing of any importance and Boone was starting to think that getting high maybe wasn't such a great idea. But then he saw a group of homeless people gathered around a tent by the Marengo exit on the 134.

"Come on," he said to the blathering Cutty. "Let's see if these losers know anything."

The two thugs got out of the car and moved towards the hardscrabble group, the car's headlights shining directly into their fearful, shaggy faces. The group consisted of three men on the older side of middle age, one of them black, the other two white. All three were wrapped in blankets and gathered around a shopping cart for some reason Boone didn't care to know. They didn't seem to be veterans or mentally ill, just a sad group who probably ended up this way due to their own poor life choices. Boone was not a man with a lot of empathy for those less fortunate than himself, but men like this—men who seemed to have no real excuse for their circumstance—were even further beneath his contempt.

"We're looking for somebody," Boone said. "White guy, mid-thirties, sandy blond hair, good-looking. Spends time with a smoking hot Latina babe. I'll give twenty bucks to anyone who can take us to where they're hiding out."

The men exchanged glances. One of them, balding with a scraggly salt and pepper beard, stepped forward. Something about him made Boone's skin crawl. He had done time with child molesters in Tehachapi, and this guy had sex offender written all over him.

"I know where they are," Gabe said.

"What in God's name is that?!"

Layne jumped in his skin, unaware that Rafaela had come out of the media room and was standing now at his side, looking on at the felt-winged horror that watched them from across the hall. Whatever it was, there was no time to explain it to her. A twitching spasm ran down the length of its considerable wingspan, a signal that Layne rightfully read as a prelude to an attack. He grabbed Rafaela by the elbow, and they ran for the nearest point of escape, which was the first floor circulation stacks. No sooner had they bolted when the thick flutter of wings followed, swooping down on them from above.

Luckily the circulation stacks were in a lower-ceilinged area, and the moth-creature found it difficult to maneuver with the flapping of its cumbersome wings, slowing it down as it awkwardly thrashed in their wake. Not that Layne or Rafaela turned around to check its progress. They kept their heads forward as they raced through the maze of stacks, heading for the back hall that led out into the parking lot. Layne figured it was better to face the streets than whatever that creature had in store for them. Nothing Boone might do could possibly be worse than what awaited them inside of those wings.

He felt a tug at his arm as Rafaela's leg glanced the edge of a stray book cart, sending her sprawling onto the carpeted floor with a yelp. Layne stopped to help her up, turning just in time to see the moth creature swoop down on her, wings folding in on themselves, shrinking its mass to accommodate the narrowness of the stack. The thing landed on Rafaela's back, a pair of mantis-like pincers emerging from the downy folds of its body, grasping on to her frayed hoodie. She screamed as the creature dove its head into her back, the horrible mandible-mouth gnawing away the already worn fabric of the hoodie.

Reacting on pure instinct and adrenaline, Layne grabbed a hardcover off of one of the shelves—one of James Patterson's endless series of novels—and hurled it at the monster, striking it right between the cotton-tipped antennae that adorned its crown. The creature shuddered, a toneless squeak sounding from inside its hideous skull. Layne grabbed another Patterson book and beaned the monster again on the head, agitating it into a flapping frenzy. It tore free of Rafaela's back and came after him.

"Run!" Rafaela screamed. Layne hated leaving her there, but she didn't stand a chance if he didn't get the creature away from her, and neither of them stood a chance if he stayed. So, Layne turned heel and ran, ran as fast as he could past the last of the stacks, banking hard right into the small foyer hall that led to the back doors of the library. Behind him the air moved in a hot rush, pushed by the flapping of large dusty wings. In moments they would be upon him, folding him into their terrible embrace.

He hit the doors hard, knowing right away that they were locked from the outside and that there was no way he was making it outside before the creature was upon him. Glancing over to his right he saw another set of doors with a punch-code lock on it, and he prayed that the codes for all the doors were the same. As luck would have it, they were. Several hammering heartbeats later he was slamming the doors to the loading bay behind him as wings struck the other side of the door like a wet sack.

Rafaela also ran, but in the opposite direction, back out into the main hall, searching the darkness for a point of escape. The closest one was a door tucked into a nook right outside the children's area, a small, thick paneled affair with the same punch-code lock she had seen Gabe use. What were the numbers again—six, two, four—of those digits she was almost certain... but was that the right sequence? Further from the door, directly in front of her by at least thirty yards was the front entryway, but if she made for those doors and found them locked she'd be trapped in a narrow foyer. Easy pickings for a hungry moth monster. Still, if they weren't locked, she'd be free to get help...

A massive shape dropped from the ceiling, making the decision for her. Another one of those creatures, this one even bigger than the other. How many of these horrible things lived in this building?! How had no one alerted the authorities or the media that the Pasadena Public library was infested with these nightmarish abominations? Was this all really happening or were she and Layne finally losing their minds from the stress of street life? God knows they wouldn't be the first.

There was no time to make sense of this now. The second creature had clearly seen her, and was rearing up from the floor as its wings spread-wide, threatening to envelop her in their musty regions. She ran for the small door by the children's area, hearing the thick flutter as the creature took to the air, closing the distance between them. She reached the door and frantically began punching numbers into the lock—six, two, four—but the knob would not turn. Her mind screamed at her as the chittering of mandibles tickled at her ear, a horrible scent of decay preceding the monster as it drew closer. Operating with blind panic she punched the numbers again, remembering as she did them that there was another number—an additional two in the code—six, two, two, four. The knob clicked, she turned it and the door opened. Rafaela tumbled into a narrow stairwell with a gasp of relief as the creature struck the door frame. She kicked the door closed behind her and the creature shrieked as a tip of its wing was sheared off by the slamming door's edge. Then she lay there at the bottom of the stairs, catching her breath as nausea and adrenaline coursed through her in sickening waves.

It took a few moments for Layne's eyes to adjust to the dim light that filtered in from the parking lot streetlamps outside the loading bay windows, casting the room in a sickly yellowed pall. It consisted of a table set next to stacked plastic crated, inside of which books from other library branches waited to be sorted into bins that sat on a long counter running the opposite length of the room. To Layne's left was a small freight elevator the size of a dumb waiter, next to it a control box with two large buttons set in a wall-mounted box, one button for up, one for down. Across the room was another door leading to what Layne assumed was the vast reading area that made up the library's east wing. There was no lock on the door, indicating that the area beyond was not restricted to employees, which supported his assumption. Aside from these observations, the loading bay was otherwise clear.

Layne entertained the idea of holing up here for the night, waiting for the safety of the morning and the arrival of the staff, but he dismissed it right away. Rafaela was still out there, and there was no way he could just sit here while she was still in danger. At present she was his only real reason for living, and the thought of abandoning her to that winged horror was too much for his soul to bear. No—he would find her, and they would ride this thing out together.

He went to the door, opening it a crack and peeking out into the east wing. Beyond lay a vast open space with high ceilings and long rows of reading tables, chairs tucked neatly under their tabletops. Far against the eastern wall were the science fiction and fantasy stacks, and the entire area was lined with shelves and shelves of mystery novels. But the library's impressive collection was the furthest thing from Layne's mind at the moment, for high above the stacks, swooping and fluttering like giant bats were more moth creatures, and least three by Layne's count. This whole cursed place was full of them, and to step out into this wing would mean a swift and certain death.

He closed the door quietly as to not draw the attention of the fluttering horrors. The creature that chased him in here could still be heard flapping outside the door to the back foyer, so that left only one other option if he hoped to escape this room and find Rafaela.

The freight elevator.

After catching her breath, Rafaela took the stairs to the second floor, finding herself in a cluster of small administration offices. Aside from some messy piles of city government memos and random books she found nothing on the tightly cloistered desks that would serve any use in her current predicament, so she moved on from the offices through a narrow hallway that led to the kitchen and break room area. Despite the waning adrenaline in her stomach she felt a desperate need to consume food, and was lucky enough to find three-day-old pizza waiting in greasy cardboard on the refrigerator's top shelf. As she hungrily munched her way to the stale crust a voice called to her from the darkness of the break room.

"Well hello, gorgeous," Boone said, stepping through the open archway that separated the break room from the kitchen. Behind Boone stood Gabe, looking every bit the guilty snitch. Beyond Gabe was a pried-open second story window, no doubt how they had managed to gain access.

Rafaela turned to run back into the hallway but found it blocked by Cutty. He must have snuck around through the hall while she raided the refrigerator. In his hand he casually fingered a switchblade.

She was trapped. A forceful hand grabbed her by the elbow, whipping her around, nearly pulling the arm out of its socket. The hot stink of Boone's breath tortured her nostrils. "You and I have some unfinished business," he hissed through yellowed teeth. "Now where's that boyfriend of yours?"

Layne stepped out of the claustrophobic freight elevator to find himself in a darkened musty hallway deep in the bowels of the library. His gut told him to head west, towards the corner of the building reserved for administration—he was certain Rafaela would have run for the safety of the closed off offices if she had managed to get out of the stacks. Now all he had to do was get there. Rather than fumble around in the dark looking for a light switch he flicked on his lighter, illuminating the narrow, cluttered path he now occupied. The hall was lined with old furniture, office equipment, book piles; just getting past all the years of gathered detritus would be a feat in and of itself. And god forbid some fresh horror should come shrieking out of one of the shadowy corners...

Best just to be ready and stay focused on the path ahead. The heat from the lighter's flame began to burn his thumb, forcing him to flick the lid of the lighter closed and allow for the metal to cool. But as soon as the darkness closed in on him, bringing with it imagined terrors, he decided to move forward, trusting his intuition and directional sense to lead him. By the time the lighter had cooled, and he was able to flick it back on, Layne realized he had made a terrible mistake.

He had wandered off course, landing in a room that housed a boiler too huge and archaic to still be in use. This entire section of the library basement seemed to have been long since ignored—furniture and light fixtures at least fifty years old sat piled against the rough stone walls, dusty spider webs draping them like something out of a 1940's horror movie set. But these spook house accoutrements were the least unsettling elements of the room. That distinction belonged to the large sagging cocoon that hung between the furnace and the wall, held in place by thick strands of webbing that fanned out in every direction, keeping the human-sized pod in a nauseating stasis.

The pod was alive and wriggling.

At first Layne thought it might be a trick of the light, shadows dancing in the flickering of his flame. But that thought was soon dispelled by thick, finger-length larvae squirming free of the cocoon, dozens of pink, wriggling worms landing in the dirty cement floor in wet plops. Layne felt a hot ball rise in his throat as he suppressed a gag, backing slowly out of the nest, his face a mask of horror and revulsion. The larvae poured from the webbing in a squirming river, piling into a writhing mass that blindly sought something, anything, on which to feed. There could be little doubt that given the opportunity the worms would burrow beneath his skin and devour him from inside, consume him faster than the rot that had settled into his soul, deprived him of all his dignity, hope...

Rafaela. She was his hope. He had to get to her.

He turned to run and slammed right into something large, winged and horrible. The mother of larvae had returned to tend to her young, gazing down on

Layne with a thousand lidless eyes. The creature emitted a chittering noise that could be interpreted as surprise, anger or both, a piercing sound that jolted a streak of cold down the back of Layne's spine. Reacting on pure instinct, he thrust the still lit lighter at the creature, not feeling the pain of its overheated metal on his fingers. But rather than reel back startled, the creature froze, mesmerized by the dancing flame. Hypnotized by its flicker.

"Like that, do you?" Layne hissed. "Have a closer look."

He held the flame to the creature's head, under the dusty filaments that coated its skull, igniting them like dry tinder. The creature emitted a soul-wrenching shriek and tumbled back as the fire spread over its sooty, flammable form, consuming its wings like tissue paper. Layne stood there a moment watching the monster flail and burn, its ashy particulate coating him like soot from a chimney. When it finally fell into a crumpled heap on the floor, Layne vaulted over the monster and ran off into the hall, following the shadows cast by the pyre-light of its smoldering form.

Having reached the stairs in a rare bit of luck, Layne stumbled on to the main floor, finding himself in a non-descript hallway in the library's west wing. To his right another set of stairs led up to the employee common areas, where Rafaela would have naturally gravitated, provided she made it this far. But Layne hadn't taken more than three steps towards the stairs when he froze, hearing the distinct cadence of voices shouting in the opposite direction, beyond a thick oak door he was certain led to the main hall. One of the voices belonged to Rafaela, clearly distressed.

After a moment of listening he recognized one of the other voices—cruel, terse, and full of spite.

Boone was inside the library, and he had Rafaela. The thug had dragged her out there in full view of the moth creatures, just begging to be attacked and devoured. It was a fate Layne would enjoy watching Boone suffer, but he could not allow the woman he loved to suffer it with him. So he stepped through the oak door and out into the reverberant vastness of the main hall.

As predicted, Boone had Rafaela hostage out in the main hall, with Cutty and Gabe also along for the ride. Boone was holding a knife to Rafaela's throat as Cutty ransacked the drawers behind the main circulation desk. Gabe was just standing there, looking like the rat bastard he was.

"It's a library, Boone," Layne said, announcing his presence. "Not a liquor store. There can't be more than twenty bucks laying around this place, all total."

Boone turned in Layne's direction, tightening his grip on Rafaela, her eyes wide and frightened. "Those late fees add up," he said with a sneer. "Nice to see you, Layne."

The feeling was not mutual. "Let her go, Boone," Layne said. "It's me you want."

Boone made a sarcastic show of considering the offer. "All right. You come back here, and I'll let your girlfriend go."

Layne didn't believe for a second that Boone would honor his word, but if he got close enough, he stood a better chance of pulling off a surprise attack and give Rafaela the opportunity to run. That was if the moth creatures didn't come out of hiding to feast. He made his way to the front desk, stepping behind it through the waist-high swinging door that acted as a flimsy barrier. Boone smiled cruelly behind the nape of Rafaela's neck. "Here I am," Layne said, raising his arms in a Christ pose. "Now let her go."

Boone pressed the flat of the blade tightly against Rafaela's throat, making her gasp, then pushed her forcefully into Cutty's waiting arms like some twisted game of human keep-away. Cutty didn't look too thrilled to be playing this game, but knowing what was good for him held up his end, holding Rafaela roughly by the arms.

"No deal, Boone," Layne said in his best tough-guy impression. "I said let her—"

Boone lashed out, raking the tip of his switchblade across the front of Layne's windbreaker, tearing a long streak but failing to catch flesh. Reacting blindly, Layne grabbed a thick hardcover off of the return cart and whipped it at Boone's face, glancing it hard off the thug's considerably wide forehead. Boone stumbled back, stunned that Layne would even attempt such a move, and Cutty let go of Rafaela out of reflex to help his boss. For a moment Rafaela hesitated, looking to Layne. His eyes told her all she needed to know – run! She pushed past Gabe and tore across the lobby to the children's wing.

Boone righted himself, putting a hand to the rapidly swelling lump growing on his forehead. He threw a severe glance at Gabe. "Go get her!" he ordered. Only too happy to oblige, Gabe slunk out through the hinged door, following after Rafaela.

Boone squared off against Layne as Cutty hung back, ready to step in if things didn't go his boss' way. The knife in Boone's hand was poised to find its deadly mark. "Where's that box cutter of yours now?" he taunted. "Let's see how it does against my blade."

Layne reached into his pocket, but his fingers did not find the box cutter. Instead they scrabbled against the cool brass of his father's lighter, and in his mind, he saw the moth creature in the basement nest staring at the dancing lick of fire, transfixed. Drawn to it.

Like a moth to flame.

Drawing the lighter from his pocket, Layne flipped the lid and flicked on the wick, lighting it. He held the flickering flame high over his head. It cast strange shadows in the vastness of the hall.

Boone chuckled. "What, you gonna burn me with that thing?" He threw Cutty a glance, who shared in his amusement. "Please."

"It's not for you," Layne said, a flash of strange confidence filling him. Right on cue a fluttering sound began to grow in the hall, the shadows cast by the flame danced in an unnatural manner. "It's for them."

A pair of moth creatures swooped in from out of the darkness, great grey wings flapping, seeking out the flickering light source that drew their curiosity. Boone's eyes widened at the approach of the flying monsters, and Layne waited until he could feel the dusty wind of wings at his back before snapping the lighter closed and ducking. There was a violent expulsion of air as one of the creatures slammed hard into Boone, knocking the wind from his lungs. Cutty—forever a man of few words—had only time to scream as the other creature descended on him, enveloping him in its wings before zipping back up into the dark recesses of the high ceiling.

As the monsters ravaged his tormentors, Layne kept low and crawled out of the desk area, through the swinging door and out into the hall proper. As he ran for the children's wing, he could hear the strangled cries of Boone and Cutty as they wrestled against the creatures' superior strength in a last wave of instinctual preservation. Then there was only the chittering sound of feasting mandibles.

Layne entered the wing to find Gabe pursuing Rafaela through the chest high children's stacks. A blind rage overtook him, blotting out the immediate danger of the moth creatures, and he raced up behind Gabe, tackling him to the carpeted floor and giving Rafaela the opportunity to land a swift kick to the old pervert's head. Layne flipped Gabe over to face him, hearing the telltale swish of liquid inside the front pocket of his tattered jacket. Layne reached into the pocket and pulled out a pint of cheap vodka.

"Is this all it took to sell us out?" he hissed. "One lousy bottle of booze?!"

"You sold *me* out!" Gabe spat back. "This was my thing and you stabbed me in the back!"

Rage boiled in Layne's gut, filling him with hot, burning hatred. How dare this creep try to turn the guilt back on him? Layne pulled off the cap of the vodka bottle with his teeth and emptied the contents on to Gabe's chest. Then he took out his lighter.

Rafaela looked on with horror. "Layne, no, he's not worth it!"

But Layne wasn't listening. The rage had overcome him. "One piece of advice," he said to Gabe as he flicked on the flame. "Stop, drop, and roll."

Layne pressed the flame to Gabe's vodka-soaked jacket, lighting the old man up like a torch. The fire spread quickly, and Layne stood to avoid being burned by it as Gabe screamed and rolled on the ground, desperately trying to extinguish the flame. That simply wouldn't do. Layne emptied the rest of the bottle onto Gabe, rejuvenating the scorching fire. That would teach the pervert to screw people over.

The smashing of glass broke Layne out of his dark revelry. He looked over to see that Rafaela had taken a kid's desk chair and thrown it through one of the windows, allowing for their escape. She glanced back at him, her eyes devoid of love or compassion. In fact, the look she gave him now could best be described as abject horror.

By brutalizing Gabe, had he lost her? Had he become a monster in her eyes, no better than those creatures out in the main hall devouring their enemies?

Then he realized the horror in his eyes wasn't directed *at* him, it was directed *above* him. Layne followed her gaze, craning his neck upwards, to the ceiling thirty feet over their heads.

It was covered in moth creatures. Smaller, child-sized ones. Younglings fresh from their larval state.

Hungry.

The moth children descended on Layne in a flurry, enveloping him in a chittering swarm, a tornado of flapping. As nascent mandibles tore the flesh from his body he looked to Rafaela, helpless to join her as she escaped through the broken window. Despite the overwhelming agony, a final melancholy pang offered him the mildest of relief. It hadn't all been for nothing. He had saved her, given her a chance to live, to go on to a better life. A life without him.

Layne called out her name, but his voice was drowned out by the fluttering of wings.

THE UNMAKING OF JENNIFER HAWKINS
BY PIPPA BAILEY

Mr Henderson clicked a button on his controller, and a new projector slide clunked into place; the stench of hot plastic wafted from a tiny fan in the machine's side. The image of Da Vinci's Vitruvian Man blurred its way onto the wall, obscured by a mottled poster of the periodic table, its edges browned and curling where the paper had disintegrated over 10 years since the classroom's refurbishment in 1976.

Jennifer Hawkins yawned and chewed the end of her pencil, fragments of black and yellow paint stuck to her teeth like she was chewing a wasp. She scrawled figures in her notebook, algebraic equations, now accompanied by a naked stick man with a tiny stick penis.

Despite physics not being one of her stronger subjects, she'd been enjoying this semester: theories about entire worlds they couldn't see, forces they couldn't yet explain, and something involving a microwave that produced some rather inedible popcorn and stank out both her classroom and several of the adjacent classrooms.

Physics was like magic, magic with numbers, shapes, and worlds beyond worlds.

Other kids passed notes beneath their desks, braided their hair, or in the case of Brandon Freeman and his friends, attempted to shoot spit-wads onto the ceiling above his desk. Jen wasn't sure if they'd ever paid much attention to the class, or even had a basic understanding of physics. The old 'what goes up, must come down.'

A wad of congealed paper flopped from its home on the polystyrene ceiling tile and mashed itself into Frankie Cox's hair, imploding his quaffed hairspray dome. He yelped, brushing the white chunks from his 'do' towards Brandon.

Jen snickered. Frankie scowled, unimpressed.

"Okay, let's call it a day, kids. Back tomorrow bright and early. You know what day it is?" called Mr Henderson in a sing-song voice.

Silence. It was as if the class assumed that by not answering, they'd not have to accept their fate.

"Come on, what day is it tomorrow?" he repeated.

The kids rolled their eyes.

"Look, I've got all afternoon, and I'm sure you'd rather be home studying."

They rolled their eyes a little harder.

"Once more, with feeling: what day is it tomorrow, kids?"

"Quiz day," moaned the class. They packed their books and pencil cases away into a myriad of backpacks: Care Bears, Teenage Mutant Ninja Turtles, and a rather large collection of Ghostbusters.

Jen was glad of the distraction, before Brandon and Frankie had turned their spit-wads on her. She ran her fingers through her cropped brown hair, which had been waist-length curls only two weeks before.

Last semester, Brandon had made it his mission to stick gum, plasters, bogies, and anything else sticky or disgusting he could find into her hair. Brian, her stepfather, had given up cutting away crusty lumps and chunks of strawberry-scented goo and had added a new rule to his list of 'Brian rules'. *Rule number 3 – Brian doesn't do hair.*

This rule followed closely behind: *1 – Brian will punch any boy he has to*, and *2 – Green food is good food*, although he did forcefully assert that gummy bears didn't count under this rule. Jen accepted the new rule and set about reducing the overall target size of her head by hacking her hair to a short, but as Brian had said, "very radical" pixie-crop. He was right; she hadn't done a bad job of it, although if her mom Angela had still been around, it wouldn't have ended up as crooked.

She'd been gone nearly two years: two years of learning how to grieve, which at fourteen years old was an alien concept. Learning that life wasn't like a VHS tape; it had no rewind.

A positive side effect had been bonding with her stepfather. Brian had been with them for four years before Angela had been beaten by the Big C. Towards the end, he was the only thing stopping Jen breaking down at the sight of her husk mother Angela, no longer the effervescent beauty she once was. Wisps of hair clung to her pallid skull, crooked veins bulged through paper skin, and her sunken eyes were so incredibly black they looked like fetid oil pools.

In life, her other life, her before life, Angela's mantra had been *'Shoulder pads and pearls make women from girls'*. A faded hand-written note in brilliant blue cursive, tucked into the frame of her dressing table mirror, bore that mantra. Brian had moved it into Jen's room as a surprise for her fourteenth birthday. She wasn't sure who'd cried more when she unwrapped it, freshly painted, with the faded note still attached and the addition of a photo of the three of them, huddled around the kitchen table at Thanksgiving, nestled beside it.

Jen dumped her bag on the floor beside her bed and collapsed into her chair. She pressed her palms against her face and slid them downwards, tugging at her cheeks, stretching the bags beneath her eyes. Her late nights of reading were starting to show.

Brian had taken to slipping books on engineering, maths, and science into her bedroom on a weekly basis since she was little, starting when she'd sat down for dinner just before her eleventh birthday and begun picking his brains on how lightsabres worked. She'd been disappointed when he'd explained that the Force wasn't real, but she couldn't let the idea go.

They built a makeshift flamethrower instead, which, when Angela spotted Jen waving it about in the yard and making whooshing noises, had gone straight in the trash. Brian had gone straight on the couch for three days and Jen straight to her room, despite her protests.

"Dinner!" Brian shouted upstairs.

Jen made her way to the kitchen and plopped down at the table, its hinged flaps creaking under her elbows. "Is it tasty?"

Brian smiled and slid a plate of meatloaf and broccoli towards her. "Ah, I don't know, but it's definitely food."

She wrinkled her nose, "Do I have to e—"

"Don't say it, just eat it. It's the only green thing you've eaten all day."

"Not true!"

"Really?"

"Really, really, I had an apple earlier."

He shrugged. "Fine, but you've still got to eat 'em."

They ate mostly in silence, other than the occasional glug of water between mouths full of veg, and whimpers as Jen attempted to stuff all her broccoli in at once and get rid of the chewed green mush with one swallow—a tried and tested method of many fourteen-year-olds.

Her empty plate clattered in the sink. She returned for Brian's and finished the washing up; she forced a dishcloth into a gap between the countertop and the sink, which was in much need of re-grouting. When she'd finished, she tossed the cloth overhead into the laundry basket.

"Whoop, two points," Brian cheered.

She rolled her eyes. "Thanks."

"So what's on the agenda this evening? Movies, music, or world domination? Oh, I've rented that *Ghostbusters* movie you wanted to see."

Jen shook her head. "Homework. I've got a test tomorrow."

Brian gave her a thumbs down. "Bummer."

She stifled a giggle. "At least I know some of the stuff. I reckon I'm the only one who does." She filled a glass of water and grabbed an apple from the fridge and headed up the stairs. "See, more green stuff."

She munched on the apple and dumped the core in the trash. Pulling Mr Henderson's recommended reads from her bag, she piled the books on her table and stared at *Geometric progressions: patterns from here to infinity*. With her sticky fingers, she flipped it open and read, stopping on a page about origami and folding paper, and tossed the paper at her trashcan.

Did you know the world record for paper folding in half is seven times?

She shrugged; seven times didn't seem all that hard. Beside an image of a woman folding a giant sheet of paper was an equation that made her eyes cross when she stared at it for too long. It showed how the folds could be completed, but it didn't make any sense, although Jen put that down to only recently having touched on algebra in maths and physics.

She tore an A4 page from a notebook and began to fold, twisting the page, attempting to fit more folds.

Six folds, six folds, five folds.

Jen was less than impressed as to how she could have lost a fold, and tossed the paper at her trashcan and started with a fresh sheet.

Seven folds, finally I'm getting somewhere.

Admiring her wad of paper that slowly unfolded, she twisted it again.

Eight... no way, seriously. Eight, that must be eight folds, it certainly looks like eight.

She placed the paper on the desk and reached for her book.

CRACK—

Something red and shiny whacked into her desk, chipping the paint, and bounced onto the carpet. A stone, it hissed and melted the beige shag-pile fibres. Jen stumbled away from her chair and stared at the ceiling: no hole, no burn, nothing. The stone hissed again; she kicked it from the hole it had melted and grabbed her glass of water, and tossed it in the stone's direction. The floor stopped smouldering and the plastic fibres began to harden. Jen reached for the stone, her gaze occasionally darting to the ceiling, trying to work out where it had come from. She picked it up—hot, but not too hot to touch—and placed it on the table, staring at it. Light penetrated the stone like it was a lump of fire-glass, a streak of red light reflecting on the white-painted wood.

"Brian?!" she yelled downstairs.

"What?"

"Something weird happened."

"*Ghostbusters* weird or teenage boy weird?" He snickered.

"*Ghostbusters* weird, I'm guessing. Wait, are you watching that movie without me?"

Brian sighed. "Guilty."

She plodded down the stairs, rolling the stone around her hand, and tried to avoid seeing the TV. "Can you..." She trailed off.

Brian paused the movie and propped himself up from where he'd been lying on the couch.

"Thanks."

"Tell me your weird news. I'm all ears."

She held the red stone out to him. "This just fell onto my desk.

"Like, fell out of your bag, or...?"

"It fell from the sky, *pop*, and it bounced off my desk and melted the carpet a little."

He peered closely at the small rock in her hand, snatched it and army-rolled onto the floor, small clumps of yellow foam popping out of a hole in the grey sofa cushion. "Meteorite!"

"What?"

Brian jumped to his feet, bashing his thighs on the couch arm as he struggled past Jen and up the stairs. "It's a goddamn meteorite. I bet it burned right through the roof."

Jen followed him up the stairs and headed into her bedroom. Brian, on his knees, peered at the burned patch of carpet and back to the ceiling. "There's nothing here."

"I know."

"I mean, how is there nothing here? A burning rock, melted carpet, but the ceiling's fine."

Jen shrugged. "I dunno. I thought you, being all smart and stuff, might have an answer."

"I don't think I have... I mean, I can't explain this. Maybe it came through at a different angle, and I just can't see the scorch."

Jen shrugged again.

Brian yawned and climbed to his feet. "This is too much excitement for this time of night. Right now, couldn't tell you where your magic rock came from. I'll look again tomorrow when my eyes are working."

He left the room, shaking his head and muttering at the shiny stone in his hand.

Jen, who still wasn't sure if this was something she'd done, plopped back into her chair and stared at a black mark the stone had left on her table. *This is seriously weird.*

Maybe she was going crazy. This, this was not a problem for right now; studying, studying was right now's problem.

She looked up at the beaming picture of herself, her mother, and Brian.

Mom would have hated all this weird stuff, but she'd have wanted me to at least come up with some sort of a conclusion.

She smiled and looked up to her mother's note, but instead found a blank space. Panic stole her breath; she looked at the frame again. Maybe she'd just missed it? Nope, not on the desk either.

Maybe, maybe, it fell on the floor when the stone appeared.

Jen dropped her knees and ran her hands under the desk, looking for the note. *It couldn't have gone too far.*

Tears streamed down her face as she patted into the dark recesses under her bed.

It must be here.

Something crumpled beneath her hand. Paper, a wad of paper.

Yes, it's—

She pulled it back from under the bed and examined it: her crinkled origami sheet.

Nope, it's not.

She climbed to her feet and unfolded the paper and placed it flat on her desk.

The sheet, which had once been A4, was now a square. Jen wiped tears on the back of her arm and flipped the paper over.

How was this even possible? She considered running to tell Brian, but the drone of his snores from downstairs told her it would be a waste of time to try. Sleepy Brian was much like stupid Brian; stupid Brian only appeared after he'd had too much candy, and he got all hyper and giggly and *unhelpful.*

She flopped into her chair, the loss of her mother's note pushed to the back of her mind, and rubbed her temples.

I think I'm going to need a better book.

* * *

Power doesn't know if it is to be used for good or bad; it only exists to serve.

Jen headed to the library before school and grappled with a few titles before dropping them onto the librarian's desk. "Do I need to check these out if I want to read them?"

"Ah, a first-timer," said the librarian.

Jen shrugged. "Yeah, I guess so, but I do like to read."

"Well, the answer is no. No, you don't have to check them out to read them, so long as you don't leave the library."

"Oh, okay, good."

She scooped up the stack and turned towards a collection of empty desks in the centre of the library; morning sunlight burned through great arched windows lining the library roof and illuminated the old scarred wood covered in decades of graffiti scrawls. Light shot in beams along a spiderweb of towering parallel bookshelves; each disappeared into the darkened wastes of the non-fiction section. Large printed signs bearing Dewey Decimal numbers marked the entrance to the book labyrinth.

"Do you need some help?" the librarian asked.

Jen jumped and dropped one of her books. She stared at the librarian and back to the open book lying on the floor, its pages folded at odd angles.

"What do you know about origami?"

Jen spread the books around her on the floor and propped her back against a dusty row of books in the American archaeology and mythology section of the library. It wasn't exactly the cleanest section; shoe scuffs and dust bunnies decorated the floor. She concluded that this was one, most probably a make-out spot, and she hoped that no one would turn up whilst she was reading; and two, no one had tried to run a mop down here in years, let alone return a book, and she was unlikely to be disturbed by fellow readers, and that was the way she liked it.

She paged through a book. *Origami for the Creative*; it consisted of fantastical arrangements of animals, paper cranes flying over folded gorillas and fortune tellers and hats, nothing particularly inspiring.

Next, please.

She dropped the book to her side and grabbed the next one; the librarian had added at least another three books to her pile, books about mathematical theory and angles, something called *The Art of the Fold*, which was as pretentious as it sounded. That one was quickly stuffed to the bottom of the pile in favour of *Paper Folding, Art or Science? Nope, still not interesting enough.*

She cracked open a peculiar little purple book: *Enter the Fold*. No author name, nor a publisher; there was only a title. It was one of those books that felt like it had been felted, but through use it had worn away to a dull patchy finish. It smelt like all good books should smell, vanilla and age. Jen breathed deeply and adjusted her back against the bookshelf panels. Something beige and crumpled fluttered into her lap, a fortune-teller crafted from what looked like pages of the same book. She opened it up and slipped it over her fingers.

Upon opening the first flap, it was lined with diagrams, which wasn't exactly what she'd expected.

Turning the flap back, there was now an image on the other side.

Wait, that wasn't there before—

An image of books, piles and piles of books, their pages warped and arranged at unusual angles. She turned the fortune-teller over and began to open it out; the paper grew and spread. It seemed impossible that so much paper had gone into making something so small. With each growing number of flaps she opened, new pages of directions emerged. Scrawled equations for creating un-named things wrote themselves in aged cursive, flowing across the paper like spilled ink.

One page showed a man intersected by a line of folded paper, his disjointed legs flailing. He smiled and waved, an unwavering ink-printed grin, but he didn't look happy.

This didn't make sense. How could this even exist?

She tried to read the notes, but they changed with her every movement. A picture of a girl folding paper into shapes, which spun on the palm of her hand, slid into view. Jen placed the unfolding mass onto the floor and reached into her bag for her scrap paper and imitated the girl, careful not to knock the fortune-teller, which now resembled a concertina map, and change what it showed. She tried to match the designs and failed, her scrap paper tearing or becoming mulch in her sweaty hands. She grunted and threw the mulch to the side and reached into her bag for more paper.

The square sheet from the night before fluttered free and landed on her knee. She stared at it for a while before snatching it up and following the already-ingrained creases. It didn't tear; it moved as if it wanted to fold, like it wanted to create the intricate patterns shown in the book, like it wanted to teach her.

The paper formed a pyramid, each page folded in on itself in a beautiful triangular arrangement. She could see no start and no end; it rotated on her palm as if atop a turntable.

A book popped free from the shelf and hit the dirty floor, sending up a plume of dust.

Crack—

Someone must have pushed it from the other side.

Jen twisted onto her knees and scooped the book from the floor, closing it in the same movement. She peered up the shelf, looking for where the book had come from; about five rows up, there was a gap. She sighed and gripped the edge of the shelf, pulling herself to her feet. Trust her to find the one quiet spot, and today is the day that Brandon and his idiots visit the library.

She peered into the gap, hoping to spot the culprit— *fire!*

She screamed.

Jets of fire coursed into the sky on the row beyond hers, flames licking the books and scouring the covers; plastic melted and pooled on the wood and pages smouldered, ashen fragments curling in the air amid the flames. Carnage, everything was being eaten by the flames; they surged towards the gap, reaching for her. A swirl of flame coursed through like an elongated arm and snatched the fortune-teller from the floor, whipping it about like a flag, the paper ignited. Jen reached for it, but the fire was quicker, drawing the smouldering paper through the gap as if through a vacuum. All that remained was a fine rain of ash that covered the shelf edge.

"AHHHH! Fire!"

Jen ran to the end of the row, trying to find her way back to the central area. Footsteps echoed through the library, growing louder as they reached her. The librarian panted, holding a fire extinguisher.

"What happened?"

Jen pointed to the row beside hers, "Fire, there," she stammered, "the books, they're all destroyed, the library—"

"There's no fire here."

The librarian stood at the end of the row and looked down either side. "There's nothing here."

"What?"

Jen ran along the shelves. There was no fire, no destroyed books; no damage at all, in fact. She peered into the gap left by the book and could see nothing but her pile of books, bag, and jacket on the floor, beside them a flat square sheet of unfolded paper.

"But there was—"

The librarian grabbed the book from her hand and shoved it into the gap. "You can't be in here causing trouble, young lady."

"I wasn't."

"Mhmm, that's not what this looks like. Libraries are for reading, quiet contemplation, and study. If you feel like screaming again, I suggest you go somewhere more appropriate, perhaps the zoo."

Jen seethed and stomped back toward her possessions.

Really, you really think I'd start screaming like a god damn idiot just for attention? So much for Mrs. Nice Librarian.

She collected her things from the floor and stuck them into her bag.

"Mhmm, and where do you think you're going with those?" the librarian sniffed. "If you want them, you'll need to check them out."

Jen was late to the test—not by much, but enough for Mr. Henderson to tut and point at the clock as she slipped into her chair and shoved her bag under the table. She chewed on the end of her pencil and set to work on the multiple-choice test that sat in front of her; Brandon and Frankie had clearly already had enough time to have a go at her test for her. Her name had been crossed out and replaced with the word *loser*, followed by what seemed to be pictures of breasts. *I guess they're feeling creative today.*

She scrubbed out their mess and added her name again, and continued with her answers.

—*Thump.* Brandon kicked her chair.

"Where were you?" he hissed.

She ignored him and circled what she thought was the correct answer for question number four.

—*Thump.*

—*Thump.*

"You were late. You're never late. Where were you?"

—*Thump, thump, thump.*

Jen slid her chair forwards, away from Brandon's foot. "Why do you care?"

He shuffled his desk and chair closer, which squealed on the floor, and booted her chair again. "Dunno, just wanted to know."

"Shhh," hissed Mr. Henderson, far too loudly for intimating people to be silent.

Brandon kicked her chair again, but remained mute.

The test went as well as it could. Jen found herself folding the edges of her exam paper and quickly flattened them out again. The fire had to have come from somewhere; she knew she wasn't going crazy. *What about the book, the paper? It must be something to do with the folding, the folding must have been what caused the fire, magic fire? That can't be true.*

Mr Henderson climbed to his feet and slammed his hand on his desk, making half the class jump out of their seats. "Pencils down, everyone, your time's up."

Jen hadn't noticed. She was already reaching into her bag for the little purple book. There had to be an explanation for the fortune-teller and the fire in there somewhere.

Brandon leant over her shoulder and grabbed the book. "Yoink."

"Hey, give that back."

The rest of the class were filing out into the hallway, the noise covering Jen's shouts of annoyance.

Frankie parked himself on the edge of her desk. "Nah, you're not getting it back until we know what you're up to. You're all different."

"What do you mean, all different?"

"Your hair is shorter than yesterday, you cut it again," Brandon chimed in. He prodded the back of her head. "You worried we were gonna make it look pretty for you again?"

"No, and I haven't changed anything."

"Yeah, you have, and you're being all weir—"

"Boys, what are we up to?" asked Mr Henderson, crossing the room.

"Nothing, sir, just chatting with our friend," said Frankie.

Brandon slid the purple book back across the desk; Jen grabbed it and shoved it into her bag.

Mr Henderson scooped Jen's test from the table, and added it to the pile in his hands. "Well, you three run along and play, then. Chop chop, I've got marking to do."

They headed out of the class and into the corridor; she knew this wasn't going to get any better and made a run for the hallway. The boys hooked her under the arms and dragged her towards an empty classroom along the hall.

"Ah-ha, not so fast." Frankie forced her into a chair. "You're gonna tell us what's in that book."

Jen gripped the edge of the chair, knuckles white. "Nothing, it's just maths stuff."

"Yeah, right, loser. Spill it or we'll tear your book apart."

She felt sick. If the librarian hadn't believed her, what would make these two any better? Maybe if she just told them, they'd call her crazy and leave her alone.

Brandon slapped her across the face. She shrieked, but Frankie shoved a hand over her mouth before she could attract too much attention.

"Shit! What'd you do that for?" asked Frankie.

Brandon sighed. "Felt like it."

"Still, it was a bit harsh."

Brandon shrugged. "I do what I want, get lost if it bothers you."

He slapped her again.

Frankie nodded, taking a last look at Jen's red tear-stained face, and left, shutting the classroom door behind him. She could see him through the glass, his face turned away from the window.

"Right, spill it."

Jen struggled with her bag and pulled out the book. "It's just m-maths and s-stuff about folding p-paper."

"Oh, stop snivelling, there's gotta be more to it."

"I-I tried one of the f-folds, and something happened."

"Something?" Brandon asked.

Jen nodded.

Brandon raised his hand.

She withered in her seat, cowering.

"It made fire. I c-can show you."

Brandon pulled his foot back and kicked her hard in the chest. She tumbled backwards off her chair and smacked against the floor. She cried out, but stopped herself and clutched her ribs. *He'll make it so much worse if anyone hears what he's doing. Just do the thing; show him, and you can go.*

"Go on, then, show me something magical," he barked.

Frankie slipped the door open a crack, "Hey, what did you—"

"You, stay out."

Frankie nodded and shut the door again.

Jen winced, gripping her chest, and snatched the paper from the floor and began to fold. Something was different; it was as if the paper manipulated her fingers, not the other way around. It twisted at impossible angles, forming new shapes she hadn't seen before.

Brandon leant against the teacher's desk and silently watched her.

A cube, but it didn't seem right. Something about the cube seemed to not quite fit. It hurt to look at for too long, and Jen scrunched her eyes.

"So, where's this—"

T-shh-t.

A drawer in the teacher's desk slid open; they both stared at it. There was no fire, no noise; Jen started to her feet.

"You stay put," Brandon snarled. He stared into the drawer, gripping the edges of the wood, and clicked his tongue against the roof of his mouth. "What did you do?"

"I did what you asked me to, it... it just came out different this time."

She started to her feet again.

"I told you..." He kicked at her, knocking her back to the floor, "to stay put."

"Ow!" she yelped.

Jen flattened herself against the floor, tears pooling on the linoleum, and watched Brandon stare into the drawer, mesmerised by whatever was there. He stuck his hand inside.

There was a loud *pop* and air rushed around the room, as if being sucked out through a huge vacuum, and Brandon was yanked half into the drawer. Too fast to scream; it folded his body in half at the chest, bones crunching as the drawer sucked harder. His limbs bent beyond reason. One arm, still free from the drawer, flopped against the desk, like a wrestler tapping out. Taut skin tore free from muscle and jagged rib spikes. His feet listed above his shoulders, flapped like deflated balloons, and then vanished. His head went last; it lolled over the edge, quivering like a nodding dog, eyes swivelling in the sockets before they were inhaled with a slurp, like someone finishing the dregs of a milkshake. And then Brandon, or what was left of Brandon, was gone.

Blood seeped down the wood, only to be drawn back up a droplet at a time until all that remained was an open drawer.

The wind died; the only evidence it was ever there were several grey fluttering blinds tapping gently against the window.

Brandon was gone.

Jen vomited and tried to catch her breath, but her body didn't want her to have any part of the air in that room. She couldn't see blood, but she could smell it, the iron tang infecting every atom of her being.

Shaking and wiping the vomit from her mouth, she rose and paced towards the drawer, her chest throbbing with every movement. Inside the drawer was blackness, a void. The abyss could look upon its self and not find darkness as such as this. The darkness wormed and undulated in on itself, reaching for her.

Jen slammed the drawer shut, holding it closed; something inside the drawer slurped. Behind her, the paper cube lay on the floor where she had once been; it slowly unfolded and returned to a flat sheet.

She looked up at the door. Frankie was still there, but he had his back to her, talking to Mr Henderson.

She ducked below the desk. They couldn't help her. They wouldn't even believe her. *How is this even possible?*

Her thoughts were interrupted by white-hot barbs diving beneath her nailbeds. She gritted her teeth and stared at her hands, her nails. Every single one was gone; there were bare stumps where the nails had previously been. She pressed fingertips against fingertips; there were no wounds, as if she'd never had any nails to begin with. They hummed with energy, each finger a lightning rod.

This was too much.

Jen attempted to organise her thoughts and line them up in order of importance, but everything crashed and jangled. She wanted to break down, to give in and quit, but something wouldn't let her. She should have been scared by what happened to Brandon, but the fear, numbed by curiosity, kept it locked away, as if behind a frosted shower door.

She wanted to know more, to see more. What else could this power offer?

Bile rose in her throat, but she bit back harder, forcing it down; she stared at the door, then the drawer, and slid it open.

The darkness had gone.

I need to get out of here.

Jen peered at the window; the ground wasn't too far below, maybe four or five feet; she could make that jump.

She grabbed her bag and forced the paper inside. She slipped the window open and leapt to the ground outside. The grass was soft, and her gentle thud didn't alert anyone in the vicinity. It smelt warm and fresh; a mower trundled in the distance, mincing the new green shoots. Memories of picnics with her mother tore through her brain, only lingering for a second before being replaced by the image of Brandon's lifeless eyes.

She regained her balance and lifted her shirt. A row of red and purple flesh lined her ribs and breast, the impression of a heel curve showing prominently. Placing a cold hand on the bruises, she leant against the wall, her head spinning. It felt like a dream; right now, everything felt like a dream. She peered at her fingers again, concentrating, as if she could will her fingernails to return.

I need help, like some serious help.

Jen walked around the outside of the building and started towards home. She wasn't spending another minute in this place, and she needed to talk to Brian.

"Brian, are you home?" she called into the house.

He popped out from behind the fridge door. "Yeppo, it's lunch, and why are you here?"

She silently wrapped her arms around him and sobbed onto his chest.

"Right, whose ass do I need to kick?"

Jen shook her head.

"Well, it seems like you're pretty unhappy."

She nodded.

"Am I going to have to play a guessing game?"

"I-I..." She lowered her head and pulled away from him.

"Hun, I can't help you if you can't tell me."

She lifted the front of her shirt and showed him her bruised ribs.

Brian slammed his fist into the fridge door; bottles inside rattled and tumbled into each other. "Who the fuck did this to you?"

She shook her head again.

"Are you in some kind of trouble? Do I need to call the police?"

"Please don't, it... it's not the bruising. Something happened today."

"Okay, if we're going to do this, I need a beer, you need a hot chocolate, and we need to sit down."

Hot chocolates were something Brian had always made for her and her mom. Things were hard when Angela was first diagnosed with cancer; for a while, it had been the only sweetness around, especially after Angela stopped smiling, stopped holding her, and eventually simply stopped being.

Jen sipped on the drink as Brian downed his first beer and started on the second.

"Don't you have to go back to work?"

"Not today I don't, you need me, and what kind of dad— step-dad would I be if I wasn't here for you? Also, did you do something different with your hair?"

Jen shook her head. "You're my dad, just...dad."

He dug around in his pocket and then held out his fist to her.

"What's this?"

"Something I made for you." Brian opened his hand. Inside was the red stone, the stone from the night before, a hole drilled all the way through; it now sat on a small silver chain. "I thought you might like to keep it, a memento of the weird, though I'm now thinking you don't need any weirder."

Jen slipped the chain over her neck and rolled the stone around her fingers, "Thank you, it's beautiful."

Brian smiled and took another mouthful of his beer and wiped his mouth on the back of his sleeve. "Right, start at the beginning."

✳ ✳ ✳

"So, he just, pop—vanished, along with your fingernails?"

"Not so much *pop*, more sort of imploded. He turned to mince and got sucked inside, and my nails, they're just gone."

"And all this was because of your paper?" Brian asked.

Jen nodded.

"Can I see it?"

She reached into her bag, "It's not the paper, though, it's the folds that are doing it."

She handed the paper to Brian, who inspected it, flipping the page between his hands. "Can you show me one of the folds?"

"I don't think that's a good idea. It seems to change every time, and I don't know what's going to happen if I do."

"Okay then, we'll take precautions."

Brian put his third empty bottle down and pulled a hockey mask over his face. "It's going to be just fine, show me what you can do."

He braced himself behind the couch.

Jen grabbed the crinkled paper square and folded it in half. Like before, it took over, morphing and changing in her hand. The air darkened; static coated her skin like a heavy blanket, pulsating like a heartbeat, tugging at the fine hairs on her arms.

This doesn't feel right.

Shadows crawled like fingertips across the floor, and in their wake, something skittered through the carpet fibres like thousand-legged spiders, riding a sulphurous zephyr.

The paper stopped, resting on her palm in a shape that she couldn't describe; it shimmered, its sides vanishing and reappearing in time with the static pulse.

"Whoo! That is insane!" Brian cheered. "So what happens now?"

Jen peered around the room, trying to play spot the difference, or spot the void. "I don't know, it's different every time."

The couch creaked and groaned; it shifted forwards as if punted along the floor by something.

"Did you do—"

"Nope!" shouted Brian. He backed away from the couch, but didn't get far. The material began to unmake itself; fibres frayed and weaved like snakes, coiling around every inch of him, pulling him against the side of it. More and more broke loose and wrapped him like a grey cotton mummy; he struggled, but his arms were pinned to his sides. If it hadn't been for the hockey mask, the fibres would have smothered his face.

FUCK, FUCK, FUCK, FUCK.

"*Get me out of here!*"

Jen threw the paper to the floor and ran for the couch, but its huge foam cushions collapsed in front of her in a wave of liquid yellow, turning the ground into a quagmire. The foam rushed up Brian's body, seeping under the fibres coating his skin; they undulated like a throat in mid-swallow, forcing the liquid upwards instead of down.

Brian twitched and shook, trying to break free.

"I can't get to you, oh God!"

THIS IS ALL YOUR FAULT, YOUR FAULT, YOUR FAULT.

Jen tried to wade through the residual foam, but her feet stuck fast to the carpet. The static pulse grew stronger, its crushing weight forcing her to her knees.

"*Help m—*"

Brian's voice stopped, followed by a retching gurgle as the foam forced its way down his throat, wave after wave of yellow vanishing from the floor.

The fibres lifted him; he hovered above the sofa frame, spiralling threads continuing to feed his grey mummified form. The static vanished; Jen broke free and ran to him and pulled at the fibres, but they wouldn't move. He was like stone, cold and still.

The cotton pulled tighter and tighter, crushing his body. Limbs crunched and twitched, contorting as bones crumbled to dust beneath the grey.

All that remained of the couch was a wooden frame that splintered and fired towards Brian's body. Several slivers hit Jen before plucking themselves free and continuing towards Brian, disappearing inside him.

Crunch—

The cotton lump seized in on itself, compressing into a tiny ball. With a blinding flash of violet light it blinked out of existence, taking what remained of Brian with it.

Jen collapsed into the empty space that had once held their couch, a square of paper beside her feet.

Jen ignored phone calls, letting them go to the bulky answering machine Brian had installed by their front door; calls from Brian's boss, asking why he wasn't coming to work. She ignored them still when they finally fired him a week later.

There was nothing to say and no one she could tell; no one would believe her. Her books and paper stayed locked away in the trunk of Brian's car; if she couldn't see them, she wouldn't be tempted to make something else. Curiosity gnawed at her insides.

Her hair had fallen out entirely at the back now, leaving nothing but a patch of puckered grey skin where her "radical" pixie cut once been.

Returning to school, she'd signed up for the free lunch program and squirrelled away extras to bring home; so long as Brian had some money left in the bank, bills would be paid, and she'd be able to keep on going. She'd even picked up a pack of false nails at the local pharmacy and glued them onto her finger stumps.

After everything with her mom, with the bullying, this, this was the lowest of the low.

With Brandon still missing, *Have you seen this boy?* posters hung on every wall at the school. She tried not to look at them, but his eyes burned into her; there was nothing she could do, she couldn't fix this, she couldn't take it back.

"Oi! Oi, you!" Frankie ran up behind her with two friends in tow. "Where've you been, and where's Brandon?"

Jen tried to turn away, but they blocked her path. "Leave me alone."

Frankie stabbed a finger into her chest, "You heard me, you freak. What happened to Brandon?"

"I don't know what you're talking about."

"Yes, you do, and you're gonna tell me, or you'll get a beating."

His friends idled to the sides, keeping an eye out for teachers.

"Fuck you!" Jen stamped on one of the boy's feet and made a run for an emergency exit at the end of the hall; she slammed down the barrier, setting off the alarm, and headed out of the school.

Frankie took off after her. "What are you waiting for, get her!"

The boys chased her beyond the school boundary, and towards the woodland at the edge of the town. More posters for Brandon hung limply from nails on trees, waterlogged photographs distorting his face.

I've got to do something, anything.

Jen tore a poster from a nail and began to fold as she ran, first into a square; she twisted the paper once more before it took over, and she revelled in it, giving herself over to whatever power this was, Brandon's face vanishing into an array of lines.

Her feet sank into the sand as she reached the lake enclave.

The boys closed in.

"There she is! Grab her!" Frankie yelled. He stumbled over a log and chased down the woodland path towards Whisper Lake.

Jen reached the water's edge and turned to face them. The paper pulsated and folded, forming intricate shapes, impossible shapes. "Stay back!"

They didn't listen, running onto the sand and reaching for her.

Darkness spewed from the palm of her hand and swallowed them. There was no sound, no light, only darkness at first. They tumbled for what seemed like forever; shards of red and violet light danced past them, firing beams of lightning. This world was a silent world, sound rejected as mere folly.

Jen laughed; her laughter rippled through her skin like sine waves, sinking beneath the surface and coiling her muscles with exquisite pleasure. This place, this was heaven, it had to be, but heaven doesn't last forever.

This was the end, and she welcomed it.

The world began to unmake her, unfolding her body from its human form. Her skin stripped into layers, peeling hairless fragments like gold leaf, each fragment disintegrating to powder, caught in the pulse of the universe and absorbed by the void. Layer upon layer sloughed away and seeped into the abyss, folding into the fabric of life itself.

The boys collapsed through a portal and hit the rocky ground with a thwack; it echoed across the walls of the dark, damp cave. Their screams joined the blossoming echo until stalagmites shook from the ceiling and fragments exploded against the ground.

Frankie pointed to the throbbing glow. "Shut up!"

Something putrid-white coiled in the dark, something that hadn't been there before, something that had come with them from the beyond.

Something that was, by now, very hungry.

Tentacles coiled along the floor, unravelling from beneath the beast, reaching for the boys. Frankie was hooked around the ankle and dragged towards the glow. He clawed at the rocky ground, slicing his fingers and tearing nails free from their beds.

Above him, two ginormous eyes swivelled like globes until they focused on his tiny, wriggling, screaming frame. The beast slid a barbed tentacle up the length of his body. It lingered above his face, darting from mouth to eyes to mouth again, stroking him with the pointed tip. Decision made, it careened through his teeth, breaking those that didn't come loose, and forced its way down his bulging throat. He tried to fight, scratching and pulling at the tentacle, but it was no use; something began to fill his stomach, something that twitched and whispered in the darkness from inside him.

GRAVE MARGINALIA

BY LYDIA PEEVER

"There's hair in my book," said the girl to a library clerk, holding up her spine-splayed copy of *Black Beauty*.

Long black hair lay like a bookmark in the centre, a tiny horsetail slinking down the fold. Thick hair with a slight wave sprouted from a dried portion of thin scalp. The clerk stifled a gag with one hand to his mouth. "What the ever-living..."

How this grotesquery dangling past the pages had been overlooked was a mystery. Bloodstains marked the surrounding pages; the embossed triangular shape of torn skin bruised the ivory paper. It had been there a long time, however it got there. Bile bloomed into the library clerk's mouth and he turned to clutch the desk, dizzy.

"It's not mine," said the girl, nonplussed.

"Fourteen bookmarks of human hair," Beth, the head librarian, read from the list of morbidity found in her building that evening after the library closed. "Two eyelids, both left and right." The clerk stood near, still needing to grip whatever solid object stood nearby to keep his stomach settled. "The spines of eleven books containing finger and toe bones." She paused for effect and allowed the visualisation to gestate among her guests: Jonah, the clerk who had turned in the first hairy book; a historian from a city committee; and the library foundation's lawyer. Beth's daughter Annie was here to drive the librarian home, also as a backfiring attempt to scare her out of attending museum studies. Her mother had thought this may chase her away, but the fascination wouldn't wash off her daughter's face, no matter how gory the details. "Seven scraps of flesh, two unidentified but related human remains alongside several fingernails, and one mangled copy of *Les Mis* containing the lower half of a human jaw." Not a breath stirred in the room.

"What do we know about these books?" asked the lawyer. They had been called in to determine any criminality in the finding.

"They aren't ours, technically, but since they *are* in the building, we own them until proven otherwise," the librarian stated, and nodded toward Jonah to elucidate.

He cleared his throat and pushed his glasses up on top of his head with a trembling hand. "Yes, the books. Not ours, as Beth said. Not stamped, not scanned, no barcode, but shelved properly at least." They waited, as if expecting more. "I'd never seen them. None of the students had ever seen them."

"How long could they have been on the shelves?" asked the historian, called in case there was any provenance to the body parts.

"No telling," he started, but with a harsh look from Beth he added, "Not long, I'm sure. A couple of the books we actually have copies of—newer ones, and shelved alongside, but..." He faltered.

Beth picked up answering questions that none had asked yet, though the police might eventually. "This was the first time anyone noticed them. Correct, Jonah?"

The clerk sputtered, "Of course! Had anyone ever..." He shuddered, recalling hair and scalp, the brownish stains. "We'd have been told, I'm sure."

"Well." Beth paused to remove her glasses, signalling the meeting as nearing conclusion. "We need a full inventory, so I suggest we all start now. And to be clear, it won't be about what we already have catalogued, but focused on what we have... recently acquired." Motioning to her lawyer, she added that they'd be in touch with a full list of the mystery books, including those marked as evidence with human remains, then saw the gentlemen to the door.

Beth allowed Annie to assist. Of all the times she'd tried to exclude her from the library and her aspiration of a career in the same, Annie belied her higher education to slog it out in the stacks. Not that library studies were beneath her, but like any mother, Beth wanted more for her unaccountably bright and well-schooled daughter. With a dual doctorate, she could be any number of places on the planet making twice the money her mother had ever made, but for some baffling reason, Annie returned here. As if the library, to be melodramatic, were a vortex pulling her back. The girl had described it as her passion, books, and her good grades being a result of that and not a passion for what she happened to be studying. So here she was, in the stacks that her family had worked for three generations, voluntarily. Not that they didn't need the help. Of the old library's holdings—excluding general fiction, children's, and audio-visual, which were so far not afflicted with the grisly discoveries—they had a lot of ground to cover. Annie had suggested a visual walkthrough of other areas of the library, and books catalogued in the first sections up to social science. All the books earmarked by hair and skin had come from books higher up in the Dewey decimal system, with the highest concentration found in the eight and nine hundreds, or literature and history. That cut their focus down from the quarter-million item collection considerably. As Jonah noted, they were shelved correctly, but if they displaced books the library owned, no one knew yet. They had little time for that, seeing as three dozen misplaced books had turned up overnight.

"If you want coffee, Jonah, feel free," Annie said, plunking down her bag heavy with ledgers, a laptop, and two tablet computers belonging to the library. "I parked my machine and pods with milk at the desk." She booted up the laptop, which housed spreadsheets noting damage, older books, access to the history of each book, and much more than the tablets could tell them. Since her mother had come around to taking the collection beyond an electronic front for members to sign books out and track late fees, they had a wealth of knowledge at their fingertips. It had also given the summer students a lot to do over the past few years, and under Beth's watchful instruction, they had done a thorough job. Want to recall that one book with a coffee stain on the first page of the third chapter? The online administrative catalogue could tell you in an instant.

Annie staged the new books in the database from Jonah's notes: books the library didn't or even shouldn't own. Books on surgery, a treatise on the diseases of the eye, the manufacture of glue, a bizarre history which ended two centuries ago, a dictionary of mineralogy, galvanism, and an obsolete manual on black bile topped the list as the oldest books. Some must be worth what she paid in rent, as they were all in good condition, save the few stained by bodily fluids. It wasn't until she had perched here with Jonah fiddling around with cups in the background that she realized his notes hadn't included what exactly was on the pages where the gory bits were found; just the page numbers.

Jonah returned to retrieve a tablet and begin the inventory, and set his coffee down on the wide wooden table Annie had chosen at the head of the rows in question. Most of the library decor was original, and little was refurbished. Luckily for her family, the shelving was the only modern thing, as it received the brunt of the public wear and tear, although it retained some old-world charm. The end caps were covered in ornate carved facades crafted by local woodworking artisans. A nice touch, and a push back at encroaching metal and plastic over the ancient wood and stone.

"Did you happen to see the pages the things were found in?" she asked, trying to not turn Jonah's stomach any more than it had been by using descriptive words.

"God, no! It was hard enough to verify what was found, let alone read along." He shuddered and picked up his cup, only to grimace and put it back down. Annie frowned, and he countered by mumbling it was too hot to drink.

"Let's call them bookmarks, for the sake of your health." She paused to offer a thin smile. "So, none of us read the pages or noted where they were?"

"Now that you mention it, every book was marked in the middle. I'd say exact centre, but we'd need them to prove that."

"And they all came from the exact centre of the library, it seems." They looked around the high ceilings, arched windows, soft pendant lighting, and it seemed right. The children's section and main doors behind them; the circulation desk sat at the far right, and reference to the left. Popular fiction sat at the rear of the building to their right as well, leaving the vast collection sitting right about the middle of the building.

"We don't know what any of this means, Annie, and really, if we have tens of thousands of books to speed through, we'd better start."

"I get that, but if we can whittle off the least likely places to look and focus, we may get more done."

Jonah sighed and slumped a little in his wooden armchair. "I'd rather not find anything more, personally."

"I'll deal with the specimens, you can just flag books that aren't ours." The prospect brightened Jonah's face a little, having the muck work off his shoulders. "The areas where the books were found are all in the same location and don't span entire sections, so if we start where the bulk of the books were found, in history and literature, and spiral outward, we may get a better idea of how broad our count has to be."

"A crime scene," he stated flatly, and was met with Annie's raised eyebrow of confusion. "You're planning it like a crime scene, which I guess it kind of is, isn't it?"

"More like an archeological dig. My mother insisted that I take more than library studies, so maybe my elective courses will pay off tonight."

"Let's hope so," Jonah said, peering over his mug at her, then over to the stacks upon stacks that would be their haystack for the next several hours.

Focusing there, Annie and Jonah found a few more books misplaced in the next hour and a half. So her hunch was proven right, and Jonah's stomach seemed to be taking it well. He noted the books and positions; she retrieved them and documented the contents. Keeping that much to herself was easy as he turned directly back to the shelves, suppressing a shudder each time. Jonah clearly wanted nothing more to do with *memento mori*.

When they hit a lull, Annie tucked her pencil behind her ear and reviewed her notes. She saw quickly that the books all dealt with the sections of the body the items were found in. That is, if you counted the literature findings of the hair, eyelids, and jawbone as the head. The rest of the portions lay in sections related vaguely to the body parts found in the books. She mused on having to keep her language so sterile for Jonah's sake. *Bookmarks*, she said; *body parts*, she meant. There was little evidence that these scraps of meat and hair were being used as actual bookmarks. Imagining a human body as we knew it superimposed above the rows, it appeared the parts would all basically fit.

"How are you doing in there?" She peered down the long row Jonah was crouched in. Despite the stools and steps they had in abundance, he was lanky enough to reach up to the top shelf or bunch down to the first row, and somehow claimed it was comfortable.

"Not bad. Nearing the end of surgery, and it dawned on me we didn't find the jawbone here."

"The layout of the books struck me too." She caught herself before saying *body* and silently applauded Jonah for saying *jawbone* without retching. "You're heading into what now?"

He froze in the row and turned slowly, a look of horror creeping up and pulling his face into a small frown. "Gynecology."

"Let's take a little break. I'm fairly sure the bookmarks are male," which bought her a grimace from Jonah, who didn't ask how she'd guessed.

Once they'd started back at it, three hours had passed, and they finished another round of coffee to keep them a little more awake. Following a hunch, Annie strolled back into the literature section, looking for any book that stood out. They had hair, eyes, and a jaw. If she were, say, a larynx, where would she be? Standing in front of the spot that had held the ancient copy of *Les Mis*, she turned to face the books behind her, then pushed the books aside from the centre, randomly. Reaching through to the next row, she took a backward book and threaded it carefully back through the gap in the shelf. This was entirely a hunch, but it wasn't that surprising to see that the book she'd fished through the row was a mid-nineteenth-century book on arias for contralto. Rounding the side of the shelf, she perused the vocal music area that book had come from until she found a suspect. Thicker than the surrounding books, the spine had no markings and was certainly leather. Slipping from the shelf, its weight impressed her, and inspecting the fore edge, Annie saw two small holes—bookworms—which the library was appropriately guarded against. The scent of the pages wafted up from the deckled edge. Cedar wood. Dust. Centuries.

Pages buckled in the centre, and she thrilled at the idea that her hunch was correct. Creaking slightly, the heavy book opened easily to the page marked with slivers of meat. Again, brown blood spread where the once sticky mess had desiccated. Quarter notes and staves provided the background for the small flaps of human cartilage and flesh. Ridges stood out slightly along the edges of weird petals.

Annie had found vocal cords.

Going over the parts they had in her mind, she walked back over to the stacks Jonah was in now, well past gynecology. She needed to map out the human body and keep stock of what they had. Then they might know what to expect.

"Any luck?" she asked when she found him in the middle of a row, a stack of books removed from the top row and piled up waist-high on the floor beside him.

Jonah gestured to one book that had been wiggled forward in the shelf above him, then stood. "Just that, how about you?"

Annie held the leather book up.

"Now, while this isn't as slow going as I thought, I found these that need cleaning. I guess they've not been moved in a while, so the dust got to them."

"Just glad they weren't... you know," Annie said, feeling badly for Jonah having to endure this.

"I just want to know how many we're going to find." The exasperation in his voice pained her further. Heading into the fifth hour, their coffee breaks would soon lead to calling it a night. He rested one hand on the stack he'd pulled out to clean. "Where is the end of this?"

Annie saw that his hands had finally stopped shaking. Colour had returned to his cheeks, and while Jonah was sometimes a little jumpy, he was either growing exhausted or finally used to the idea that they were hunting for what amounted to a chopped-up human in their library. She decided to not mention how the more parts they found, the more fresh and bloody they seemed to become.

Looking to his hand again, Annie thought she caught movement. Maybe, if he was still on edge, they ought to stop. Then she realised the movement wasn't his hand at all, but under it. The brown casing fabric of the book's cover swam in her vision. Annie's eyes weren't moving, but the book itself. Just as she opened her mouth to speak, Jonah snatched his hand back from the stack of books, making them jerk away, both seeing the same thing. The book cover warbled as dust motes caught in a river of smoke rising from the cover. Swirling upward, the small plume of warm air and dust carried more of the book scent of cedar, mulch, and coffee. As suddenly as it began, the air was then still, with a different book now set on top of the stack. As if pushed up from the volume below it, the new book was its grandfather: the same size and width but older, darker, and heavier, making the stack teeter for a second. Annie reached out to steady it with her now shaking hand, and the warmth could be felt through the cover as she stabilized it.

"Warm? Is it warm? My hand was warm. My hand was, my hand was on that, that," Jonah was staring, mouth working but not finding words to describe what they had just seen. "That... thing!"

Bells rang out, a shrill alarm, and Jonah screamed. The bell stopped as abruptly, and they gasped in unison. Once more the bell rang out, tinny and long. Jonah clamped one hand to his mouth, then muttered through it, half questioning, "Telephone?"

Annie made a move to pick up the book, but decided to leave it there. Jonah backed away as if the stack was infected, and followed her toward the front desk to see who was calling.

"Annie?"

It was Beth, calling to see how they were getting on, but right away Annie could hear tension in her mother's voice. This was unlike her, both as a head librarian and as the strong, serious woman who had raised her.

"Mom, is something wrong? You sound—" Annie's mind reached for words other than *scared*, *troubled*, or *weird*.

"I can't sleep. I want to go down there, but I keep going over this in my mind, and I think there's something you ought to know." Exhaustion caught up with Annie for a moment and dizziness rocked her, mind reeling with whatever her mother had to say. Leaning on the desk, she held her breath a moment as her mother spoke. "And I don't know if this is exactly what's going on, but something sure as hell is, and it's the sort of thing that sounds crazy even without actually saying it."

"Yes, mother, you're swearing." Which was a rarity, and they both knew it, so something was definitely wrong. Jonah sat on the desk, as close as he could, to hear the call too, and perhaps for a little primitive safety.

"In the basement they found a body when I was young."

"In the basement they found a body when she was young," Annie parroted for Jonah. "And you think this is what we're finding? How?"

"I don't claim to understand, Annie. They found the body and just left it there. They poured concrete. It used to be a dirt floor, but they found it when I was little and my grandfather had them cover it up."

Thinking rapidly, Annie recalled three times they had resurfaced the basement that she knew of, the first by her own grandfather. "All the times the floor was re-poured here, there was a body under it?"

"Yes, and my father had it done twice before you were born."

"That makes no sense," Annie said. "How many times can we lay concrete before the basement stops being a basement at all?"

"It's sinking, or something. I don't know. Listen, honey, all I know is that when we found the body, everyone panicked. The library had just gotten a grant, all eyes in town were on the family, and they couldn't afford to let that get out."

"We, when you say *we*, who found it?" Jonah had hung his head but was listening, perhaps trying to make sense of one end of the conversation.

"I did. As a girl. Maybe five? I was young, but I remember. Under the front of the library, the basement was an earth floor, and the back half had been finished for a meeting room and storage. Mother had raked the dirt away, making sure it was dry after a storm, and I noticed what she thought were smooth rocks. A week later he began to surface."

"He, who?"

"We don't know. He'd been broken at the wheel. Quartered." Annie had an image of the antique torture practise.

"And you saw this," Annie said.

"Then, and every time he surfaced. The first time he was a little more together. We took the wheel out and buried him again as best we could. The body fell apart. Oh, Annie, it was horrible! And you can't blame me for not telling you these horrible things. The next time I saw him, the body was in pieces. Legs, arms, ribs. Just awful. The last time"—Beth's voice hitched once on the other end of the line, drawing breath to push out the words—"it was all bones."

"You mean to say this body just keeps rising to the top of the dirt, the concrete?"

"And the truckloads of chipped slate I had dumped in there before we poured it last. I salted it, Annie. I salted the earth where he lay, and I prayed." Of all the revelations, this one silenced her. Never had Annie heard her mother resort to prayer, or wishing to or thanking God or any other form of a higher power. "I prayed it was over and that you would never have to see this. We never knew who he was or why he had died so horribly. We never knew why he was buried under our library!" The anguish in her mother's voice took over and Annie could hear her breathing quicken, fighting back so many old and fearful emotions.

Jonah took the update remarkably well. Having a mythological body with a will of its own under the foundation sat better with his stomach than finding the actual body parts.

"I've been thinking," he said, after Annie finished relaying what her mother had told her. "We're gaining a book every hour or two, and have over the past day or two. The shelves were dusted last weekend over there," and he pointed to the furthest section the books had been found in. "This side hadn't been, but we did sand that patch of ceiling that we had to spackle after repairing that skylight."

Annie's gaze followed the ceiling to the section they were digging through last. "So there was dust, but no drywall dust on the book from the top shelf?"

"Exactly. And the students."

The students had been all over the library, replacing plastic slip covers in the reference section over the weekend as well. Any oddball book would have been noticed, and any book sitting longer than that would have been dusted and noted, or had dust on it. That was the weekend, and this was Wednesday.

"So we've had nearly thirty books show up over as many hours?" Annie said.

"More just today, I figure," and a small shiver proved he still did find this as unsettling as he had when first handling one of the books. "At an increasing rate."

"In the shape of a man."

"You judge that by where we find them?"

Annie nodded, still staring at the shelves as if waiting for something to move. A shifting, a whisper, or the sound of pages shuffling.

"So let's see if we can't hurry this along."

Confused, Annie looked to Jonah, who had certainly found some courage behind his fear, but was still visibly shaken by the whole ordeal. "What do you mean?"

"Come on," he said, sliding off the desk he had sat on beside the phone, and heading toward her mother's office. "I've got what may be a terrible idea."

Of the little modernization the old Carnegie library had undergone, none had touched the office of the head librarian. Orange oil and tea scents lingered in the dark, hollow room. It featured a handful of large leather chairs that had always been there, as far as Annie knew. The desk was original, as was the woodwork, and the huge Persian rug underfoot had kept its threads and rich hue despite the years, thanks to the heavy curtains that cut out most light. Jonah tugged the chain of one green glass lamp and laid his hand on top of one short stack of books that dotted the top of the desk.

"I thought the lawyer took them!" Annie was more unsettled than she ought to be, having the books in one spot, and more than a few volumes.

"And I thought they'd take the remains, at least, but no. As we left, I heard your mother discussing a warrant if police became involved."

"So they're here until..."

"Until she lets someone take them. If she ever does."

"And your terrible plan is?" Annie asked.

"We lay them out on the floor out there. In the shape of, well, roughly and as best we can. You know, how they want to be."

"Jonah." Annie faltered; not because his idea was terrible, since it was brilliant and simple as the best plans are, but because she suddenly couldn't recall how many books there ought to be. "Two books an hour is based on thirty books?"

He counted visually, then suddenly took a step back as one stack grew before their eyes, one book higher with a small swirl of smoke rising between them

"Fifty books. We should hurry."

At first, she feared Jonah wouldn't fare well if they had to open and inspect the flesh and bone in each book, but as they laid them out, he fell into his position as circulation clerk. He read the titles and handed them to her, and she used her knowledge of anatomy to place the books in the shape of a human body without much guesswork.

In some places, like the head, heart, and other major organs, the books overlapped slightly. Brown, red, black and tan; it reminded Annie of a pixelated image or a tangram of a man. Through blurred vision, a shape indeed took form.

Halfway through, before the copies of *Les Mis* and *Black Beauty* joined the piles, they stepped back as another book appeared. Much like the last ones, there was a soundless puff of smoke and a stirring of heat in the air. As the book sank upward from nothing on the floor, they moved tentatively closer. There was no marking on the cover, as with most of the books, and the spine was thick dark leather. With the toe of one black canvas sneaker, Jonah flipped the cover open to reveal woodcuts and indecipherable Latin. Had it been a religious book, they might have been able to pick out a word or two. He made no further move to touch the book, so Annie bent down to see why it had appeared in the middle of the supposed torso. Her thumb found purchase about thirty pages in, and she flipped the onionskin leaves over to reveal another woodcut: a kitchen scene, and animals of various shapes skinned and drying over a roiling fire. Another thirty pages or so she flipped together, and kitchen tools appeared.

"A cookbook," Annie figured. "The stomach..." and she heard shuffling behind her. A glance back, and she could see Jonah's sneakers now pointed away. He'd turned his back so she could take a moment to verify they were still finding body parts.

There was little she needed to do to guess where the middle was. A small buckle was apparent in between the pages, dead centre. Sliding the tip of her finger in, she flipped the book open wide. Blood and bile stained the pages, sticking many together where it was once wet through. Rot and vomit reached her nose, as well as a faint odour of shit. The c-shaped flattened piece of anatomy was immediately familiar to her. The duodenum, so not the stomach at all, but the next organ in line, heading into the small intestine. "Back up a little, Jonah, it smells." Annie heard him taking measured breaths through his mouth as he stepped once, and again, further away. Slipping her pencil from behind her ear, she used it to lift an edge of the dehydrated tissue. Nudging the sharpened tip under the skin, she could hear it pop with a small wet sound as the edge slowly lifted away from the paper it was stuck to.

Rustling sounds rose from the head and arms of the paper body on the floor. Annie jerked back and lost her balance, tumbling to the floor on her butt, hands behind her. She could see several books shaking. Jonah scrabbled at her shoulders suddenly, and roughly pulled her up and away. Books jostled on the floor, barely moving but enough to see and hear. The heat hit them. Wrapping her arm around Jonah for balance, they took quick steps back with wisps of smoke rising here and there from the arms and legs. A book that sat in place of a hand jumped toward them. Only by a half inch, but enough to make them both cry out, terrified.

"What did you do?" Jonah barked, pulling her another step away.

As quickly as the movement began, it stopped. The warm aura around the piles dispersed, and the books lay still again. Annie loosened her grip on Jonah, realizing she had a handful of his shirt, mumbling, "I didn't mean to! I just wanted to see if it was stuck to the pages or if it would come out."

Pacing a few feet away and back, Jonah apologized for snapping "Let's just not do that again. Don't, for God's sake, touch any of it." His hand went to his stomach again, and the slightly green look had returned.

"I'm sorry, it was just..." Annie trailed off at first, then simply said what had come to mind. "I want to put him back together."

"Not like that, you're not." Jonah's voice was strong, and he stared hard at Annie. "We keep the cadaver in the books," he said, slowly and clearly. "We keep the books together. We put the books in a fucking box and we put the fucking box in the god-damned ground."

Eyes locked on his, Annie pondered his fear, his clenched jaw and rationalizing though terror. How the insanity of what they had just witnessed had steeled him against it and toward containing it. She took in what Jonah had just said, and it clicked. The god-damned ground.

"Mom, it's me." Annie had dialed fast and was talking faster, cutting off her mother's curt greeting. "We need a box. A coffin, or something like it. There are fifty books now." Her mother whispered *fifty* back to her in disbelief. "What's left of him might be all here now, or most of it. Burying him might stop it, and we can't put him back."

"Perhaps no grave would take him," her mother said, somewhat lost in thought. "I thought of that. Many times. My father once joked that he hadn't paid his overdue fines, and that was the punishment. That was the last joke made about it, believe me. We never knew what this ground was used for, but there are two churchyards close enough to make our property sit outside of one. Unconsecrated ground. Where to bury him now, that's the question."

"He's staying here, mom."

Jonah shook his head, mouthing the word 'no,' and her mother began a verbal flurry of protest. Annie closed her eyes for a moment, not listening to a word, not hearing Jonah begin suggesting otherwise; what her ears picked up was a faint shift of paper on the floor. Opening her eyes, she could she another book perched where the heart ought to be on the body of books on the floor.

"What we have now is a magnet, pulling the parts of this man from the very ground. We don't have a crime scene, we barely have a body, and if we keep the books together, maybe that will be enough."

"Together where?" both Beth and Jonah asked at the same time.

"Right here. In state."

"In what, though?" her mother asked "We can't have piles of books with bones and hair lying around in the middle of the library, and a coffin would be out of the question."

Jonah had stopped shaking his head and sat listening to follow the conversation as best he could.

Annie planned as she talked. "We keep the books in something inconspicuous up here. No more buried body in the basement. We can keep an eye on him, and if we need to, we can talk about burying it another time. It's late, and we have this under control. The library can open, and nothing is amiss if we can keep this contained and discuss this in the morning."

"What to put it in?" her mother said, agreeing with her voice that they were all tired and the idea made what sense it could.

Annie looked to Jonah, who was finally nodding his head, agreeing.

"I know," he said, loud enough for Beth to hear too. "Under the card catalogue. The wood base it's on is just a big hollow waste of space. No one uses the card catalogue anyway."

"*I* use the card catalogue!" Beth's voice squelched through the receiver loud enough for Annie to have to hold the phone away.

"No, you don't. I took the cards out months ago. It's just a big empty wood box now."

"Where did you put the cards?" Annie asked.

"In the basement," and with a small smile he added, "so it's like a fair trade."

The base of the card catalogue basically was a squat coffin. It was a solid and heavy piece of furniture even without a hundred pounds of card paper in it. Taking out each drawer to lighten the load made it manageable. Then, they lifted the heavy frame off of the base it sat on. For years it had perched at the top of the stairs, untouched for most of that time. No students were trained to use it or instructed to update it. Constructed in two parts, Jonah had discovered the hollow base under the series of drawers after having to move the monstrosity for carpet cleaning. The whole piece stood about four feet high, and the base was only there to keep people from crouching to the very ground when using it. The last time he'd moved it was months ago, and that was when he'd removed all the paperwork to lighten the load. Half of his intention was to make a correlation project for the students; the other half was to see who noticed them missing, if anyone would at all.

With the top off and set aside, they were faced with a lidless box. Annie began laying the books in, one by one, in the exact order they had come from the floor. Jonah was done touching them entirely and had gone outside for some air before they both had to lift the catalogue back onto the base.

It wasn't long before she laid the last book in and felt a draught of cool night air as the heavy front door creaked open and closed. Jonah joined her, then looked across the books in the coffin with a glum expression.

"Well, I may not be religious," Jonah said, holding out a handful of sand, "but that doesn't mean he wasn't." Dry dirt fell out as he tipped his hand over the box and scattered it, hitting the books inside.

"From the churchyard?" Annie asked.

Jonah nodded. "From under the largest tree."

With a bit of effort, they placed the base on the floor in the middle of the room, roughly above where the body had been buried originally.

Lifting the base back on, they had to nudge it a little so the top fit into the base snugly, as it had been before. The books shifted a little inside each time, and each time they winced, studying one another in case this was the wrong thing to do.

Once the card catalogue was in place in the centre of the room, they moved carrels and tables around. It looked good. It looked planned. It looked centred, as any pulpit does in a place of worship. A secret reliquary hidden within, commanding unspoken admiration. This library was more a place of mourning than most now, being usually only a repository for the words of the dead.

She pressed an ear up to the wood and listened; then Jonah turned to go. Annie waited another minute after the big main door creaked shut. Hollow shuffles finally sounded from inside the box, and she felt strangely comforted, as if whatever had begun with them would finish by itself. Following Jonah, she turned out all the overhead lights, shrouding silent rows in darkness for the few hours left until dawn.

Annie let the creaking library door close behind her, unlocked.

ABOUT OUR AUTHORS, ILLUSTRATOR, AND EDITORS

AUTHORS

Pippa Bailey lives north of the wall in the Scottish Highlands. Principally a horror writer, YouTube personality and independent reviewer at Deadflicks with her partner, Myk Pilgrim. She's known for supernatural horror with a vile sense of humour, and you can find her and Myk's collections Poisoned Candy, Bloody Stockings, and Rancid Eggs through all good book retailers. You can spot her drinking too much tea, making terrible puns, and bothering the local wildlife

Sebastian Bendix is a Los Angeles based writer and musician, as well as host of a popular midnight horror film series, *Friday Night Frights at the Cinefamily*. He attended school at Emerson College for writing and has had fiction and non-fiction pieces published in both in print (*Mean Magazine, Sanitarium Magazine* and *Xchyler Publishing*) and online (CHUD.com, *Encounters Magazine* and *Grinning Skull Press*). Bendix self-published his first horror/fantasy novel *The Patchwork Girl* in 2013, and his second novel, *The Stronghold*, is a ripped-from-the-headlines thriller that has been published and is available as an eBook and in print. Also an avid film lover, Bendix has a sci fi/horror script that has been optioned and is in development.

C. Bryan Brown writes to avoid going to jail and to provide himself with stable mental health after being hit with a dirty plunger at the age of seventeen. The plan succeeded beyond his wildest dreams; he's married, has three wonderful, intelligent (and sarcastic) sons, a trio of grand kids and he manages to hold a steady job that lets him stay in debt up to his ears. He's living that so-called American dream and wishes he'd wake up soon.

K. B. Goddard is from Derbyshire, England. She is a former Open University student with a lifelong love of mythology and old ghost stories. She has released several collections of Victorian-Inspired, supernatural fiction. Strongly influenced by the subtlety and elegance of classic ghost stories, she likes to craft tales that focus on the mysterious and wondrous aspects of the genre. Her first novella, *The Girl with The Roses: A Tale from The Haunted Auctions*, came out in 2017, and her latest collection, *Tales Of The Macabre And The Supernatural*, came out in 2019. Her work has featured on both *The Lift* and *The Wicked Library* podcasts as well as in *The Lift*'s first written anthology. The episode of *The Wicked Library* featuring her story "Shadows" won the 2017 Parsec Award for Best Speculative Fiction Story: Small Cast (Short Form). She also penned the opening episode of season 2 of *The Lift* podcast "The Lost Library", Which was a finalist in the same category. She has also contributed to *Shadows at the Door* and *The Spooky Isles*.

Lydia Peever is a horror author, web designer and news design professor living in Ottawa. Her debut novel, *Nightface*, was published in 2011 and short stories have appeared in *Postscripts To Darkness*, *Dark Moon Digest*, *For When The Veil Drops*, *Memento Mori*, *The Wicked Library*, and her small collections, *Pray Lied Eve 1* and *2*. In her spare time, she updates the new releases section of the Horror Writers Association website, co-hosts a podcast called *Splatterpictures Dead Air* and talks horror books on Youtube at typicalbooks. Being a big fan of horror music, books, and film; anywhere there is blood, you will probably find her lurking somewhere in the corner.

Kelli Perkins is an author and horror fan. If you like your fantasy dark and full of video game references (and Queen), then Kelli is your girl. She spends much of her time with tongue firmly planted in cheek, a podcast in her ear or with a cat or ukulele in her lap. You can find her novel, This Mortal Coil, on Amazon. Kelli clutches her blanket against the encroaching darkness in rural south-central Ohio with her newlywed husband Cory and three rotten kitty-pooks, Fenris, Sirris and Teemo.

Myk Pilgrim is a horror writer, or at least that's what he likes to tell people. He lives in a tiny village just north of the wall, where he spends his time sharing cappuccinos with his inner demons, binge watching bad horror movies with his Pippa, shaving his head, annoying the locals, and generally just counting down the days until Halloween.
Also, sometimes, he writes stuff.

Nelson W. Pyles is a writer and voice actor living in Pittsburgh PA. His latest novel, *Spiders in the Daffodils*, is available from Burning Bulb Publishing. His first novel, *Demons Dolls and Milkshakes*, was re-released in 2019, and the sequel is in progress. He is also the creator and original host of *the Wicked Library* for the first five seasons and has stayed on as an executive producer and voice of "The Librarian". He has written and performed on *The Wicked Library, The Lift, The Private Collector*, and *Wicked Fairy Tales* podcasts.

Meg Hafdahl is a horror and suspense author, and the creator of numerous stories and books. Her fiction has appeared in anthologies such as *Eve's Requiem: Tales of Women, Mystery and Horror and Eclectically Criminal*. Her work has been produced for audio by *The Wicked Library* and *The Lift*, and she is the author of two popular short story collections including *Twisted Reveries: Thirteen Tales* *of the Macabre.* Meg is also the author of the two novels; *Daughters of Darkness* and *Her Dark Inheritance* called "an intricate tale of betrayal, murder, and small town intrigue" by *Horror Addicts* and "every bit as page turning as any King novel" by *RW Magazine*. Meg, also the co-host of the podcast *Horror Rewind* and co-author of the forthcoming books distributed by Simon and Schuster; *The Science of Monsters* and *The Science of Women in Horror*, lives in the snowy bluffs of Minnesota.

Christopher Long is a writer hiding out in the end of his thirties, where he spends the majority of his free time sending out ghost stories to help deal with his own morbid paranoia. Chris has released two novels, six novellas and three collection with KGHH Publishing. His stories have featured in Sanitarium and The Ghastling magazine and have appeared on The Lift and Wicked Library podcasts, one of which was nominated for a Parsec award. Along with these, he's had a story on the first series of the new Shadows at the Door podcast, based on one of the ghost stories for Christmas he contributed to their website. Last year he also had the honour of appearing in the latest Infernal Clock anthology, Deadcades. He lives in the UK with his wife, Sam, and is currently working on his third novel.

Jessica McHugh is a novelist and internationally produced playwright running amok in the fields of horror, sci-fi, young adult, and wherever else her peculiar mind leads. She's had twenty-three books published in eleven years, including her bizarro romp, "The Green Kangaroos," her Post Mortem Press bestseller, "Rabbits in the Garden," and her YA series, "The Darla Decker Diaries." More information on her published and forthcoming fiction can be found at JessicaMcHughBooks.com.

Aaron Vlek is a storyteller who works with the trickster mythos in its role as bringer of delight and proponent of disquieting humors. Some of her (yes, her) stories center around the goings on of the jinn, and of a universal imagining of the Native American character, Coyote. Some works are historical in setting while others occupy a contemporary and urban landscape. She also indulges frequently in the reimagining of classic themes of horror and the occult. Aaron is a graduate of SarahLawrence College. "13" appeared in The Wicked Library Live Halloween Special, October 31, 2016. "The Accursed Lineage" appears in the Alban Lake anthology Miskatonic Dreams, November 2016, "Dear Cousin Gavin" appears on The Wicked Library podcast #622, March 2016. "Twice Per Annum" appears in Ink Stains Anthology #1, March 2016. "The Black Meal," a work of speculative horror appeared in the October 2015 issue of Outposts of Beyond. "Some Thoughts on the Blind Owl" appeared in the Surreal Nightmares Anthology in April, 2016, and "The Wet Man" appeared on The Lift podcast in July 2016. "The Dreams of Which Ghouls are Made" appeared in the Ghost's Redemption anthology in 2016. "Domine Canè," a short piece of speculative horror with a historic theme, appeared in the April 2015 issue of Bards and Sages Quarterly, Vol. VII, Issue II. Additional stories have been accepted for publication throughout 2016. Aaron is also the author of each episode of The Private Collector, our premier, member only, audio drama for supporters of the show at the Private Collector level of support. This show explores The Librarian's true mission and delves deep into the occult and mystical realms in a way sure to give you the whim-whams.

Stephanie M. Wytovich is an American poet, novelist, and essayist. Her work has been showcased in numerous anthologies such as *Gutted: Beautiful Horror Stories,* *Shadows Over Main Street: An Anthology of Small-Town*

Lovecraftian Terror, and *The Best Horror of the Year, Volume 8* (edited by Ellen Datlow). Wytovich is the Poetry Editor for Raw Dog Screaming Press, an adjunct at Western Connecticut State University, and a book reviewer for *Nameless Magazine.* She is a member of the Science Fiction Poetry Association, an active member of the Horror Writers Association, and a graduate of Seton Hill University's MFA program for Writing Popular Fiction. Her Bram Stoker Award-winning poetry collections, *Hysteria: A Collection of Madness, Mourning Jewelry, An Exorcism of Angels,* and *Brothel* earned a home with Raw Dog Screaming Press, and her debut novel, *The Eighth,* is published with Dark Regions Press.

ILLUSTRATOR

Jeanette Andromeda is a lifelong artist and storyteller. A passion for theater in high school led her to earning a BFA in Technical Theater Design at UCONN. Afterwards she production designed her fair share of Horror Movies for the Sci-fi and Chiller channels. Currently, her focus is on a career in illustration. Her work can be seen on YouTube.com/jeanetteandromeda, in various seasons of *The Wicked Library* and *The Lift,* in the Lift's first written anthology, *The Lift: 9 Stories of Transformation, Volume I,* as well as in The Wicked Library's first written anthology, *The Wicked Library Presents, 13 Wicked Tales.*

EDITORS

Scarlett R. Algee's fiction has been published by *Body Parts Magazine, Bards and Sages Quarterly,* and *The Wicked Library,* among other places. She is a regular contributor to the horror flash-fiction site *Pen of the Damned,* as well as to *The Lift;* her short story "Dark Music," written for *The Lift,* was a 2016 Parsec Awards finalist. As an editor, her work includes the bestselling *Explorations* anthologies; the *Survivors* series by Nathan Hystad, and the *Lucky's Marines* series by Joshua James. She's also managing editor for JournalStone Publishing, where her projects have included the Bram Stoker Award®-winning novel *The Rust Maidens*, by Gwendolyn Kiste. She lives in rural Tennessee with a Hound of Tindalos cleverly disguised as a beagle, skulks on Twitter at @scarlettralgee, and blogs occasionally at scarlettralgee.com.

Daniel Foytik is a teller of interesting lies who explores his love of story in all its forms through writing, narration, and the creation of multiple award-nominated and award-winning audio drama podcasts including, *The Lift*, *The Wicked Library*, and *The Private Collector*. His short story "Buying America" appears in *The Lift: 9 Stories of Transformation, Volume 1*, and his short tale, "A Little Light Gets In" appears in *Shadows at the Door, An Anthology*, which he also narrated along with Cynthia Lowman. He is the co-creator of *The Lift* and has written a number of episodes for the show, but considers himself to be as much Victoria's creation as she is his. Daniel lives in Pittsburgh, Pennsylvania, for now, but has a strong desire to move to the mountains and disappear onto a farm surrounded by deep, dark woods.

THANK YOU

Many people are involved in breathing life into a collection this nature. So many, that if we attempt to list *everyone* here, we'll leave someone out, which would be worse than Wicked. So, we'll instead name just a few, and mention the rest as part the groups they belong to. Know that if you've be a part of this experience, we are deeply thankful to you.

To start, we must thank you, who have given your ears (and now eyes) to The Librarian. He's thankful to have so many useful body parts in his collection. Thank you to those who have donated to the show, bought this book, and written so many amazing reviews sharing your love of the show. Your appreciation and support are why we continue to make the show. That, and the fact that the Librarian demands it of us, and his dark tomes are hungry for your fear.

We also wish to thank Jeanette Andromeda for her amazing work on the illustrations and cover, and Scarlett R. Algee for her help in editing all of the stories herein.

Of course, there would be no podcast and certainly no anthology without the work of the authors. We hope you'll find their other work and buy it – that's what ensures they will keep making more.

Finally, we wish to thank all of the composers, the artists, the voice actors, and everyone else who has been a part of making *The Wicked Library* more than the sum of its parts. All of you have been a huge part of this project. It would not exist without you.

Daniel Foytik and Nelson W. Pyles
October 2019

Made in the USA
Columbia, SC
17 March 2020

89409335R00190